Praise for

STRANGERS

"You can tell V has an incredible grasp of who these characters are and we benefit from that right away. There are so many snappy bits of dialogue and interaction, there is what I call great over the shoulder moments that turn us around and look back at this or that, and there is this underlying tension that really is handled so well in the writing. It's nice when an author treats its audience like grown-ups. I also love that this story gives us just enough when we need it and so much just when we think we are about to settle in. It's easy to picture all this in your head, very cinematic, and a great puzzle as well."

-Joe Compton, author of *Amongst the Killing*

and for

TRAVELERS

"I think I'm in love with this series. Grounded in the solid bedrock of real archeological techniques and experience, it takes off from there into the fantastic. I love it the way I love Tony Hillerman's writing: it challenges me to research new areas of study without once losing the draw of a gripping narrative. Even better, it shows truly rounded queer characters whose sexuality is just one facet of a complex and engaging personality. From page 1 Nel tromped through my imagination with a screw-you-too grin and a trowel in her back pocket. Her description of the field life feels incredibly real. This book rocks."

-O. E. Tearmann, author of *The Hands We're Given*

"The whole concept this story is based on and built around is fascinating, the way V.S. Holmes has written the characters and plot is brilliant... a suspenseful read with lots of surprises, a touch of romance, and a whole lot of promise..."

-Serena Yates of *Rainbow Book Reviews*

OTHER BOOKS BY
V. S. HOLMES

NEL BENTLY BOOKS
Travelers
Drifters
Strangers
Heretics
Fugitives
Emissaries

BLOOD OF TITANS WORLD
Smoke and Rain
Lightning and Flames
Madness and Gods
Blood and Mercy

SHORT FICTION
"Nowhere Fast" (*We Came to Dance*)
"Starfall" (*Vitality Magazine*)
"The Tempest" (*Out of the Darkness*)
"Disciples" (*Beamed Up*)
"Familiar Waters" (*Love and Bubbles*)
"Mere Primordium" (poem, *Mystic Blue Review*)

HERETICS

STARS EDGE: NEL BENTLY BOOK 4

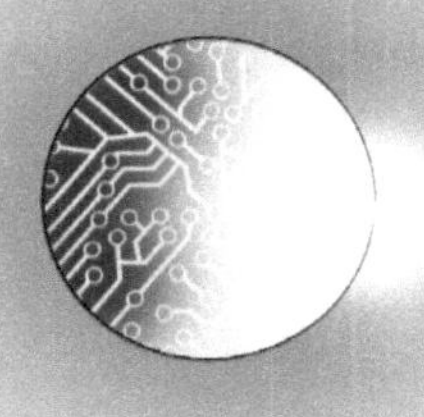

V. S. HOLMES

AMPHIBIAN PRESS

Amphibian Press

www.amphibianpress.online
www.vsholmes.com
ISBN : 978-1-949693-67-6

For those with bonfire hearts.

AUTHOR'S NOTE

This series combines archaeology with science fiction. Doing so is a hazardous road, particularly with the advent of television like "Ancient Aliens" and the fourth Indiana Jones film.

This book is a work of fiction, and something to be enjoyed as entertainment. I wholeheartedly believe we are far from alone in the universe. That being said, I am an archaeologist by trade, and I know humans are ingenious and resourceful enough to build pyramids and other architectural wonders all on their own.

ONE

Nel glared at the message blinking beside her bracelet. Her nerves were shot. The elevator's whispering hydraulics sounded closer to sandblasting the hull of a crashing ship. Soft phosphorescence flickered sickly green over fresh pink scars and the white threads of old wounds on her arms. She wished for the comfort of sleeves.

The decision to disband audio messages was unanimous, at least until *Odyssey*'s sonic bloody mystery was solved. Her shaking hand fumbled with the holographic buttons until the unread message appeared in the air above her wrist. Nel preferred texts anyway.

I'll be there soon, talking with my mentor.
Can't wait to see your outfit!
-L

Nel glanced at the faux-silk front of her vest. Even without the distortion of the elevator's curved aluminum, she doubted she'd recognize her reflection. At least the available fashion offered something suitably androgynous—high-collared vest and thigh-hugging pants. The soft faux leather of the boots cupped the aching place where her toes once were. *Even if they aren't steel-toed.* Woven translucent pads covered the sand burn and nicks Samsara left across her exposed biceps and forearms. Hopefully she looked closer to Ellie Williams than, well, herself.

She had hoped Lin would meet her outside the hall—feeling nervous was impossible with someone that beautiful on your arm. *C'mon, Bently. Get your shit together.* This wasn't an exploding planet or deadly soundwaves. Her lip curled. She'd take either over a gala any day.

The elevator passed from its metal tube to a glass cylinder, treating her to a view of the hall. The guests who arrived on time already ranged about, a sea of rich colors and glittering accessories. Nel flexed her hands. Copper and burnt sienna were as subdued as she could go. She was used to archaeology conferences, mingling with too much alcohol and too little professionalism. She could hold her own with glorified shovelbums. Surrounded by space scientists and cultured extraterrestrials? She was a turkey among peacocks. *Fake it till you make it.* The platform slowed and she plastered her favorite cocky smirk on her face.

Murmurs and soft laughter filled the hall. Somewhere the sound of water trickled, though Nel couldn't say if it was recorded. *Hopefully not.* She rubbed the base of her skull and stepped out. Several gazes glazed over her as she edged through the crowd. Did they dismiss her because they didn't know who she was or because they did? A handful of folks clustered by what she prayed was a buffet table. Anything to occupy her hands. If it wasn't for the promise of snacks and getting a moment with Emilio, she wouldn't have bothered to come at all. *Okay, and maybe to see Lin in a fancy dress.*

As it was, she had barely managed to say a dozen words to the secretive Los Pobladores leader since he glitched into Samsari airspace four days ago. *And you still haven't told me that damn story.*

Curiosity dragged her focus to the glass bubble pressing into the forest at *Odyssey*'s center. It was shadowed by the mighty boles of jungle trees, vines draping the lower segments of the glass. Two more levels rose above, but Nel cared more about occupying her fidgeting digits than mingling.

Hors d'oeuvres and drinks drifted by on hovering platforms. Nel maintained strict eye contact with a platter of cheese as she navigated the surprisingly sparse crowd. *It's a gala for the Samsara project. It's not like engineering should be here.* Still, the scarcity may have been as much an illusion due to the sheer size of the room. Someone Nel recognized but couldn't place offered a smile and wave, but their expression faltered when Nel attempted to return the gesture. Perhaps smirk wasn't the look to go for.

Nel's attention returned to the table. Edible containers housed each snack, meant to complement the flavors or act as a palate cleanser. While the majority of the protein was made of insects, she was relieved to note not a single prickly leg among the smorgasbord. *Fancy suit aside, you're an embarrassment to anthropology, Bently.*

Nel glanced at her wrist and thought about typing Lin a message. Instead, she let her alien boots wind their way through strangers and plants. She paused by another buffet table just long enough to shove some sort of tapenade into her mouth. She apparently dawdled too long because a figure loomed over her when she turned to make her exit. "Annelise!"

Nel cringed, wiping a hand on her pant leg quickly before offering her hand. "Ah, Nel, please. Or Bently. Anything really, but that."

"Yes, yes." The man pumped her hand repeatedly, grin vacant. "I was just speaking to your colleague there, Dr. Arnav Patel. He said you were present for the planet's ah…rearrangement."

"Rearrangement," she responded, voice flat. "Yeah, I was. Didn't feel like rearrangement from there, though. More like Armageddon."

"I can imagine."

Her eyes narrowed on him, doubting very much that he could imagine anything like

Samsara's implosion. "Who'd you say you were again?"

"Apologies! I'm Komodor McNally." He shook her hand again, gaze pausing on her bolo. "Oh, that's delightful! Meteorite, yes? Do you know which one?"

"Not a clue. But yeah, meteorite. My—Letnan First Class Nalawangsa gave it to me." She seized the excuse, still trying to extricate her hand from his. Sweat dampened her palm. "Have you seen her, actually?"

"Last I saw she was with the Nalawangsa boy."

Dar hasn't shown his face all night. "Gotcha, thanks! Better catch up, she wanted to show me the," she glanced back, searching for anything to fill the blank drawn in her mind, "forest. It looks amazing. Great to meet you!"

She wove through the crowd, annoyed enough to don a furrowed brow in hopes of preventing further conversation. She didn't trust slimy, middle-aged men at archaeology conferences—or any conference, really. Space conferences were no different, it seemed.

"Scuse," a low voice remarked. An arm reached across her to a bowl filled with vials of clear and faintly orange or blue fluid.

Nel glanced up into an open face under an elaborate swoop of pale blonde hair. "Hey, you're one of the tech people, right?"

"Yep! Teera." The smile was bright. "Want one?" She offered an alarmingly large tube.

"No port," Nel explained, showing her bare arms. Curiosity warmed her gut. "What are they?"

"Mingle-ease. Calms the nerves, lowers inhibitions, settles the stomach a bit."

"So, IV beer?" Nel suggested. "Guess my awkwardness is that obvious, eh?"

"No, but I remember my first gala. They don't get easier." She wrinkled her nose.

"Thanks for the thought. I'd kill for Black Pond's jalapeno saison though." As if in answer, the pastry she popped into her mouth smacked her tongue with smoky heat and a sweet bite. She hummed in approval and grabbed another. "Man, the food is almost good enough to keep my feet off the ground forever."

Teera laughed and cringed. "Doesn't make me feel any better about whatever I'll be eating once we're planetside."

"I heard something about beer."

Nel turned to see Arnav hum up. The rims on his wheelchair were decorated to match the elaborate caps to his sleeves. Angular structures rose from either side of the back of his chair, framing his head.

"Dude, you look badass," Nel remarked.

His mouth quirked. "Thanks. Just for your kind words..." He opened the draped front of his jacket and produced a heavy flask. It was battered, the metal covered in dings and the wrapping soft and warm.

"Shit, this what I hope it is?"

"If you're hoping for grade C recycler distilled starshine, then yes, yes, it is."

Nel knocked back a sip, then a second before returning it with a pleased shudder. It was burning ice in her gut, setting off the fire of whatever spice she ate a second before. "Fuck, that's good. You've made a best friend of me, that's all I need tonight."

"You're welcome to it, I've another in my pack, but I'm starving—what do they have out? Anything good?"

Nel shrugged. "Don't know what half of it is, but this spicy stuff is nice. I've my eye on that fruit thing that looks like caviar."

Arnav laughed. "I honestly wonder what the Nalawangsa girl is doing with you, upbringing that she had."

"Opposites and all that—maybe I'm good for her." Nel offered a wink, belatedly realizing she was already slipping up on the professionalism. She scrubbed a hand through her gelled hair. *Dammit, now I'm gonna look like a cockatoo.*

"Where is she?" Teera asked. "I'm always dying to see what the elite end up wearing."

Nel's gaze was pulled up to the upper levels. "Haven't found her yet. Sure she's busy though. I'll rescue her later from some boring intellectual nightmare."

"Oo, well it looks like the department heads are already at it," Arnav groaned. "I swear verbal sparring over ethics is the only joy Dr. Ndebele gets these days."

"Best be off before she realizes I've holed myself up over here." Teera flitted off, gossamer cape and fascinator bobbing above the crowd.

"This is all very space fairy," Nel decided. "Odd food, ephemeral costumes, highly educated."

Arnav laughed. "I don't know, this is just a piece of it. Everything looks pretty on *Odyssey*. How well do you know your Homer?"

"Enough, why?"

"Well, the *Odyssey*? It wasn't easy. Took a long time and a lot of blood." His gaze followed a cluster of people that seemed to move over the crowd instead of through it. "And more than a few monsters."

Nel followed his gaze, caution flitting up her spine. She was tired of distrusting, but nothing surprised her these days—warring space factions? Sure. Exploding mechanical planets? Just another Tuesday. "I hear that." She itched to ask him more, but surrounded by gleaming strangers made her feel more than a bit out of place. "Except I'm pretty sure the fae have to tell the truth."

"Only if you're asking the right question," a deep voice rumbled from behind her.

Zachariah leaned on the delicate metal support beam. His bare arms were decorated in gleaming phosphorescent paint, and his collared vest seemed to be of the same style as Nel's, if several sizes larger and made in black. The top half of his hair was caught back in a clip, but the bottom half was loose, one finger already twirling a lock absently.

She flashed a smile. "If I remember undergrad correctly, the only question I asked was 'you want a drink?'"

"Seems like it's the only one you ask now, too," Arnav quipped. He nodded to Zach. "Ramadan Mubarak."

"Thank you. You ready to return to Samsara next week?"

Nel blanched. "We're going back? It's a gate—how're you going to excavate anything? Plus, I thought we'd be locked in debates with the Flounders for the next month at least." She glanced at the ceiling as if the artificial sun would tell her the season or time. "Or whatever."

"I'm going back," Arnav clarified, "with a small forensics crew and a lot more weapons."

"Plus, noise-cancelling headphones, I'd hope," Nel sneered. "I envy you."

Arnav grimaced. "I'd rather have the time to breathe, to grieve."

Nel flushed. Apparently even space alcohol didn't prevent her from awkwardly inserting her foot into her mouth. "Right. I guess I'm a throw-myself-into-work griever."

"That's fair," Arnav offered, though his next smile didn't reach his eyes. "Just makes me think they're more scared than anyone is letting on, if they're risking even more of us to look for answers."

Zach hummed in response. "I think after this performance is through, we'll all be headed somewhere. I was called in to discuss my workload and remote service capabilities a few days ago."

Whatever question she had for Zachariah stalled on her tongue when a tall figure ascended in the translucent cell of the elevator. She moved into the crowd, hand relaxing around the flask until Arnav caught it from her limp hand. Only after a dozen steps across the crowded lower level did she realize she was moving at all. A patch of darkness moved through the soft greens and gentle mints of most of the other guests. Apparently, she wasn't the only one who felt glitter and gossamer weren't for her.

Perhaps it was Arnav's words, or the sheer grace with which Lin crossed the floor, but Nel's pursuit stilled. She was content to trace the soft illumination down the curve of Lin's throat and watch the black fabric turn iridescent when Lin paused at a table. A thin vial slipped in her port and after a moment, her shoulders dropped back with relaxation.

This room, this woman, seemed so removed from Nel's world. Even with the burn of cheap booze in her throat and the flutter of nerves, this place was firmly rooted in the unfamiliar. A week ago, their reality had exploded in sand and sound. Now gentle music and the trickle of artificial streams filled the air. Delicate bundles of tiny phosphorescent lights made the very air glow. Futures were bandied between high-tech minds and extraterrestrial politics.

In that moment, though, Nel didn't really care.

Her entire focus trained on the woman gliding between officers and department heads, cheeks gleaming as she scanned the crowd below. Then dark eyes settled on Nel's and narrowed in a smile. A metal bracelet clipped to the edge of her split skirts raised them just enough to appear as if she floated down the stairs to where Nel had stilled.

"Hi," Lin's smile broadened to a beam. "I guess the dress was a good choice."

"I'd say." Nel cleared the rasp from her throat. She opened her arms and did a flourish. "What do you think?"

"I think you might be one of four people wearing brown."

Nel grimaced. "It was supposed to be copper and reddish, but I forgot all the green lights. I'd kill for my cargos and tanks."

"I suffered your miserable Earth fashion; you can survive a night. Besides, it makes you stand out. Reminds us where you're from. It's fitting."

"So I was imagining the disdain?"

"Well, I can't take my eyes off you." The low note in Lin's voice shot straight to Nel's core and she swallowed the fluttering.

"I was just over there, with the food. You hungry?"

"Not yet," she gestured to her port. "Waiting for my nerves to calm."

"I thought this would be normal for you. Pretties, politics, and parties."

Lin grimaced, but on her made-up face, even that looked artful. "Hardly. My parents were all about these when we were little, but it's been a long time since they were close enough to join in. This is more Dar's speed." She glanced behind her. "I'm surprised he's not here yet."

"Probably has better things to do. I know I wish I did."

"C'mon, anthropologist—I'd think mingling with the locals for a celebration is exactly what you were into."

"I prefer my subjects dead."

"Arguably, you thought we were."

Nel laughed. "Okay, and not having just threatened to court martial me in an army I was never really a part of."

"They were never going to go through with it," Lin dismissed. "They're all bluster up here."

Nel didn't need the memories of her few hours of imprisonment to know bluster was nowhere to be seen. But even she knew a gala was not the place to start an argument. She reached for Lin's hand. "We alright with PDA here?"

"PDA?"

"Public displays of affection," Nel clarified. "You know, holding hands, kissing."

Lin frowned. "Unless you're planning to undress me with more than your eyes, I don't see why it'd be an issue."

A strange twinge of longing shot through Nel's chest. As much as she missed home, she had to admit this version of humanity made some wonderful advances. "That's the one part I'll miss when I go back. The freedom to love whomever I want."

Lin's face lit up and her long fingers curled over Nel's callused ones. "Well, you're always free to love me."

Nel blinked away panic at the word. "So, you people dance or what?"

Lin tilted her chin at the second tier. "There's a cleared area up there. But it's mostly for mingling. I've got a pass for one of the alcoves, if you'd like."

"Please—I'd rather not have all eyes on me."

Lin's long fingers laced with hers and the taller woman turned to the edge of the second level. What looked like glass bubbles extended out from the floor, furnished with low, plush couches, spaces for hoverchairs, and a few tables for drinks. The third alcove from the right was deserted. The entryway glimmered with what Nel could only guess was a security shield. Lin raised her bare hand for a moment, then, grasping both of Nel's in hers, drew the archaeologist into the muffled privacy of the room.

Nel scanned the architecture with curiosity. "So, sound dampening?" Glancing back with a wink, she added, "Any chance this glass is one-way?"

Lin's laugh was bright and loud in the small space. "Hardly. It's treated, so no one can read lips or screens through it, but that's about it. You'll have to get your voyeuristic rocks off another way."

"If I was an exhibitionist, I wouldn't care how clear that glass was, Lin," Nel remarked, cheeks hot with a blush. Despite her devil-may-care attitude, something in Lin's eyes struck right to her heart when she teased. "It's just been a while."

Lin drew her down onto the couch, hands softening in Nel's grasp. "I know. The past week feels like months."

"And the months like years." Nel shook her head. "I was hoping to have a bit of recovery time before diving into another mission." Her mood darkened. "Though if Arnav is right, it sounds like I'll have nothing to do with Samsara now."

Lin's dark eyes softened. "I'm sorry, Nel. We have a lot of resources up here, and it stings when you're not considered a necessary one. But I think we'll need you more when we return to Earth. I know I will."

Nel felt her cheeks pink further. "I'm just antsy." With Lin's warmth pressing against Nel's palms, her dusky lips hovering just above the place between Nel's unkempt brows, she could almost forget a black vacuum yawned beyond the thousands of tons of aluminum and steel. For a moment whatever spinning, baleful monster she woke in Samsara's heart didn't glare from the void in her chest.

"I just have this nagging unease," Nel confessed. "There's so much wrong, so much to worry about. I'm exhausted and we've done nothing but be debriefed and stare at screens for the better half of a week."

Lin lapsed into silence, her gaze fixed somewhere over Nel's shoulder. Something dark crept into the rich brown of her eyes. "I'm worried too, you know."

"About?" Nel prodded. As much as she liked the other woman, she knew better than to assume their concerns lay anywhere close to one another.

"*Odyssey*. Whatever happened to Ada. What's wrong with Dar."

"Wrong?" Nel's curiosity sat up at that observation. She didn't know Dar well—or at all— and suspected very few people did. But despite the nervous drumming of his fingers the only time they ever exchanged words, Nel wouldn't have thought to worry about him. *He's her brother. Of course she worries.*

"He's been removed lately. And he's not here. Usually he arrives early, officer's cloak gleaming, and entourage already laughing at his cruel jokes."

Nel mimed gagging. "No offense—I get that family is family—but I don't imagine he and I will ever get along."

Lin laughed. "No, I don't think many people I've been with did." Her expression sobered. "Still, it's unlike him. And gala aside, this feels tense."

Lin's gaze dropped to the deep V-neck of Nel's vest. "You're wearing the bolo I gave you."

Nel grinned. "I figured it would blend in nicely here."

"It looks nice on you." Lin's beige fingers lifted it gently, her dark eyes unreadable. "I'd love if you wore it more often."

Nel frowned but pushed the voice in the back of her mind away. "I will. Wore it on Samsara a bit. Just so worried to lose it—I'm rough on my things."

"I'd say you are at that."

Whatever followed Lin's suggestive quip was overshadowed by the appearance of a familiar Chilean face by the projection panel just past the private chambers. Nel dragged her attention back to Lin to find the other woman's dark brows were arched in poorly concealed amusement. "Sorry, I just—"

"Oh, I see, you're not interested in mingling with anyone but your fellow earthlings," Lin teased.

Nel slipped her hand around the back of Lin's neck and pulled her down for a hard kiss. The moment their lips softened into the invitation for more, however, she pulled away. Lin's eyes glittered and passion flushed under the pearlescent makeup on her cheeks. "I'd like to remind you that you and I did far more than mingle," Nel murmured. "If I wasn't determined to set eyes on one Emilio Sepulveda, apparent interstellar traveler, then I'd take you up on that offer right now."

"Go, I know he's the real reason you showed up tonight."

"If I'd known about the dress, I wouldn't have been as reluctant. But I'll find you later, alright?"

"If you'd known about the dress it wouldn't have been nearly as effective," Lin theorized. She stepped back with a smile. "And I'm supposed to see Dar later, go over some things, but tomorrow?"

Disappointment flickered, but Nel ignored it. She could honestly use a decent night's sleep. "Well, if you're free, come find me, 'kay?"

"Promise. I'll look for any topiaries or statues with an orange shadow."

Nel rolled her eyes and slipped from the room before she lost sight of Emilio. For now, the wall displayed scattered stars. A looming glow in the top corner told her planet rise—or gate-rise, she supposed—was imminent. The faint gold light cast Emilio's weathered face into stark relief. She sidled up to the projection, but her determination faltered. If she stared long enough, would she catch the echoes of Chile's hills on his features?

His dark eyes flicked toward her and his broad mouth curved in a subtle smile. "Bently."

"Hey." Nerves overwhelmed her and her hands clenched. *Fuck it.* She closed the distance, wrapping her hard arms around him. The structured, faded fabric of his outfit hid bone-thin shoulders and what was once a barrel chest. "Sorry."

She made to pull away, but his arms locked around her for a moment longer. He smelled of fresh air and warm sun. Did all those born of Earth smell of the sunshine and soil and rain their bodies incorporated into their bones?

"It's nothing." When he pulled away, Emilio's eyes held a new softness. "It's good to see a familiar face."

Nel followed his lead and slipped into Spanish. "Few and far between out here."

"It's good to see you," he clarified a moment later. "Never been this far out."

"Me neither," Nel remarked, taking a sip from the glass he offered her. It was sharp and sour, but from what she could tell, devoid of alcohol. "But I didn't have a fleet of—" she frowned and borrowed the English word before returning to his native tongue, "—spaceships at my disposal. Or a gate."

His smile bloomed and his gaze settled on the projected image before them. "I wondered how long you'd wait before bringing that up."

"I admire the theatrical arrival, but it left me with more questions than answers. I think I've been pretty patient, waiting almost a week."

"Only you would think a week was indicative of patience."

She glanced over, looking at the new lines on his face, and was abruptly aware of the new years separating them. "How are you? Truly? Last I saw you were being bundled into a prison, framed for Lin's murder spree."

"Ah, well," he drew a slow breath. "Cryo is another layer of privilege, I suppose. Removed from pain and time and age for however long."

"Maybe you're right. I guess like a lot of privilege, it doesn't always feel like it from this side. Missing moments. Years. Gaps getting bigger." Nel glared down at her soft boots. Anger sizzled down her limbs and she wished she could rip all the ethical, clean, sustainable fabric from her skin and just be imperfect and human again. The feeling passed after a moment and she sighed. "You didn't answer me."

"I'm well enough. Reeling a bit, in the wake of all that happened on Earth. But there's not enough time to really focus on it. Just running forward hoping whatever we're racing toward isn't worse than what's closing behind us."

"I know that feeling intimately."

"I imagine so." His smile returned. "But look, we're both here and alive and have enough breath in our lungs and fire in our veins to keep running for now."

Nel's concern nagged at her manners. "Emilio, about Earth going dark—"

"I told you when you first boarded—Earth is alright. Not safe, not yet. But with your help and IDH's resources, she might be."

"Right." Her eyes fixed on the growing glow of the gate as it rose into view on the projection. "Why were you the only one I could get through to?"

"Because radio silence is all that's protecting them for now. We've broken it only a few times. They'll explain all in detail tomorrow during the briefing—I assume you'll be there?"

"If they don't invite me, I'll just show up anyway."

Emilio smiled. "I have fewer answers than anyone wants, I'm sure. But I do have a plan. While you all were up here playing *Starship Troopers*, some of us were cleaning up your mess."

"My mess—"

"IDH's mess, then."

"I'm not IDH," Nel muttered, glowering at the empty cellulose glass in her hand. It was already softening in the warmth of her palm. "Don't know if I ever will be."

"Looks a little different from where I'm standing."

Longing tugged her heart again. Maybe there was no place she would ever fit again, not without Mikey as her counterpoint. "Think I'll be heading home soon?"

"For all our sakes, I hope so."

"Why's that?"

"We need people like you. Like me." He fixed her with a pointed stare, as if he had reached into her gut and pulled out her deepest fear. "People who don't quite fit in either camp."

"At last!" The voice cut through what Nel realized had been whispers.

A panther of a man padded from around the corner. If IDH had business casual, Nel guessed his attire would have fit perfectly. The soft glimmer of an electrosuit peeked from under the gathered sleeve of his shirt. Nel would have bet cold cash that it was real linen. *Is that a sign of wealth or poverty out here?*

Light brown skin gleamed under the gentle lighting. What hair he still had was dark and shorn close to his long skull. His hand was elegant against hers as they shook. "You are the ineffable Dr. Annelise Bently."

"Please, just—"

"Call you Nel?" His gentle smile broadened before he turned to Emilio beside her. "Of course. And this is the incredible Munshi Emilio Sepulveda. An honor, sir."

Warmth faded from Emilio's eyes. "And you are…?"

Other than a simple metal pendant, the man wore no decoration or hint at any rank. "Ah, forgive me. My excitement gets the best of my manners. Harris, admirer of both your work. It takes a mighty man to counter IDH and still receive an invite to an event such as this." His long fingers captured the whole affair with a single gesture. "I hope you feel welcome here. Your opinions are greatly appreciated as we navigate these waters."

Nel found a smile on her face. His gentleness reminded her of Zach, excitement tempered by perhaps twenty years. "I'm just glad IDH is broadening their metaphorical horizons."

"Will you be coming to the Committee tomorrow? Surely, we would benefit from the account of one who contributed so much."

"I don't think I'm invited." Nel frowned. Until Emilio mentioned it, she hadn't known there was any meeting. "I assume Lin will relay whatever I need to know—they don't seem overly fond of me. Or my temper."

Emilio attempted to conceal his snort beside her. "Is anyone?"

She glared at him.

"Oh, a pity. Many hands, light work, two heads and all that." Harris's broad mouth curled and Nel caught a glimpse of the carefully concealed cleverness behind his angular face. "I was wondering if I might borrow our dear Munashi Sepulveda for a bit. I have some questions we need not bore the important people with tomorrow."

Disappointment shuttered Nel's excitement. *But I have questions too.* She pulled a carefree grin on instead of arguing. "Of course! But Emilio, let's find a time to catch up soon, alright?"

"There's time on the journey home." He patted her shoulder, wordless ellipses transferring from his hand to her bones. Nel watched the two men climb the ramp to one of the alcoves suspended over the forest. Her eyes found Arnav surrounded by several people Nel didn't know who oozed power. It was the last place she wanted to be, but she'd brave anything for another sip of starshine.

TWO

Phosphorescence eased from the golden warmth of candlelight to the soft sage of forest dapples. Even here, in the memorial bay, modern efficiency blended with sacred tradition. A few dozen people were gathered, and Nel slipped into the back of the bay, wordlessly finding Lin.

"Hey," Nel murmured. "Glad you made it."

"They moved the briefing to accommodate it, thankfully." She didn't meet Nel's eyes. "I'm sorry they aren't including you. I'll tell you everything they say tonight, though, promise." The woman squeezed her hand but let go a moment later to stand at what Nel assumed was attention. Her sharp jaw jutted out, muscles bunching. Was she biting back tears?

Nel dragged her attention to the gleaming canisters set along the innermost wall. There were three, engraved with names and dates. Words too small for her to read spiraled over the metal. Epitaphs perhaps, or memories.

Nel caught sight of Arnav at the front. His head was bowed and his shoulders shuddered. Grief welled in Nel's chest, overwhelming the numbness of oversleeping, the fog of a hangover. She was exactly where she needed to be. *These were your people, your crew, for a time.*

Someone emerged from the crowd and pressed their hand to Gretta's canister. They could have been the woman's double, but for another few inches in height and the thin blonde braided beard. "I am Klus Wagner and I stand for Kapten Gretta Wagner. I share the blood from which she was birthed, and so I will commit her back to our community, to the living we create, and to the dreams and hopes we protect, here and among the stars."

Murmurs rose as the crowd repeated the last five words. Klus's massive shoulders rose in a long breath, falling as he exhaled and depressed the lever beside his sister's coffin. Hydraulics hissed and the coffin sank into the wall. In a year each of them would be spread across the central forest, feeding the insects, plants, and fungi that were their bread and breath.

Next a row of officers read the achievements for Kapten Orso, and a weeping older woman, his mother, relinquished her son to be recycled within the space station's walls. As the coffin disappeared, the bay door opened soundlessly, and Dar entered. If he had attended the gala, Nel would have assumed he still wore his gala finery. His officer's robe was immaculate and as dark as the circles under his eyes. He moved to stand beside the final body. A silent moment passed with his hand resting on the canister.

"I am Komodor Muda Dar Nalawangsa, I stand for Dr. Paul de Lellis. I am the bond to which he was welcomed. The blood from which he was birthed is far, unable to join us today for safety, to protect all of us from the same terror that took Paul from us. Instead, I will commit him back to our community, to the living we create, and to the dreams—" His voice broke, but when he began again his words rumbled with rage. "To the dreams and hopes we protect, both on Earth and here among the stars."

This time, Nel's whisper joined the affirmation rising around her. "Here and among the stars."

Dar drew a simple strand of red rosary beads from his suit. "Like many of us, Paul carried a second faith from the doctrine of our mission here. He was a Catholic man, and his family on Mugdha 3 will be offering his funerary rites in their community's prayer center at this time. I ask that you stand in silence for a moment to honor their grief and Paul's sacrifice." Dar's face was rigid as he mouthed words, caressing each bead before moving on to the next.

Nel bowed her head, not looking up until she heard the lever depress and the casket click into the wall. As different as their worlds were, grief was universal, loss a quiet shroud over life. The crowd let out a collective breath and Nel glanced up at Lin. Her face was pale and her smile wan.

"It's odd, usually the rear wall is lit with family and friends stationed elsewhere to stream in. I always felt that was isolating. Sad. But I think missing it entirely is worse."

An errant fear of missing so much—funerals, births, weddings—while out here or in cryo flashed through Nel's mind. "I think so, yes. Have you gone to many? Funerals, I mean?"

"A few. Mostly remotely, though." She frowned at her wrist. "Ten-minute warning for the committee meeting, and I gotta lose the fancy coat."

Nel caught the woman's cheek as she made to drop a kiss on it, searching Lin's eyes. "Hey, I'll see you later, alright?"

"Promise."

Nel was almost back to her room when her own wrist comm flickered into life. It was an internal message from Phil, devoid of anything other than a projected path to the high-level conference rooms and a single line:

DON'T BE LATE, DON'T GET CAUGHT.

She grinned. Though she missed his unnerving conversation, she'd settle for silent help if it got her closer to the action.

The committee hall was packed when Nel slipped through the side door. Nel's stare settled on Lin's shoulders, drawn as if by the gravity of the other woman's appearance. She turned, scanning the crowd, and Nel pressed back against the wall, putting the bulk of a tall man between herself and discovery. As much as she wanted to take the empty seat next to Lin, there were still many rules the Letnan refused to break, especially now while on tenuous probation. *Because of me.*

Many of the debriefings had been held in smaller rooms, filled with scientists and medics. Already she recognized more than a few high-ranking military officers. *But no Emilio?*

A hologram waited, glowing and blank, for the meeting to begin. The sheer number of moving parts that any IDH mission required was staggering.

"Hey, Dr. Bently."

Nel winced and glanced at the young medic, who slipped in just behind her. Their hair was shorn this time, but Nel recalled the benevolent expression as her consciousness swam out of cryosleep. "Hey, ah, Jem, right?"

"Yeah. Good to see you." Their dark brows curled in. "I didn't think you were on the roster for this one."

"No, um—"

Jem nudged her with one of their muscled shoulders. "Don't worry, I won't tell. Gonna grab a seat, though." They wound through the back rows to find a chair.

A sharp cough demanded attention. Now that the group had settled down, Nel saw a line of officers standing a step behind a Black woman with a high-ranking badge on her shoulder. The metal rings decorating the collar of her electrosuit were etched in delicate circuits. The name across her breast was Ndebele. Nel frowned. *Like the people?*

Her confusion over the head officer's name dissolved when she caught sight of the man at the end of the line: Harris, with his hands clasped gently in front of him. His officer's jacket was as starched as the others' but lacked any colored trim denoting his department. *What are you, special ops?*

Dr. Ndebele stepped forward. "Most of you are familiar with our task force officers, and time is of the utmost value. We won't be wasting time with introductions. Your itineraries should cover most questions, and any others I expect to be directed to your immediate supervising officer. Firstly, let's address the supernova in the room: we will be going to Earth to attempt to solve the mystery of Samsara. Yes, it will be a dangerous mission and yes, we will be working in collaboration with the organization known as the Founders. Your loyalties to IDH are expected to remain a priority, and our relationship with them is complex. Those antagonizing that relationship or fraternizing with Founders operatives will be disciplined."

Tension puckered between Nel's shoulder blades. *Be nice, but not too nice.* She didn't like anyone who demanded loyalty, even under the guise of protecting her home. Besides, if all of their information came from Emilio and his team's hard work, why did none of them rate an invitation?

"It has been brought to our attention that a signal—akin to what happened on Samsara—was broadcast at certain locations on Earth. It triggered various tech malfunctions and, unfortunately, several fatalities. While the grid was shut down quickly, we are still uncertain how much this attack has to do with our own mystery.

"Departure from *Odyssey of Earth* will commence tomorrow morning at 1200, with prep at 0900. Our departure will coincide with that of our sister task force headed to the Samsari gate to study the event there. And yes, we will indeed be using the technology to shorten our journey." She held up a hand at the rising murmurs of concern. "The risks and benefits have been examined by our top analysts, including our current senti-comp Philos, and it is not under discussion. If you have concerns, you may apply for transfer to our local team staying on *Odyssey*."

Nel's pulse thundered in her throat. They were leaving tomorrow? She wasn't certain how the gate worked or how long it might take, but she didn't care. *Home. I'll be home soon.*

"Our itinerary on Earth is rudimentary and that is by design—our data from the planet, even with the added information from our new allies, is limited. Our plans may well change, and indeed, I expect them to." Her finger twitched and the blank projection dissolved into a hologram display of

Earth, with dots of light marking places across the globe.

"Upon touchdown at our newly installed Bakjeeri Aerospace port off the coast of Mumbai, we will board the high-speed rail to Ahmedabad and then travel west via the Trans-Arab rail—"

"We're not flying?" A leggy man with a pilot's badge sprawled in one of the seats in the second row.

Dr. Ndebele's features tightened. "As I stated, any concerns should be brought up with your supervisory officer, Kapten Lesu. The new high-speed rails are more reliable and don't require radio transmission to safely arrive or depart. While I agree it lengthens our mission significantly, speed alone is simply not worth the risk currently inherent in the AV communications required for flight, at least until more data surfaces."

Her tone softened only slightly as her attention returned to the room as a whole. "These sites are, interestingly, the locations of our ancestors' first contact with the Teachers, and where the root of our division with the Founders began. We can all assume this isn't a coincidence, but the exact reason is one we hope to discover."

A dozen points across the globe bloomed brighter. Nel pressed forward, ignoring the glare from the man beside her as she bumped him. *I know those.*

KV-H 4, Damnoni IX, the Jefferson cluster. Every site was groundbreaking or controversial and contemporary with one another. All papers she had read. Her eyes stilled on the point along Chile's coast. *Or written.* Chills erupted over her body. Perhaps it was because the sheer might of space was a bit difficult to wrap her hard head around, but the scope of IDH never seemed larger. Part of her wanted to punch the air, cheering that so many people had rejected these first attempts at galactic colonialism. Another larger and more spiteful piece wanted to just punch all those who claimed humanity couldn't have gotten as far as they had without some extraterrestrial involvement. *We did, not because of the Teachers, but despite them. All on our very own.*

"Excuse me, Dr. Ndebele, but I feel this is something only you are qualified to answer," Lin interrupted.

The officer's full lips pursed in displeasure, but she nodded for the young woman to continue.

"Have we considered the possibility that it is, indeed, the Founders behind this? As many of us can attest, these sites have also been the locations of modern vandalism and guerilla warfare."

"Those with more resources specific to those concerns are, indeed, investigating that line of speculation; however, we are operating under the assumption that they are, indeed, our allies in this." Dr. Ndebele smoothly slipped back into her previous topic. "Our first point of focus will be near Founders' North African headquarters in Qena, Egypt. Our trajectory will be finalized there, but we intend to visit each point where the signal was released if necessary to examine what evidence there may be as to what happened to cause the blackout and assess the risk of it occurring again." Her tone implied they were most concerned not with it occurring again on Earth, but rather among IDH's far-reaching scattered holdings. Murmurs swelled briefly, but her single finger-twitch silenced them. The projection flickered to display a long list of ranks, names, and departments.

"Any questions regarding roles or our general organization, both for our field task and analysis forces and those remaining here, can be addressed privately."

Nel peered closer, scanning the departments.

Field Task Force
Intelligence
Transport
External Relations
Internal relations
Communications
Technical support
Medical
Domestics
Intelligence
External Relations
Communications
Technical support
Miscellaneous resources

There, under the final category, she found her name. Lead slammed her gut. Not only was she barred from returning to Samsara, but she wasn't leaving *Odyssey*. Earth was under attack and she was relegated to this glorified moon lightyears away. *And my girlfriend gets to go in my place.* The buzzing of anger in her ears was louder than even the murmuring crowd. Screw Zachariah's suggestion to count before opening her mouth, screw the fact that she wasn't even invited to this special elitist meeting.

Before her last shred of common sense outweighed her temper, she shoved aside the man beside her. "I'm sorry, Dr. Ndebele, but this has to be a mistake."

Thirty-odd heads turned to stare. Her cheeks were fire, but it was too late to rephrase and certainly too late to keep her mouth shut. Even though she forced her focus not to waver from the chief officer for even a second, her periphery caught the utter horror on Lin's face.

Dr. Ndebele's face hardened in deserved cold fury. "Dr. Bently. I see you've decided to join us despite," her gaze flicked to the security officer at the door, "multiple measures to keep this classified meeting private."

"Well apparently that's just the tip of this exclusionary iceberg since, despite the fact that I ran the excavation on Samsara, I'm apparently listed as nothing more than a 'miscellaneous resource'. I can't save my home just 'cause I'm not part of the cool kids' club?"

"Due to the unpredictable nature of both this mission and your involvement in the events on Samsara, you are considered temporarily relieved from duty. Were it not for your arguably limited data and experience, I would have shipped you off to a labor station the minute the *Thunder-bump* docked."

"You're fucking kidding me."

"Dr. Bently, this is an official briefing," Dr. Ndebele interjected. "Since you're incapable of not only remaining professional but following any sort of order, I suggest you step outside."

"Oh, I'm capable," she spat, jaw working. "This whole shitshow just seems about as professional as the average high school yearbook meeting."

"I wasn't asking."

Nel shot a last glare at the woman and stalked from the room. Her outburst was childish, and she knew it. And Dr. Ndebele had more than a fair point—this was hardly new behavior. Right now, though, Nel didn't care. She didn't care about any brilliant doctor's opinion of her, even if IDH controlled everything from her mortgage payments to her life support in cryo. *Let them fucking disappear me. Nothing matters if I can't go home.*

Her fury left in a wave of despair and she slumped onto the floor, head thumping back against the gleaming walls. The words cracked over her fear and frustration. "I can't go home."

The door hissed open around the corner and a moment later, Zach settled beside her.

"I don't want to talk about it," she snapped, "or my feelings."

"Didn't expect you to," he responded. "Sometimes it's nice to have company when we sit with our demons. Or our tempers."

"Most people don't like to sit with mine," she muttered. "Myself included."

"Part of my job, archaeology princess."

She snorted. "Your nicknames crack me up."

He smiled, still politely looking away, twirling his hair. "We could all use creative compliments."

"Listen, since you're going home, do you think—"

"I don't know how it's going to be when we get down there, Nel. But I'll do my best."

"You didn't even know what I was gonna say."

"Make sure your family is okay, right?"

She nodded.

"It's my home too. If it weren't for my religious teacher sending me a vid-call shortly before blackout, I'd be just as worried."

She frowned at her IDH-issue boots. In that moment she hated everything about them. "It's not just that. It's all of this. I think I got in over my head chasing a cute chick. Half the time I feel like I got dragged into an inter-planetary mob, you know?"

He hummed thoughtfully. "I can see how it appears that way. What are you going to do about it?"

"Don't know. Not much I can do. Wait and see how things play out. But they're nuts if they think I'm just going to sit back and watch while my planet and family are threatened."

"No one expects you to do nothing—at least, no one in that room who knows you at all. There's plenty to be done and researched and pieced together without being on the investigative team itself."

"Yeah, but seems like anyone who has any say would rather I sit around with my thumb up my ass."

"I very much doubt Dr. Ndebele thinks about your ass at all. Letnan Nalawangsa on the other hand—"

"Hey now," Nel teased. The expression on Lin's face flashed through her mind, erasing her warmth. "I don't even know much about all that either."

"Still a commitment-phobe?"

"Still a therapist?"

He chuckled. "You're filled with a lot of questions, Nel. Good ones. Important ones." He rose with a sigh. "Just make sure you're asking the right people, alright?"

Nel watched him disappear back down the hall. Between Zachariah and Phil, she was starting to feel like everyone was in on some big secrets and just expected her to discover the answers on her own. *Maybe that's the ticket to the cool kids' club. Gotta solve the newest boxcar mystery.*

When the meeting let out, Lin trailed the cluster of officers. Her lips were a thin line.

Nel shoved herself to her feet, wiping sweaty palms on her legs. "Hey."

"I cannot believe you!" Lin hissed. "Sneaking into a meeting is one thing, but you made a total ass of yourself—both of us, actually. And you completely missed the local mission details."

"I wanted to stay—"

"Well maybe you should have just stayed quiet then!" Lin snapped.

Nel rocked back on her heels. "I'm sorry, okay? I get it, I fucked up. But I need to be on that ship home. You heard them in there!" she protested. "That's my planet on the chopping block, you know."

"We're from there too, Nel, and we share the same species, as much as you like to pretend we don't. And the losses on Samsara were ours."

Nel looked away. She always hated the "boys are from Mars" joke, but it seemed she was spinning a parallel falsehood each time she distanced herself from Lin's community. *Organization.* "I'm sorry. You're right. I think I'm just really amped up. Between missing my mom and everything that's going on—both like big picture and in my head." She heaved a sigh. She couldn't shake the image of Paul's skin bubbling in Samsara's corrosive atmosphere. "I'll be helpful,

I'm just really fucked up lately. I was framed for your crimes. Signed away two years of consciousness. I wasn't close to Paul, but we were friendly. And he was my responsibility."

"We're not saying those sacrifices don't take a toll. They absolutely do. What we're saying is you need to recover—"

"We," Nel intoned.

Lin glanced over, then at her shoes. One lithe shoulder lifted. "Yeah. Me too. Me maybe most of all."

"You broke me out of detainment, Lin. You admitted that maybe you were too trusting."

She closed the distance between them, but only to hiss, "They are all we've got right now and at least they approach it rationally. You're reckless on a good day." Lin stepped back, reserved features awash with disappointment. "And this really isn't a good day."

"I'm sorry. I've been an asshole." The frantic fight bled from her body, leaving embarrassment and confusion. Both pissed her off almost more than her lack of agency. "Can I see you tonight? If you're leaving tomorrow—"

Lin flinched, raking a shaking hand through her black hair. "I can't even think about that right now. I have to go get my health scan." She disappeared without another word.

Before anyone more official could appear and—rightfully—embarrass her further, Nel found the nearest service elevator and palmed it open.

When the doors opened it was onto the sweet air of the core. She stepped into the forest, breathing deeply. She strolled through the densely packed ferns, moving from cloud forest to scrub jungle to high desert. Even there, organisms flourished. Her hand pressed into the coarse sand. Did they make it? Bring it from Earth? Mine it from some asteroid? Pain pinched at her chest at the thought of Paul's mining family.

Tiny insects crawled over the grains and she watched the floor teem with life as night fell. Her eyes inched upward to the dimly glowing orb suspended high above. The senti-comp had been eerily quiet since the events on Samsara, following the order for radio silence like the rest of them. *Did you find what you were looking for?*

"Hey, Phil, you home?" Her voice boomed in the quiet biome, and she glanced across to the bubble of the function hall emerging from the jungle biome. It was far enough away that it was hardly more than a glimmer, a silver dollar on the manufactured horizon.

Her wrist flashed and she scanned the message.

"Evening, Dr. Bently."

She grinned. "Do you think I can stop by before we leave?"

"I'm using more processing than usual, and I fear even the increase in temperature from your biological form will impact my cooling system."

"You could have just said you were busy," she teased.

"I have as many processing units as most of those on Earth combined, Doctor. I don't really get busy."

"I wanted to see how you were. If you'd made any headway." The pause was lengthy, exponentially longer than it would take a supercomputer to consider his words.

"This puzzle is complex. And I fear each answer uncovers worse news. But yes. I am making headway. If I can hardline to other senti-comps it will be easier. And how are you doing?"

"I know you could just scan Zachariah's notes."

That'd be rude.

"Okay, I guess. Tired. Frustrated. Homesick. Can I help at all?"

Not in this particular moment. But soon. There is something for you to do—not for me, but for yourself.

She glanced up, as if he could see her gaze from there. Maybe he could. "Yeah?"

You've been lonely before.

She frowned. It was an odd statement, one more intimate than she felt their relationship warranted. Dread weighed her stomach, churning with the starshine. "This more of your pattern-recognition pre-cog shit?"

Pay attention—you will feel more alone than you have in a very long time. Isolated. Without allies. But you won't be.

"You gotta give me more."

The rest is up to the choices you and a hundred other people make over the next few weeks. Why don't you get some rest.

"I'll try. Phil?" She stared at her hands, still dipped in the sand. The cursor blinked on her comm, waiting. Expectant. "Are you lonely?"

Good night, Dr. Bently.

Her shoulders slumped under the weight of his unspoken answer. "Night."

She didn't return to her room. How could she? It was as much hers as any hotel room she had taken over during her shovelbumming days. As much hers as the dorm on Samsara had been, or the tiny pod where she spent two unconscious years crossing star systems. She didn't know where home was anymore. Would her ranch house still be there? Surely it would need a new coat of paint by now. Was the lawn mowed? Did they rent it out for her or just pay the mortgage until she returned?

She leaned back, pressing herself into the packed sand. If she closed her eyes perhaps even she, like the insects, would believe this was Chile. Or the boreal forest. Or whichever fabricated ecosystem she picked from the greenery arching over her head. She sank into the memory of pulling into her driveway, hearing the grind of old asphalt under her tires and the tick of her truck's engine when she turned it off and sat for a moment. Every moment she could remember since blasting free of Earth's atmosphere she had spent longing to go home. But now, hesitation tangled her homesickness.

Her key might still fit, but would she?

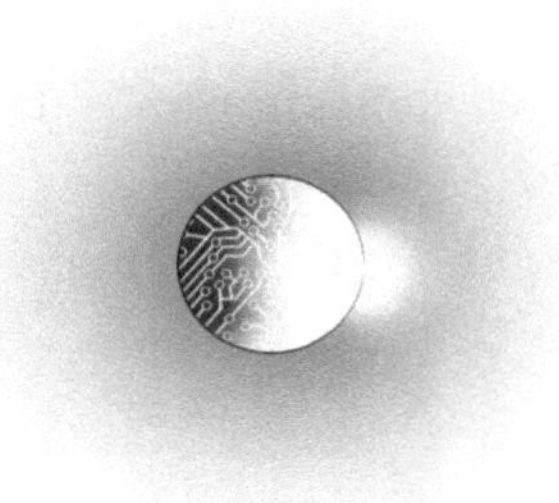

THREE

Stiffness woke Nel. She rolled her neck with a groan. "I don't think I have the body for camping anymore," she muttered, peering against the sunlight bathing her face. Somewhere above, a hideously cheerful bird chirped, and she fumbled for her sleeping bag zipper.

There was no sleeping bag. Or tent. Sunlight was beaming from mirrors and lamps just overhead. The chirping continued and she glared at the holographic message displayed over her wrist.

REMINDER: Shuttle Departure for *Le Fe De Amor* in T-105 minutes

She peered at the glowing red letters for a moment before parsing that if she didn't hurry, she might miss saying goodbye.

"Fuck fuck fuck!" She scrambled to her feet and bolted to the nearest elevator shaft. Shoving through the doors, she jabbed at her communicator. No messages from Lin or Zach, or frankly anyone. Only one unread thread blinked in her inbox, and it was the four system reminders that she had apparently slept through. She swiped it clear and bounced on the balls of her feet, trying to blink exhaustion from her bleary eyes.

"C'mon," she muttered to the elevator as the floors rolled past. Weight draped over her as the capsule hurtled outward. Another two seconds and it hummed to a halt at the residential level. She broke into a jog. Whatever she and Lin had was complicated, made even more so by the layers of their increasingly complex world and Nel's own mercurial temper. *But I'll still miss her.* More than she'd like to admit.

Tense voices slowed Nel's steps as she rounded the last bend to Lin's room. Shrinking back against the wall, she peered around the corner. Dar lounged beside Lin's open door, feet crossed at the ankle. Despite the relaxed stance, a dark glare knotted his features. Lin blocked her doorway, arms crossed.

"I don't really care what you think," Lin snapped. "And I don't want to get into this at all, let alone here and now. Just because you've suddenly grown some emotions doesn't mean I have to put them above my own. You had your chance to see things my way years ago. You had another chance back on CE7."

"I'm not suddenly interested in 'seeing things your way,'" he spat, "I'm interested in my baby sister's safety! I'm concerned this rabbit hole, this obsession whatever it is, will get you killed. You were on track for a promotion—"

"You demoted me! I could have been Ndebele's intern—"

"I had my reasons. What kind of person follows someone across fucking space—" he hissed.

"Dar, language."

She never corrects my cussing. So why was she bothering with her brother's? Lin's voice was tired but tense with something else. *Fear?* Nel fought back the urge to rush from behind the corner and wedge herself between them. Except Dar didn't look like he was going to hurt her.

"Lin, please just think about it. Ayah and Ibu are worried too, you know."

Lin's hand slammed into the wall with a sickening thud. Tendons bunched in her throat, but Nel couldn't say if it was pain or fury. "Is that why I haven't heard from them in months? You're holding them over my head until I sharpen up and fly straight?"

Dar looked away and his gaze halted on Nel, tucked by the door. She opened her mouth to apologize, but his head shook almost imperceptibly.

"You know I haven't heard from them either. But they mentioned it before. And again, when Nel's transfer docs came over their screens this morning. Associating with her is going to get you killed." He shoved off the wall and made to reach for her shoulder but stopped a few inches shy. "Please, just consider it."

Nel jerked out of sight again. A second later he almost collided with her as he strode around the bend. His gaze pinned her, but he said nothing, boots stomping long after he disappeared up the hall.

She peeked at Lin's door again. It was shut, the corridor deserted. Dar clearly felt she threatened Lin somehow. *Why do I feel like he just entrusted a huge secret with me?* Drawing a deep breath, she stepped up to Lin's door, heart hammering. She pressed her brow to the door, palm spreading across the gleaming metal. *None of them want me here—fuck, I don't even want to be here.*

And every nasty comment her exes' bigoted parents spat at her now drifted in the space stations recycled air lightyears from home. Intellectually she knew it wasn't anything to do with sexuality—not if she was to believe Paul's anecdote about his relationship with IDH's hotshot Komodor Muda Udara Dar Nalawangsa.

She pressed the private intercom. "Lin?"

Silence.

"Sorry I'm late. Can I see you before you go?" Still nothing. "I saw Dar in the hall, looked kinda pissed. Do you—"

"Nel?"

She whirled to see Lin striding down the hall. Her gleaming electrosuit was perfectly fastened, long hair braided and tucked carefully away in preparation for the helmet of her space suit. The shadows under her warm eyes rocketed Dar's words to the forefront of Nel's thoughts. *"What kind of person follows someone across fucking space?"* She pulled a smile she didn't feel onto her face. "Hey, babe. Just looking for you."

"Me too. You weren't in your room."

Nel stared after her for a moment. They hadn't kissed since the gala. "Sentimental" was the last word Nel would use to describe herself, but the undercurrent of exclusion gave her new sympathy for all the exes she ghosted over the years. "You sleep okay?"

"Not really. Been up since 0500." Lin frowned at Nel's half-done suit. "You packed?"

"What?"

"Is your comm on? Did you get the messages?"

Nel glanced at her wrist. "Just a bunch of updates about your mission—"

"Our mission," Lin interrupted. Her expression might have been a smile, were it not for the hardness in her eyes. "As of 0200 today you've been transferred to the Field Task Force."

Excitement blasted through every one of Nel's more complicated emotions. "What? Thank you!" She wrapped Lin in a tight hug. When it was only reluctantly returned, however, she stepped back. "You pulled strings?"

"Not me. Harris, I guess. Said he wanted someone like you on his team."

Confusion dampened Nel's thrill. She barely knew the man. What about the woman who almost single-handedly destroyed their second home appealed to him? *Cut the shit, Bently, and be grateful.* "Any idea what I'll be doing?"

"I'm not sure. Maybe research? They'll need data on CE7, Los Cerros—"

"Yeah, I know the abbreviation." At Lin's closed expression Nel forced tenderness into her voice. "Sorry, just got a bit of mental whiplash. I'm happy to help any way I can." Tagging along behind a stranger was better than nothing, but it was far from ideal. *But I could try to find Mom. And Tabby. And Annie.* And everyone else who went dark. It could be just the radio silence, but the shadow behind Emilio's eyes at the gala and Lin's extra avoidance frayed Nel's tenuous trust.

Both their wrists flashed. "You better get ready," Lin suggested. At long last, something close to amusement graced her regal features.

Nel backed toward her own room down the hall. "Don't let them leave without me, okay?"

No sooner had her door hissed shut behind her than she was yanking her case from under her bunk. "Christ, Bently, your only chance to fast-travel back home and you're about to miss it." Her bags were mostly packed—honestly, she hadn't really ever unpacked much more than a few items. She was triple-checking that both her father and Mikey's cremains were tucked safely into her bag when the final call flashed on her wall screen. She shoved her last things into her bag and did a final sweep before jogging to the nearest outward-bound elevator.

It took a span of seven minutes to cross to the designated departure bay. To Nel, it felt like hours and a single heartbeat. *Home.* After having the possibility ripped from her, she wasn't quite sure she believed she was actually going. Maybe she wouldn't believe it until her boots were on terra firma.

A dozen shuttles awaited, hundreds of crew members and mechanics swarming their undercarriages. Even with her limited experience, Nel could tell these were nothing IDH had created. She glimpsed styles that were surely inspired by Russian and U.S. space tech. Instead of the modular, efficient equipment *Odyssey* usually hosted, these bore clunky heat shields and battered landing gear.

Emilio jogged up, a loose button-down open over a bulky black electrosuit. "Morning, Bently. Well rested?"

Nel smiled, but her expression must have been too somber to warrant teasing. "What's the deal?"

"You'll be on my shuttle. We'll get you loaded up and head out, then you'll be checked into the med bay for cryo-prep. I'll be up front, but I can walk you over, if you'd like."

Nel frowned. "Cryo? You guys beamed out of that gate like fucking Solo. You telling me I still have to be locked in a tin can for this?"

He chuckled and led her to the third shuttle from the left. "Gate-passage is dangerous and takes far longer than it looks like from where you were."

Nel's hopes sank. "So what's the point?"

"I don't know about you," Emilio confided, "but I'd take a two-week flight over two years."

"Wait, I thought black-hole stuff looked like it took forever from the outside and was fast inside."

"I'm no ah, ingeniero aeroespacial? But I believe this is closer to a wormhole."

Nel groaned. "Can I opt-in to being awake? I'll wash your space dishes or whatever you want."

He strode up the loading ramp with an apologetic smile. "I'm sorry, we already have a busboy for the mess, but we'll find you some busy work once we land. I promise," he winked, "we'll be home before you know it."

A klaxon blared from somewhere in the shuttle's bowels and he swore. "Med bay is down that hall to the left. I'll see you when we're planetside."

Nel trailed off in the direction he indicated, counting her breaths in a failing attempt at maintaining control. *Fucking cryo.* Emilio may have been her one nebulous tether to Earth, but with the high-tech words rolling off his mouth as easily as his Chilean Spanish, that connection was fading fast.

Lin emerged from the large room that smelled of antiseptic and pulled her into a service alcove. "Hey."

"Hey," Nel responded, uncertain.

Lin pressed her brow to Nel's, eyes fluttering closed. Nel forced her eyes shut and gripped the other woman's hands. Steam hissed. Boots clomped on metal grates. A dozen different languages shouted instructions and warnings.

"You alright?" Nel whispered. She wished Lin would ask her the same but had no idea how she'd begin to answer.

"Yeah. Just nerves. It's been a strange few months. Years. I miss my family."

"Me too." Nel squashed the bitter voice chirping that she had a lot more change to contend with than Lin. It wasn't a competition. "We'll be okay, though. I'll try to be less of an asshole. And I'll help, promise." She tried a chuckle, but it fizzled between them. "I'll have the home court advantage."

"Home court?"

"I swear you have the strangest gaps in your understanding of Earth lingo. It's a sporting reference. Familiar ground gives us an advantage…" She trailed off. "Never mind."

Somewhere outside engines screamed to life.

"Am I going to see you again before we get put out?"

Lin shrugged. "I don't think so, but I put in a request for our pods to be next to each other."

Nel laughed and squeezed her hand. "Well, have a good trip. Miss you."

"You too. And you'll wake up before you ever miss me." Lin dropped a kiss on Nel's lips before backing away into the med bay with a last little wave.

Nel tilted her head back against the battered corridor wall. *It's just cryo. You did it before.* But she couldn't remember the moments beforehand. She barely recalled the days leading up to it, even now, months after waking. Had she been afraid? Cool-headed? She jerked herself upright. According to Mindi, from the moment Nel slid squalling and furious into the world, she had never been cool-headed.

"Dr. Bently?" A dark face peered through the doorway. "We're ready for you."

Nel tried a friendly smile, but by the pity on the tech's face, she figured she looked closer to constipated. "That makes one of us."

Heavy hooks and anchor rings lining the bay told Nel it had once been used for cargo. *Or at least, I hope that's what those are for.* Cellulose curtains cordoned off each cubicle, though most hung open and vacant by now.

The tech stepped into one, pulling the curtain closed once Nel followed. "It's simple, and we give sedatives. Just a few questions and scans first."

Nel hopped up on the table, recognizing Jem. "Oh, hey again. Do you need me to strip?"

"In a moment. For now, you're fine." Their eyes crinkled. "Nice job playing it cool in the committee there."

Nel winced, face heating. "Playing it cool is something I've never been good at."

"Well, some of us space folk don't mind when the officers get hardballed. When was the last time you were on Earth?"

"Ah, a couple months ago? You were there when I came out, actually."

The tech glanced up and smiled. "I was, but this is as much about what you recall as facts."

"Well, very little. I lost the whole week before cryo, except for flashes."

"That's probably the sedative. I can lower it this round." They made a note on the holochart and turned a dial on the bank of fluids hanging from the wall. "Any chance you're pregnant?"

Nel snorted. "I'm a lesbian."

They held her gaze. "That tells me about your preference, not your genitals, or those of your partner."

"Right. Um, no chance, no." Nel shuddered. She liked her friends' kids well enough, she supposed, but the idea of tethering her life to another person was uncomfortable enough when they were both independent adults. She had little interest in making or caring for a pink raisin of her own.

"Good. Any underlying conditions? Chronic illness? Tachycardia? Anxiety?"

Zach's analysis of her mental state flickered in her mind, but she shook her head. "Not that I know of. This more dangerous if I did?"

"Depends, but it's always good to know the whole picture. Cryo lowers your body's systems, and if some of yours work differently we need to adjust levels."

"What happens if you die in cryo?" The question was out before Nel realized she didn't really want an answer.

Jem glanced up from their examination of Nel's forearm. They paused, meeting her eyes. "I'm told it's like going in your sleep."

"I see." Silence hung between them while Jem returned to their notes.

After another moment they looked up. "Alright, ready to get wired up?"

Nel tugged off her suit, folding it carefully on the exam table before turning back and raising her chin. She blanched at the cold cleansing alcohol and the pinch of the needle. A moment later the injection burned. She didn't dare look down at the gentle tugging of Jem inserting the mainline through her carotid. *It's fine. Just needles. Just cryo.*

"Dr. Bently?" Jem asked.

Nel hummed.

"Can you look at me, please?"

Nel's gaze flicked down to the tech's. "What?"

"I need you to take a few long, slow breaths. In through the nose—"

"Out through the mouth, yeah, I know this one." She was too distracted to regret the snapping tone. She obeyed, however, fixing her attention on the rings of the cubicle curtain. The edges of her vision darkened. "Aren't I supposed to be in the tin can before I go under?"

"I've just given you some sedatives. Why? Dizzy?"

"Just vision's tunneled a bit." She licked her lips, mouth tasting of metal and sawdust. "Bit woozy. Feel like I'm having a heart attack."

"I see. That's pretty normal when you're nervous. Keep breathing, I'm almost done. Let me know if you think you're going to pass out or vomit."

She forced her hands to unclench from the exam table's covering. "Just been a wild few weeks."

"You can say that again," Jem muttered. A few careful movements later and they were withdrawing the needles, leaving the mainline taped and coiled. "Alright, let's get you bundled in."

Nel slipped her suit back on, letting Jem attach the port to its twin above her left breast. When she stood her knees trembled, but her legs held. Each of the smaller rooms lining the outer edge of the medical bay held twenty cryo pods and Jem led Nel to the nearest one.

Sure enough, Lin was already in repose, eyes fluttering with relaxation. Her lidded gaze caught Nel's and her fingers fluttered in a wave. "Sweet dreams, love."

Nel offered a numb smile and climbed shakily into the neighboring pod. *Fuck all of this. Next time I'm pacing the ship's length for two years instead of this nonsense.* Jem's deft fingers had already hooked Nel up and were fiddling with dials and buttons.

Nel glanced up. "Shouldn't I be feeling something? Sleepy?"

Jem shrugged. "Hits each of us a little different. Your adrenaline is fighting it, though. Can you think of ways to relax? Any history of anxiety?"

"Nah. Usually pretty chill under stress. I can try the breathing thing." She forced her eyes closed and thought of Chile.

Soft air whispered from the tiny holes lining the pod. Thick tepid fluid dribbled into the bottom, enveloping her in an utter lack of sensation. Her heart pounded faster. Beeping increased and her eyes fixed on the glowing readouts that, based on her limited understanding of human physiology, seemed too high for someone minutes from chemically forced unconsciousness.

"Dr. Bently—"

Beeping. Static screaming turned up to eleven. The suit's warning trill, moments before Paul ripped his helmet off.

Get your shit together, Bently!

"Nel!" Jem's voice left no room for argument, but Nel's rampaging fear barreled onward, the tech's voice fading in the face of flashbacks. Their voice rose. "I need a doctor at unit 34."

Thirty-four. How old was she, again? By Earth standards? Weight pressed on her chest, squeezing the will to struggle from her muscles. Still, her breath heaved and her stomach threatened to vomit up the breakfast she hadn't eaten. Would she forever be keeping track of her perceived age in parallel with how many years she'd technically lived? How wide would that gap be when she eventually died? *What happens if you die in cryo?*

"Does she have an assigned psych?" The new voice was low and deep.

"Yeah, but he's about to go under too, unit 75. And audio-comms are locked for safety. We launch in T-10."

"Pull up her chart."

"Doctor, that's against—"

"Excuse me, Doctor."

Nel's blurred vision settled on a new smooth, long face. "Hars," she slurred.

"Yeah, it's Harris. Nel, I'd like you to just focus on me. You're having a panic response. The human system can only panic for twenty minutes. Just ride it for another five, alright? It might feel like you're dying, but you're perfectly safe. Your body is just being an overachiever. Based on what I've heard that's pretty on-brand for you." His face curved in a smile. "You've got your girl right over there too— just picture your hands clasped. She'll anchor you here."

Blaring alarms made her eyes fly open, but his face still hovered in the shadows over hers. "Just preparing for launch. By the time we take off, you'll be asleep. It'll be summer in the northern hemisphere when we arrive. Can you remember summer at home for me?"

"Cicada," Nel rasped. Her eyes felt heavy now too, and her lungs slowed, exhausted. "Fucking bugs everywhere. Sunburn. Dirt. Beer."

"I can smell it already," he murmured. "I've always been an IPA man."

"From Earth?"

His smile warped, swam. "Indeed. Just another minute more and you'll be in dreamland."

Darkness encroached, but this time it was a soft descent into twilight. Rushing air was replaced by the slow billow of her own breath. "Dream in cryo?"

"You'll have to tell me when you wake up. They say it's impossible," he patted the glass and stepped back, "but I always have."

Darkness became the rich indigo of the forest at night. Soft soil cradled her bare feet as she padded to the edge of the meandering river. It was the Connecticut, or maybe the Susquehanna. A canoe ghosted by, a single hulking silhouette in its hull. Water burbled along its fiberglass sides. The man leaned against the oar, pushing his craft upriver in the darkness. Nel edged to the crest of the embankment. Rocks skittered down the slope in her wake, plinking into the brown bathwater warmth.

His shoulders bunched as he heaved against the current. The wooden paddle groaned with the effort. He did not turn, but she knew those arms, those battered hands. She knew the hang of his short, fuzzy locs.

"Mikey?"

Her heart hammered and somewhere in the rearmost corner of her skull, wailing rose. Sharp rocks exposed in the eroding bank bit into the meat of her palm. She ignored the sting and stumbled into the churning water. "Mikey!"

It was only at the river's bend that he turned back. His face was shadowed, but she saw shattered cheekbones and torn flesh where a crowbar had cracked features better suited to smiles than screaming. His full lips parted, and river water tumbled from his putrefied mouth.

FOUR

Decay coated Nel's tongue. She grimaced and probed her teeth. Hopefully whoever was warming her back wouldn't judge her for the worst morning breath in human history. Air eased from her chest in a groan as she stretched. Her arms hit hard, smooth warmth. Her eyes flew open, blinking against the dim orange lights flickering over the glassy surface inches from her face.

Muffled chiming drifted through and bubbles rose around her skin. Fluid drained and the scent of clean air replaced its warmth. Above, familiar features swam into focus. Lin's face broke into a beaming smile. A beige palm pressed to the glass.

Nel choked back a sob that dreamed of laughter and lifted her hand to push it against Lin's. "Morning," she rasped.

Lin's words were faint, but Nel caught enough. "How'd you sleep?"

Her nose wrinkled. It was odd to pretend something so alien, so unnatural, was akin to being tucked in by a parent, but Nel supposed it was what kept most cryo-hoppers sane. "I think I had weird dreams. Don't remember them, though. Can I get out?"

"Almost. One more step."

Figures milled about behind the woman, and air rushed in. Nel winced as her ears popped. Her memories were blurry, but images filtered back in. A funeral. Dar's glare. Buzzing insects—or was that her dream? The lid bounced up as it unlocked, then rose slowly. She sat up, half expecting dry ice vapor to billow out, a theater geek's imagining of a lesbian space Dracula. Laughter bubbled from her throat, followed by burning bile as she vomited.

Lin's soft hand wiped her mouth. Portable, opaque screens provided privacy. Nel perched on the edge of her cryo bed, wishing her deep breaths drew in more than the bright stench of emesis or the dry, powered scent of medical equipment.

Jem handed her a foil blanket, then held up a small syringe with an apologetic smile. "Helps with the sick."

Nel shuddered as cool fluid spurted into her vein. "How about you? Sleep okay?"

Lin smiled. "Good. Always feel refreshed afterward. Looking forward to a proper shower, though."

Nel groaned. "Me too, now."

"I'll get your suit if you want to clean up."

"Please." She fumbled with the damp cloth Jem folded over the pod's side, grateful her nerves hadn't allowed her to eat before going under. *Maybe our stomachs are always empty when we wake.* Did people digest in cryo?

"Here, babe."

Nel took the suit from Lin with a wan smile. A memory nagged at her, another pet name as Lin went under. She shifted with discomfort. *Babe's preferable.* The suit was looser, barely. "We gonna wear these down there too?"

Lin shook her head. "Depends. Just another few hours and you'll be back to your tank tops and cargos."

Nel's fingers stilled at the throat of her suit. Hours. The reality of where she was exploded what remained of her groggy state. "Windows. Now."

Lin's deceptively thin arms levered Nel up. It was then she realized gravity no longer existed. Rather, everything drifted, in stasis until its course was altered. She finished fastening her suit and nudged off of the cryo pod after Lin.

"Can't you hear it? Screaming!" A naked man flailed into them, babbling in a half-woken panic.

Nel's pulse spiked, but Lin squeezed her hand. "Just woke up on the wrong side of the pod."

Nel averted her eyes, backing up until the medics retrieved him. *He said screaming.* She shuddered and followed Lin through a doorway. Neither spoke as they wound through the milling techs and doctors. A far more organized throng of officers and engineers filled the ship's main bay. Lin's fingers laced with Nel's to keep them from losing one another as she propelled them along the edge of the room.

"Oi! Sci-nerds!"

Lin paused halfway up the obsolete stairs at the voice booming from the gangway above.

"Back to the med bay. You've seen the vids of zero-G yak. Don't need cryo sick gumming up my ship."

Nel's face flushed and her mouth opened to snap back, but a tan hand pressed on the officer's shoulder. Emilio shot her a wink and muttered something in the man's ear.

The officer's jaw worked but his sneer parted enough for his amendment. "Make it quick, eh?"

"Yessir." Lin glided the rest of the way up to the next level. Two turns and a narrow, grease-stained passageway later, they drifted into what Nel assumed was a tiny emergency pod. The view pitched Nel's balance to the left and up and she threw a hand out to steady herself. Her teeth clenched. She'd be damned if she proved Officer Barked Order's concerns right.

"Man, gravity is underrated."

Lin laughed, sliding the door closed behind them. It muffled all but the loudest machinery.

Nel slipped closer to the window. She spread her fingers on the window, peering up at the swath of tan and marbled white that was Saudi Arabia. Except there were no borders. Just a smattering of earth grounding nine billion feet as they all rocketed through the void. Perhaps it was a delayed reaction to waking, but tears sprang to her eyes. "What day is it?"

"Early August, I think. We'll touch down at Bakjeeri spaceport at 3:45 p.m. local time. I'm told it's a nice day."

Hopefully tears didn't damage spaceships. *Home.* She could live a thousand cryo-lengthened years and never grow sick of seeing the precious marble. She could live a thousand more and never want to leave again. Somewhere down there was her mother. Her friends. Everyone she had ever known for the first thirty-odd years of her life. *I'm coming,* she vowed. *I'll fix this, somehow.*

A heavy clunk shook the ship and a distant alarm began.

"We ought to get back."

"Yeah, thanks for humoring me," Nel agreed, backing up, but unable to look away just yet. Lin's thumb brushed moisture from Nel's cheek. "Bit woozy is all. Delayed reaction to waking up, I think."

"I get it." At Nel's skeptical glance, Lin clarified. "I have a home too, you know."

"Right." *But you were raised knowing there were thousands of you scattered across the sky. Knowing there was a contingency if it all went belly-up.* Nel shot a final look over her shoulder at the brilliant blue ball. She wouldn't let her home be amputated in some galactic fight for a healthy humanity. Or whatever IDH claimed this was.

"Nalawangsa, Bently!" Harris floated in the mouth of a service corridor. A gleaming officer's robe drifted over his meticulous suit. "Get settled. Docking is in T-15 minutes!"

"Sorry, sir!" Lin called.

"I knew he was an officer," Nel muttered, aloud this time, as Lin towed her into the passenger area. "So, how long until we can wander around? I have no memory of being on the ISS from before."

Lin blushed. "I doubt we'll be able to wander much. We have nine hours here. Usually they try to give us at least twenty-four to recover from cryo sick, if we need to. Weather and timing made them cut it short though. Going from the stasis of cryo to the G-force of reentry can really—"

"I don't need the details, thanks though," Nel interjected. As much as she enjoyed traveling to a dig or back home after a summer abroad, the added danger of space travel—even when conducted by people raised there—just pissed off her empty stomach.

Lin looked down, apologetic as they waited for a train of cargo bins to drift by, propelled by a tech with propulsion boots. "Sorry, I find research and knowing all the facts helps me when I'm nervous."

"Me, not so much. At least with this stuff. Maybe you can distract me in other ways," Nel amended, running her finger up the inside of Lin's forearm.

The other woman jumped but smiled. "These things are ticklish, you know, when paired."

"Oh, I hoped so."

Lin grabbed her hand and pushed off, turning back toward the med bay. At some point during their flight it had been converted into bunks. The flimsy 3D printed walls were more a suggestion of privacy but were better than nothing. A flashing sign on the wall cycled through various bulletins, including the time until the shuttle for Earth launched and the location of the space station's medical wing, which would replace the makeshift one used prior to launch.

"Shouldn't we be suited up or something?" Nel asked. "In case something goes wrong?"

"I thought you didn't want to know the details," Lin teased.

"Well, I guess just the most important ones."

"No, this is a sealed compartment. All the airlock doors are closed for docking. If a hatch blows, the liner melts and seals us in this self-contained life support—" Lin stopped herself. "No, we're alright here. We're just not supposed to be drifting about." She paused outside one of the cubicles. "This is me. You've your own."

As friendly as Lin had been over the last few hours—*okay, few weeks, technically*—slippery anxiety still dampened the intimacy they had found on Samsara. She hesitated, then all her exes rolled over in their metaphorical graves at her next words: "Do you think we could talk?"

Lin's smile may have been small, but its warmth was genuine. "I wouldn't mind company while everything gets settled."

When the door had shut behind them, Nel made to sit in the folding chair clipped to the floor before realizing there was really no point in sitting anywhere without gravity.

"Hey, I don't bite." Lin gestured to the space beside where she hovered just above the cot.

Nel moved closer, heart pounding. "I want to apologize. For the briefing. For not keeping my mouth shut."

"You already did."

"I know, but still. Dr. Ndebele is your mentor, right?"

"She is. She headed my mission in Chile when you and I first met."

"Right. Well, I don't want to start burning bridges you still need to cross, you know? But I'm a lot better at burning bridges than I am at repairing them. Working on it. And my temper."

Lin's expression softened. "I get why you're angry. I've spent a lot of my life angry too—mostly at Dar's aloofness and how close he and my mom are. The Samsari connection was much stronger with them."

"Wasn't that by design?"

"Yeah, but when you're a kid it feels more like favoritism." She shrugged. "I know IDH screwed up a lot, especially with you. I know you don't trust them—and to be clear, I don't either. But I trust this mission and the officers leading it. I trust their goals and their concern. And I also know that we'll get a lot further with them if we don't piss off every commanding officer within the first few days."

"Bit late on that one for me, I'm afraid," Nel muttered with a dark laugh.

"It's not—the fact that you woke up in a cryo pod orbiting Earth today instead of on *Odyssey* is proof they're giving you another chance. Or, at least, Harris is."

Nel nodded. "Not sure what he sees. I'm starting to worry the reason IDH chose me was as much to do with the reputation of my shitty temper as my curriculum vitae. Hot temperaments make fantastic scapegoats."

Lin shrugged. "Just give them a chance, okay? I really want this to work—not just IDH, but us too, you know?"

Fear zinged through Nel's body. She wanted this to work too. Badly. More than she could admit. But she wasn't used to having something other than her fear of commitment standing in the way of happily for now. In an attempt to calm her nerves, she flipped open her tablet and pulled up the mission details.

"Hey," Lin's soft voice cut through her frown, "what're you looking for?"

She sighed. "There's a lot to catch up on. Feel like this hasty alliance is gonna crumble the minute we set foot on Earth."

"I think you're not giving any of us enough credit."

Nel grimaced. "I dunno, I just keep remembering you and Bas's firefight across my fucking site."

Lin's mouth thinned. "So much for you working on trust."

Nel's gut got cold. "I do trust you. It's not about you. Just how nervous all of this makes me feel."

"All of this meaning IDH? Space?"

Nel chuckled. "Honestly? The feelings I have for you are scarier." She fiddled with the sheets.

"What's so scary?" Lin asked, hand brushing over Nel's fingers. "You're fiddling."

"Trying to keep myself from running out the airlock." Her eyes were fixed on the dim lamp overhead, picking out every imperfection in the 3D printed ceiling.

"It's that bad that death-by-vacuum is better?"

The memory of Lin, naked, in the hull of the *Thunder-bump* seconds away from rescuing Nel from death by massive space gate flashed through her mind. "No, more like it's the realest thing ever and you're this colossus of grace and I'm over here not knowing what to do with my hands."

"That's good, though."

Nel sighed. This was the longest she had stayed after a hookup. Sure, physically she stayed, but she never mentally stayed. She dared not relax, but she could unclench her death grip on the bedding, maybe. So far nothing had exploded. "Why, you like me scared? That your kink?"

"No, more like if you're scared, then you're breaking new ground in here." She tapped Nel's chest with one long finger.

She tucked her head against Lin's shoulder, feeling the adrenaline of waking transform into exhaustion. It had been a long time since Nel broke new ground without a trowel and shovel and work boots. *Maybe the first time ever.*

Soft blooming light woke Nel. Her whole body ached from sleeping on the cot and her left arm was numb from the pressure of Lin's head on her bicep. The weight of her every molecule seemed to press down, down. *Guess we're docked now.* Wincing, she extracted her arm, replacing it with the thin pillow they had discarded earlier. She rolled her wrist, listening to the bones pop. The sound was visceral against the mechanical aural backdrop. Whatever number cubical she had been assigned was a mystery, and she wasn't about to try to discover its whereabouts in the middle of the night. *What time is it, even?*

She tapped her comm, hiding the bloom of cold light as it awakened, casting 0417 across the floor. The light reminded her why she woke in the first place. A tiny icon popped up in the corner.

SENDER: Picklestein's Monster
SUBJECT: safe keeping

Adrenaline splashed her tired brain. A glance at the closed bathroom door told her she was alone enough to read it. The name was obviously an alias, and equally obvious was the fact that it was Phil's.

There was no message, only a single, massive attachment: polyana.thk

Nel didn't know what a "thank" file type was, but it seemed like Phil neither needed nor expected her to. Frankly, she was more concerned with the fact that a massive supercomputer needed to send her something for "safe keeping." Phil controlled every system on the space station without a second's thought. So what was he afraid of?

Further speculation would require caffeine and a notebook. She flicked the display away and donned her suit in the dark. It was too late to bother going back to bed, with the reentry that morning, and too early to risk waking Lin. Nel's brain was loud enough without the emotional chatter the other woman's presence caused.

She slipped into the makeshift corridor, padding barefoot through the ship. Whirring engines. Whispering air. Cycling systems. She wondered briefly whether a senti-comp piloted *Le Fe De Amor*. The ship seemed to breathe. Not in the way *Odyssey* did, massive mechanical lungs in place of Phil's meat and bone. *Does he think of them that way?*

She turned a corner and was met with a clear acrylic door. Within, bright, warm lights cast a sun-like glow over hundreds of planted tanks. She nudged the door, half expecting it to deny her access. Instead, it slid open and she stepped inside. Fish meal and the bite of running water greeted her nose. She bent over, peering into the tanks. Through the cloudy depths a tan face appeared, distorted by acrylic and water.

Nel shrieked, stumbling backward into another bank of tanks, sending water sloshing. Anger flashed in the wake of fear. "What the fuck!"

Emilio raised his empty hands as he straightened, a faint frown flitting across his features. "Bently. Just me."

"You scared the shit out of me! Your face in the tank, I thought—" she cut herself off. What had she thought? That someone had left Emilio's body bobbing in the ship's hydroponic system? *Get a grip.*

"It's alright, I was down here fiddling with one of the filter valves. I didn't mean to startle you." His face eased into a cautious smile, though whether he was afraid of her or that he might upset her further, she didn't know. "Ships get, ah, fantasimal?"

"Spooky."

"Spooky at night."

"Yeah. Whole new set of sounds too. From the station. I was just trying to figure out if this thing had a computer like *Odyssey*'s."

"Ah." He looked back down at the hoses in his hands. "It doesn't."

"I didn't think so. It doesn't feel—"

"Alive?"

She grinned. "Aware. So you know about the senti-comps?"

"Oh, that old puzzle." He shook his head. "I know enough to be certain my hang-ups with IDH's ethics are fully justified. I mean, really now: heads in jars?" He squinted at her. "You knew that bit, yes?"

"Yeah."

"And where does Dr. Bently sit on the matter?"

"Iffy would be an understatement. But not like, at them. I mean, they're already here so we can't debate whether we should have done it in the first place. I can't decide if I pity or fear them."

"Pity?"

She shrugged. "That existence. I like Phil, actually, as a person. It's just a bizarre idea. How do you get from AI to sentient pickle?" She shuddered, head tilted to see the naked underside of a plant. "So, explain this to me?"

"I assume you don't mean the hydroponics." His eyes lighted on her, steady, stern.

She glanced up, then straightened. "I mean, that's cool and all. But no. I mean the ship. The fleet. Showing up out of literally nothing while the planet imploded. I can barely wrap my head around the fact that it took a moment but for you it was weeks." She shook her head. "I never had the brain for physics."

He chuckled, brown fingers cupping a delicate leaf. "If you were one of Los Pobladores, then you would know the whole story. We didn't forget, you know, when the Teachers arrived and promised everything, when they took our people from us in the name of altruism. Those stories lasted longest of any of ours."

"How did I study you for years and never hear about it?"

"Because you found what we wanted you to find. That's very colonial of you, by the way, to think you could possibly know our deepest history, our most sorrowful secrets after studying a handful of years where you were most likely equally, if not more, intrigued by the backside of the student in front of you."

"Nah, it was my teacher's, actually," she joked, but her voice grew quiet. It was easy to think she was a hotshot when an intergalactic organization asked her to run their space dig, but she'd be fooling herself if she thought it wasn't just cosmic nepotism. "You're right."

"I know." His tone held little judgement. "We knew our cousins would return, knew when they did, they would be as if gods. And if they held the violence of their teachers, then we wouldn't stand a chance." He peered into one of the tanks of plain fish. "So we advanced too. It's easy to focus on IDH. They're sparkly, flashy, filled with hubris and gleaming determination. But just as they have fingers in every organization from NASA to the former Soviet government, so do we."

Nel's brows rose. "So the vandalism on Los Cerros Esperando VII—"

"Was stamped in three nations and sanctioned by a member of the UN."

The laugh that barked from her mouth held more incredulity than mirth. "Holy shit, man."

His dark eyes narrowed. "You seem surprised. More than when you learned about IDH?"

She looked away. "I would have pretended to believe anything Lin said for a night. You know that. By the time I could critically evaluate the mess, I was racing the feds through New England wilderness with a reticle on my back. Didn't really have time to question whether it was the most plausible action-movie plot I'd ever heard."

"And now?"

"I think you could rip your head from your neck and show me you're actually an alien named Blergh and I'd hardly bat an eye." Nel returned to the issue at hand. "I'm more surprised that IDH didn't know."

"Oh, they did, here and there. They'd catch us, just as we would them. A space race between paleolithic astronauts and those they left behind." He grinned, nudging her with his round shoulder. "C'mon, even you'd watch that blockbuster."

"Maybe," she teased. She moved down the line of plants, examining the delicate roots reaching for moisture. "So tell me how you got here."

"We'd been building a station for years, completed a few months after you left for Samsara. My contract was bought out from IDH by the Founders—their Egyptian branch, actually— around that time and I was transferred here."

"Fuck, man." Nel shook her head. "And they've got you fixing goldfish tanks?"

"They're catfish. I helped grow half the food at my restaurant back home, you know. So now I help out with the food production here. It's what I did before I was a liaison. We knew open contact with IDH was only a matter of time."

"Everything seems to be going smoothly," Nel observed.

"I suppose." His mouth quirked. "I prefer the fish."

"I would too." She watched the sleek brown bodies glide for a few more moments. "I should get my things in order for the landing. Reentry. Whatever you people call it."

"Homecoming?" Emilio suggested. When their eyes met again his smile was gentle and as sad as she imagined hers to be.

"I suppose," she echoed. Raising a hand, she slipped back out of the room. Flight crew and those who were, judging by the grease on their faces, mechanically inclined, were beginning to stir. Nel floated along the hall, now understanding the ridged design of most spaceships. *You need something to propel from in zero-G.* Lin was awake by the time Nel returned to the tiny cubby where they'd spent the night.

Her face brightened when Nel poked her head inside. "Was wondering where you got off to."

"Just insomnia. Had to snoop around in the dark like usual." She grinned. "Be happy I came back, usually when I take off in the dead of the night, I don't even leave my number."

Lin scoffed and nudged Nel's elbow with hers as she fiddled with her electrosuit. "I guess I'm special then."

Nerves shot a chemical command to run up the small of Nel's back. She fished her bag from under Lin's cot with a tired laugh. "Guess so."

A knock pounded on the door. "Oi! Letnan, we're strapping in. Bently with you?"

"Yeah."

"No!" Lin answered simultaneously.

Whoever was knocking paused, probably to stifle a laugh. "Whatever, both of you need to be ready in five!"

An alarm blared and Nel's shaking hands dropped her bag. "Fuck!"

"Just the minute warning. Better get moving." Lin dropped a kiss onto Nel's mouth. "You alright?"

Nel barely heard her through the buzzing in her ears. The alarm weaseled through her head, almost drowning the echo of screaming. *"Get it out!"*

"Nel? Nel!"

She blinked and looked up into Lin's concerned face. "Sorry. Hey."

"You alright?"

"Just the alarms. Makes me jumpy." She drew a breath. "What'd you say?"

"I asked if you were okay. I'd like to talk about last night. Your feelings. Breaking new ground. Once you have time to adjust and we're back on Earth."

"Yeah, for sure," Nel lied. She flashed a smile and hastily did up the throat of her suit. "See you in the shuttle!" She was out of the door before Lin could pry any more.

The raw emotions nagging at her for the past week were gone. Sated perhaps with their arrival or maybe just muffled by adrenaline. One thing was for sure: landing brought far bigger concerns than having The Talk with Lin.

She jogged down the corridor, raising an apologetic hand at the tech who tossed her a full space suit with annoyed impatience. Thankfully, he had the sense to remind Nel how to fasten the ports properly.

Once her suit was on and locked, she clomped into line with the rest of the passengers. She caught a glimpse of Zach's towering silhouette. Virtually everyone from Samsara was clustered in the corridor, weaving from the space station to the waiting shuttle. She found herself counting breaths, counting steps, picking out every hose and wire trailing along the rounded halls. The suit's insulation turned her heartbeat to thunder in her ears. *Man, if someone wanted to blow us up and cover their tracks, this would be a great opportunity.* She hated that the thought popped into her head, but it was there now, and there was nothing she could do about it.

The view from a small porthole to the left brought a distracted smile to her face. The shuttle was docked at a right angle to the rest of the massive ship, which was in turn docked onto a space station. Nel's thoughts were too disorganized to recall whether it was one of Los Pobladores, and her memories of the ISS were too fuzzy for her to be able to recognize it.

Nel tilted her head, peering at the waiting shuttle's lines. "That could be from the planetarium."

"Don't fix what's not broken," a tech remarked.

"Oh for goodness sake, even our cloud-jumpers have reusable heat shields. This is...is just a controlled bonfire plummeting into the sea." Lin's voice was pitched high with nerves.

Nel slowed her pace and reached a hand out. "Well, considering, we have a pretty good track record."

"Yeah, Nalawangsa." The tech winked at her. "Let's see you fly a controlled bonfire without killing anyone."

"I'd rather not fly at all, thank you very much."

For a moment, curiosity distracted Nel enough to ignore the deceptively thin joints of the docking mechanism as they crossed from ship to shuttle. "You're afraid of flying?"

Lin's lips pursed in discomfort. "I just find the cavalier attitudes of most pilots disconcerting in the best scenarios and disastrous in the worst."

Recalling Bavin's boisterous nature, Nel grinned. "Yeah, I'd agree with you there. I love flying, but this is a bit different now." *Now that technology and audio can kill us in seconds.* Voicing that to the rest of the passengers wasn't fair, so she bit the words back.

Nel tugged Lin onto the gangway, blocky, padded hands bumping into one another more than interlinked fingers. Banks of seats filled the shuttle's narrow belly. "So where are we landing again? Canaveral?"

"Spaceport Bakjeeri."

"Right." Nel frowned, then shook her head. "So spaceports are a thing now?"

"Two are—this one's just best timed for weather and orbit." Lights danced over the smooth surface of her space helm, like a halo of manufactured stars. Nel suppressed the urge to tap their glass domes together in a helmed good luck kiss. "Once we land I guess we'll have a briefing on the situation."

The craft lurched and Nel gripped the arm of the chair. Lin chuckled, then tapped the helmet. "No sound once we uncouple. I'll miss you."

HOLMES

Nel fingered the lock of the suit around her neck. In the space of every blink her vision flickered with Paul's blood splattered over her face. Glass or no, she swore she could feel the heat of it. She squeezed her eyes shut, grasping for some prettier mental image. Someplace safe. Maybe the hot flash was just nerves and not some violent echo.

When she opened her eyes again the window was filled with the hazy blue-black rind surrounding Earth. It was horrifyingly fragile. *Climate change is a small wonder.* They twisted in the air then, though she could only tell by the view spinning outside. Now they were belly down, she supposed. Then the roaring started.

Rumbling shook the seat beneath her, as much a sensation as a sound. Muffled howling took over, searing flames spouting along the windows as the heat shields did their job. Weight pressed on her chest, pushing her back. If she could have lifted her hand, she would have linked fingers with Lin. The other woman's eyes were closed, lips thin and tight in fear.

Atmosphere burned away their shields, enveloping them with vicious welcome. Juddering continued, increasing. If alarms sounded, Nel didn't know. Then the fire was gone and the window cleared. Nel's heart faltered. Home. G-force dampened her cheeks and her heart thundered with relief. For the first time since arriving on *Odyssey*, her mind was quiet. Outside the air was hers, the ground was the same she had first crawled on, first shoved into her mouth with a baby-fat fist, the soil she dug her first trowel into. The soil that held Mikey's remains, her father's remains. *Most of them.*

Another minute of shuddering and the shuttle leveled. Below, clouds cleared and the brilliant green of the Sanjay Gandhi jungle appeared. Nel could not tear her eyes away. Even from the height of however many thousand feet, the Himalayas were massive. Everything else might have been softened by the sheer scale, but not the crags. *To think, I crossed star systems before I ended up in India.*

With the lessened pressure, she turned to look at Lin. The woman was peering out the window too, but her dark eyes flicked to Nel's. Her smile was small in her nerve-pale face, but genuine. Though Nel couldn't hear her, she recognized the words the woman mouthed: "Welcome home."

Nel spent her adolescence running. Running from home, running from bigotry, running from anything that tried to pin her down. University, from undergrad to doctorate, was one big race to being the best, the most interesting, the most qualified. Now, she realized, all she was racing toward was home. Mindi. Whatever was left of her battered life. A holographic sign flickered onto the bare white surface separating them from the cockpit:

WE HAVE SUCCESSFULLY ENTERED TERRESTRIAL ATMOSPHERE. OUR CURRENT ALTITUDE IS 19 KM. WE WILL BE LANDING AT SPACEPORT BAKJEERI IN ABOUT THIRTY MINUTES. LOCAL TIME IS 1837.

Nel's tears began in earnest. In thirty minutes she would be on proper soil. She didn't care for IDH or the Founders, frankly, but tomorrow she would commit everything she had to helping them protect this blue rock. Tomorrow, tomorrow, tomorrow.

Lin's hand rested on hers. Maybe, if it weren't for leaving, for Lin, for meeting Phil, she would never have known how much there was to love about Earth. *Or all the precious, insignificant assholes down here.*

FOR THOSE OF US TRAVELING *FROM LE FE DE AMOR* AND *ODYSSEY OF EARTH*, WELCOME, WE HOPE YOU ENJOY YOUR STAY. FOR THOSE OF US FROM EARTH: WELCOME HOME.

FIVE

The shuttle alighted with a screech on a swath of bright black tarmac. Heat haze thickened the air, and the plump peach of the sun hung above the western horizon. Bundled in her suit with several layers of aluminum and insulation separating her from proper air, Nel still swore her blood sang with familiarity. The shuttle taxied to a halt at a causeway. Her heart pinched, wishing for once to climb down onto the runway. *Gotta take advantage of the rare occasion when kissing the ground is justified.*

Despite the sprawling modern building, theirs was the only aircraft in sight. Weeds sprouted through cracks in the otherwise pristine pavement. The arching bridge to the mainland, visible beyond the tangle of jungle, was deserted. Lin caught Nel's hand as it rose to unfasten the helm. "Decon first!" Her shout was muffled by the glass and she jerked her head toward the shuttle door. "C'mon!"

Nel dropped her hands. Outside the shuttle door, two glowing signs directed those native to Earth to the left and the rest to the right for what was, Nel assumed, additional screening. Gleaming steel and crystalline acrylic cubicles greeted them. Nel fought her impatience with increasing difficulty. *Can't I just run screaming outside and French kiss a continent I've never been on like the weird-ass white chick I am?*

A figure in a clean suit directed her to the nearest empty cubicle. Sterilizing chemicals hissed out, bombarding her atmosuit. The next room provided racks to deposit suits. After a moment's entanglement with her wires, she extracted herself and exited. Nel stepped aside, watching as someone pressed a compact object against Lin's upper arm in another clear room. Based on her wince, it contained a needle.

Immunizations?

"Ma'am, your arm," Clean Suit requested, brandishing an injector of his own.

Nel glowered at him, but extended her arm. "Couldn't we just have this done while in cryo?"

"With an immune response in stasis and your body already flooded with a dozen chemicals?"

"Good point." The device clicked and a deep burn spread through her deltoid. "What is it?"

"Had a few outbreaks in the last couple years. IDH helped us develop the vaccines, but they aren't required unless you're making planetfall. Have a good visit." He turned to the next passenger, and

Nel was left with her own complicated feelings at not being immediately recognizable as an Earthling.

Rubbing her arm, she exited the decon rooms. Four continents, a dozen countries, and countless flights were under her belt. This was the largest Arrivals terminal she had ever seen. Eerie stillness gripped the typical warren of customs lines, moving walkways, and security points. It was then that she noticed the signs along each wall and the friendly stickers on the floor reminding travelers to maintain distance and wear surgical masks. New concerns weaseled between those about space invasions and homicidal audio. *Mom was always pretty healthy,* she promised herself.

Nel heaved a sigh and shouldered her personal bag. Conversation was muted in the early hours of the day, and Nel turned onto the concourse amid relative quiet. The group funneled along the bright hall and descended an escalator into the bowels of the building. Gleaming tile hadn't had enough traffic to even collect dust. Instead, the whole thing had a stale chemical odor, as if carpets still outgassed.

Below, she glimpsed the silver snake of a train, ribs cracked open to permit the few dozen interstellar travelers. Nel deposited her bag on the cargo cart and drifted to the crowd gathering on the platform for their briefing. She pulled up the mission itinerary on her comm, scanning the events with disinterest. The light rail would depart at midnight, apparently, leaving them yet again with an awkward amount of time to fill. Her gaze snagged on the date, blinking unassumingly at the top of her comm's projected screen. Three years ago she was in Chile with Mikey, full of certainty and fire and beautiful ignorance.

A moment later IDH staff swarmed through the door from their extended time in decon. The idea that this little ball of dirt posed more danger to them than a routine trip to *Odyssey* ever did for her brought a smile to her face. *We may be small, but we are fierce.*

Lin emerged, long strides keeping pace with Dr. Ndebele, much to Nel's horror. She fought the urge to duck behind the nearest support column. Lin listened to the mission operative's words with an almost feral concentration, nodding every few seconds. Nel could almost see the thoughts darting between neurons. The woman clapped Lin on the shoulder before disappearing onto the train. Lin stepped aside, making several notes on the open screen of her communicator before scanning the room. Her eyes alighted on Nel and she grinned before jogging over. "Sorry that took so long!"

"You're fine." Nel jerked her chin at the stickers suggesting a two-meter distance. "What's with this? Needle-dude said there were outbreaks?"

Lin shrugged. "Seems to have dissipated, since no one's enforcing masks or whatever with us."

"Or they just have bigger issues to focus on," Nel muttered darkly as she fell into step with the rest of the passengers.

"If there was a pandemic, they wouldn't be risking us," Lin promised.

She meant to be reassuring, Nel knew, but the unspoken undercurrent was hardly comforting. *Would you just let us all burn down here?* "I hope to show you a bit more of Earth while we're here, you know."

"I'd like that. There's a lot I didn't really get to see last time." Lin's gaze slid back to the notes still lighting the space above her wrist and she typed a bit more.

"Yeah, murder charges have a way of hindering plans," Nel drawled.

Harris stepped up to the front of the crowd, which stilled at his stern expression. "Welcome to Earth. While most of you attended the previous briefing—whether invited or not—" his gaze flicked to Nel, "there are several additional details of which to be aware. Effective immediately, there will be no auditory communication. Period. Noise-canceling headphones await you in your cabins and will be required for all missions. Those of you who use auditory readers due to blindness or other visual disabilities should see our tech staff, who will be happy to set up external blocks on your devices."

"Excuse me, can't we just put those on everything?" a young man piped up.

"No. Please save questions until afterward, and direct them to your group officer." He crossed his arms. "Lists of both your occupational and domestic groups have been uploaded to your communications device. Any questions, again, should be taken up with your officer, who is listed on your grouping notice. Some faces you're going to want to know: I'm Harris, Chief Field Operative. Dr. Ndebele you know, Chief Analysis Operative. The aforementioned Technical Officer Teera Mak, Head of Computer Engineering. Munashi Sepulveda is our Founders liaison.

"As with all missions, chores will be assigned according to ability first, then equally among us. Scheduling conflicts will be considered, but otherwise we all pull our weight around here. We recognize some of you have never been to Earth before, and we respect the curiosity. However, recreations off-base will be strictly supervised and generally prohibited." He paused, gaze falling to her boots for a split second. "IDH is public knowledge. But we are not liked. We are not trusted. We are tolerated as a curiosity and necessity at best. You stay within our supervision, otherwise your safety is your own responsibility." He cracked a thin smile. "Dismissed."

Nel tucked herself into the angled metal flashing along the wall. She had been here, waiting for a departing trip on the floor with hundreds of strangers many times before; it was easy to fall back into those patterns of navigating liminal space. These days everything seemed liminal.

She glanced over to Lin, half-baked plans of dinner on rooftops and summer beers fizzling at the distraction in Lin's eyes. "So, we got some time to kill—once we're all through, want to poke around?" Nel suggested. "I'm dying for some fresh air."

"I don't," Lin dismissed. "Have time, I mean. The preliminary data from the Samsari mission just got in and we're going to cross-reference it with what the Indian government has for us."

"I thought we couldn't send messages—"

"We can't. No Wi-Fi. But a courier is meeting Dr. Ndebele in fifteen minutes." Lin frowned and reworded something before closing the screen down. "I'm sorry everything's been so busy." Her intensity belied the apology.

"Busy and chaos are my norm lately," Nel assured. "So, know when you'll be free?"

Lin's face brightened. "I should have some time before we leave. See you soon?"

Nel lifted her chin to catch Lin's brief goodbye kiss, then watched her go. Between the few hours until departure and Lin's brisk attitude, she was, once again, spinning.

She popped open her pack, discarding its deceptively light, gleaming case with relief. *Is this what Lin felt, back on the* Promise? *On* Odyssey? Righteous relief. Her remaining toes worked into the soles of her boots. Sure, she'd rather have her own gear, clothes, be recognizable for herself and herself alone. But it didn't matter. Beneath her shoes, beneath fire retardant floor tiles and cracked pavement the soil was made of the same minerals as her bones. She was of this place.

Even as her finger hovered over her mother's messages, the warning flashed over her screen:

NO AV CALLS

NO AUDIO CORRESPONDENCE OF ANY KIND

It was repeated in Mandarin, Cyrillic, Hindi, Spanish, Arabic. English was third on the list. Nel found her smile fading. Even if her feet were solidly on honest-to-fuck Earth, she wasn't home. This was a strange world she had never experienced. Her eyes ached. Her bones dragged. She wondered if terrestrial bones made her more brittle than her star-born counterparts. It could be the renewed weight of gravity. Or a new gravity all her own, seated in the hollow between her billowing lungs.

Overwhelmed by the newness and the sameness colliding, she drew her field book from its pouch and flipped through the last few written pages. Notes on Los Cerros Esperando VII, sketches and a map from running from the cops. Thoughts on Samsara. Somewhere along the line her field notes took a turn for the conspiratorial.

Finding a blank page, she wrote the date of their departure from *Odyssey*, and today's as well.

What do I even say? The pen felt clumsy in her hands. Even if she wasn't aware of the time since she last wrote longhand, her fingers were.

"Dr. Bently."

She shrank back as she turned to face Harris's banal expression. "Hey, Officer…I'm sorry, I don't know your rank."

"Harris, please. I was going to look at the view. Thought you might appreciate some fresh air."

"Fresh air as in outside?" Her heart hammered to life.

"Indeed."

"Fuck yeah." She faltered. "Do I need my badge?"

"You're with me. But in the future, you might want to carry it with you. Earth's a dangerous place these days." He extended his elbow. "Shall we?"

"Keep the chivalry, Harris, but sure." She locked her hands behind her back to dissuade any more contact and fell in beside him. "I didn't know we were allowed out, otherwise I'd already be there."

"You would be long gone, I'd imagine. Or off to the spaceport bar."

"Ah yeah, I was considering that." Nel chewed on the inside of her cheek. "Though I probably shouldn't have told you."

"It's not my spaceport," Harris rationalized. "I don't concern myself with other people's business unless they pay me to."

"Seems like a good policy." *So who's paying you now?*

"It's worked so far."

"Thanks, by the way. For pulling whatever strings you did to get me here."

"So you found out about that."

"Lin told me. I hope that's okay. Whatever you need help with, I'm yours. This means, well, the world."

He held open a door emblazoned with EMERGENCY EXIT ONLY, flashing his card at the reader just inside the stairwell before the alarm even began. They walked in silence for a few moments, his steps a soft echo of her clomping stride. They reached the top of the stairs and he shoved open the rooftop access, holding it open for her to exit ahead of him.

She stepped into the hot, humid air of the sunbaked rooftop. She didn't care that drawing breath was like sucking gelatin through a crazy straw or that she had never been within a thousand miles of Bakjeeri before now. She was home. She rushed to the edge, leaning over the wall. A parakeet fluttered from its nest several paces away. Nel tilted her face to the sky, eyes squeezed shut against tears as much as sunlight. Until that moment she hadn't realized how afraid she was of never feeling Earth's daylight on her face again.

Another lungful of air brought her the sharp musk of distant forest, the warm stone of the mountains, the bite of hot tarmac, the tang of sea salt. "Thank you," she whispered, eyes fluttering open to take in the view, blurry through the haze of heat and emotion. "You grew up off-world?"

"No." His eyes settled on the glitter of the city, several miles away. "Valladolid. It was an idyllic childhood followed by a lovely adulthood that ended abruptly." His smile held no mirth. "Not everyone thinks this place is worth saving, Dr. Bently. Forgive me if I find my motivation for this mission elsewhere."

"Different paths, same goals. I can feel you there." She followed his gaze and hoped she was being as subtle as possible. "So was overriding their gatekeeping just about shutting me up?"

"This isn't gatekeeping, Dr. Bently. This is just assignments. You're still here, your expertise is still needed, and surely Lin appreciates your being here."

"Eh, she's pretty into the mission stuff. I guess Dr. Ndebele is a hero of hers."

"Her mentor, yes." He lapsed into silence again, seemingly aware of her gaze but content to let her stare.

Nel took him up on it, following the set of his jaw and the unreadable expression of his eyes. As much as she was growing to like the man, the very IDH mysteriousness made her second-guess her trust in him. He reminded her of someone, but each time her mind came close to grasping who, it slipped away. "So your role is, what, reconnaissance?"

"I am very good at finding things," he demurred. As always, even his seemingly bald confessions were carefully imparted. "So are you, if you just keep that temper in check. Luckily IDH has a larger ego than it does a sense of retribution. Most of the time." His eyes crinkled with mirth, however, that told her he didn't share their qualms.

"You don't think I was out of line?"

He did not smile. "I respect you."

"But you don't like me."

"I do not like much of anyone, Dr. Bently." Shadows clung behind his eyes, ones that were new to Nel. Those filling Lin's eyes were left over from events Nel couldn't imagine. The darkness in Harris's, however, was from things she didn't want to. "You've a part to play in this, and I look forward to discovering what it will be."

The sun slunk lower, its brilliance pierced with the jungle canopy, a popped yolk bleeding pigment across the clotted clouds.

Harris's wrist comm flashed, and he stepped toward the door without checking the message. "Duty calls, Bently, but you're welcome to stay. Close the door behind you."

"If I stay out much longer, I'll never come in," she explained, following him to the door. They didn't speak on the descent back into the bowels of the hulking spaceport, and he disappeared into the crowd with nothing more than a polite nod goodbye.

Taking permission from Harris's disinterest, Nel decided to spend the rest of her evening exploring the hulking mass of the spaceport. The bank of main doors proved locked upon her firm jiggling, but several yards down a brick propped open a service door.

As a teen, whenever her mind felt too close, she had taken off into the woods, exploring until the wilderness of her thoughts seemed tame once more. The service hall split, hooking left toward what must have been an employee lounge and time clock, while the main corridor continued on to meet with the security check. She moved down the concourse, listening to the soft tap of her IDH-issue boots on the gleaming tile. The forgotten reminders of whatever flu wracked the place were eerie warnings that anything could change.

She rounded a corner and the hall opened up into a massive lobby. Like your average big city mall, the three stories of terminals opened into a massive food court. The hub of intergalactic hopes and dreams. It was empty and smelled faintly, comfortingly, of mildew. She tilted her head. Somewhere the sound of rushing water echoed off the gleaming steel and glass. Most of the restaurants and stores were barred with metal grates, but enough weren't that Nel could almost imagine it bustling. Streamers still hung from opening day.

The sound of water emanated from the huge fountain in the center. A botanical garden's worth of plants and trees tangled the space on the ground floor, branches reaching toward the glass dome overhead. Vines curled around every rail, and epiphytic orchids and plants were tucked into every crevice Nel could see. Was it by design, or had nature already claimed its place even here?

Abandoned wasn't the right word. Not really. The decor was both outdated and progressive at once. Held gently in stasis until something changed. It wasn't even overgrown or reclaimed in the way every post-apocalyptic movie led her to expect. *Probably because we're not to the "post" part yet.* And they wouldn't ever be, if Nel had anything to say about it.

A restaurant bar extended along one wall on the second floor, and Nel jogged down the stationary escalator to try the staff door. It was locked, as she expected. Instead, she hopped up onto the bar itself and dropped behind.

"Jackpot." She cradled the almost-full bottle of El Capo Anejo with a lover's tenderness. She fished a glass from the rack and blew the dust out before pouring a few fingers into it. Of course the fridge was empty—mercifully so, considering the power was off—so she knocked the drink back straight. It burned in all the familiar, right ways, a trail of seductive fire down her throat. "Oh sweetheart, it's been too long."

"I thought you only talked to me like that."

Nel glanced up to see Lin leaning on the end of the bar. The high collar of her electrosuit was undone, the gleam of sweat on her beige skin set off by the cold blue and black of the electromesh. Even as pissed as she was, Nel couldn't deny the draw of that open fabric. "Hey. Thought you had a meeting."

"Cut out early." Lin rapped her knuckles on the bar. "In the movies this means I want a drink. That true?"

Nel laughed. "It was, at one point. Never been to India in the 2020s before, though, so my social cues are probably a bit antiquated." Playing roles was a relief, even if contrived. Bartender she could be. The rest of the world was too confusing for her to have the energy to try to figure out who she was on top of everything else. She gestured to the array of bottles behind her. "What'll it be, ma'am?"

"You don't remember my drink order?" The hurt in Lin's eyes was feigned. *At least, I think it is. Mostly.*

"Scotch. Rocks. Expensive. Well, as expensive as Jerod's bar got." She glanced at the options and whistled. "They got Macallan 18. 'Bout as fancy as it gets down here." She grabbed a dusty glass and tested the bar sink, surprised when bright clear water splashed across the stainless steel. "Should I warn you about Earth's gravity or altitude and the potency of alcohol?"

"I think I'll be fine," Lin assured. "You forget we abuse our chemicals as much as you. We just prefer to use ports."

Nel shook her head. "IV drug use was never my thing, despite being part of the DARE generation."

"Dare to what?"

"Never mind. Just some anti-drug propaganda that backfired pretty hard." She splashed scotch into the glass and slid it across the bar. "Fridge is out. So here's your scotch on the rocks without the rocks."

"I don't mind." Lin grinned. "You look better. Happier, I mean."

Nel took a slow pull of her tequila, rolling it around her mouth before swallowing to answer. "Harris took me to the roof. Fresh air does wonders after a few years. And I'm glad I've a few allies—or whatever the fuck he is."

"I think allies is right. I'm sorry I didn't stand up for you more. I'm still on probation and I figured it was safer having one of us here than rocking the boat and risking neither of us being included." Lin's jaw worked. "That doesn't make it easier, huh?"

"It just is starting to feel like it's on purpose, is all. The excluding."

"I mean, it's on purpose because it's not your job, you know? You don't get mad at being excluded from *Odyssey*'s waste recycling meetings."

"The fate of my planet is a little different than space shit, Lin. I know I didn't make Dean's List at Space U, but c'mon, I've got a lot of insight to offer. If only because I'm from here, you know?"

Lin took her hand, eyes still refusing to meet Nel's. "I know, babe, but it's not me you have to convince."

"Dr. Ndebele? I'll be lucky if she thinks I have two brain cells to rub together." She scowled at Lin's patronizing sympathetic look but drew a long breath. "I'm sorry, too. Just edgy. And sick of not sleeping. You'd think I'd have gotten enough in cryo. Does that count as rest?"

"Depends on your definition."

Who was supposed to apologize first? Usually in these situations it was always Nel who had done wrong, whether it was not calling someone she should or kissing someone she shouldn't. This time she wasn't sure. Catching the shuttered look in her girlfriend's eyes, Nel scrambled for common ground. "So, what do you like about scotch?"

"First drink I learned to order."

Nel's brows rose. "Those are some pricey training wheels there."

"Pricey is a bit of a different game with IDH." She swirled the drink gently on the bar, watching the red liquid splash gently. It was a practiced gesture, one Nel recognized from a hundred pop culture broody scenes. Was there anything Lin did that wasn't meticulously curated and rehearsed?

"Where'd you have your first drink, Tatooine?" Nel prompted. Lin seemed to be in the telling mood and she wasn't about to waste the chance. *That attraction or self-preservation speaking?*

A giggle erupted from Lin's full lips. "This isn't *Star Wars*."

Nel barked a laugh. "I told you at the beginning I hate all this sci-fi shit. Give me a normal dark comedy or thriller any day. Preferably with Gillian Anderson."

"I don't know who that is—"

"Sure you do—Scully. *X-Files*."

"Oh, yes. I liked her. I wanted to be like her."

"I wanted to do something else with her, but yeah." Silence swelled between them and Nel made a show of wiping dust from the bar top.

"Mugdha 3. Mining outpost on an asteroid. I was seventeen circadial. Dar was a few years older, can't remember. He'd persuaded our parents to let me tag along with him for some transit mission. He was already clawing his way up the ladder and I wanted to see the mines. They're really neat and isolated. I already knew I wanted to study our origins, and I felt like the isolation of the mining outposts might help me understand our ancestors a bit more."

"Did it?"

"I spent most of the trip drinking with two of the mine-rats my age. We drank scotch on the rocks—though there it was actual rocks, chilled in the vacuum of space. Can't be wasting water on drink ice. We got drunk every night and went space walking."

"That sounds horrifyingly dangerous."

"It was. But fun. Spinning out there in the nothing while your brain was on fire. I swear I could have seen God if I looked hard enough."

"Yours is way better than mine. I was fourteen and this girl and I were hanging out. We went to middle school together, but we hated each other then. Few years later she watched one of my softball practices. After she asked if I wanted to take a walk. Spent almost every night together that summer, drinking cheap spiced rum and Smirnoff Ice by the swamp behind the school. Drank enough that we didn't care about the mosquitos. She told me what she'd do when she became a famous musician—she was in her church choir—and I told her I was going to find a famous archaeological site. The next pyramids."

"Did you date?"

Nel shook her head. "It was more like a love affair. Secret and torrid and finite. Her parents decided I was the bad influence for making her gay—not her, for getting me into booze. Went to a different school that year and never heard from her again. Kept drinking though," she laughed. "Did you get in trouble for the drunken EVA?"

Lin shook her head. "No one cares about mine- rats. My parents were influential enough at the time that no one said anything to me and Dar was wrapped around this guy." She paused, a faint smile fading slightly. "It's when he met Paul. I thought it was pathetic at the time, his devotion to this dude who he'd only just met."

Nel frowned at their hands, both resting on the polished bar, inches from one another yet seemingly lightyears distant. She knew she was supposed to ask Lin if she still felt that way, ask if she saw parallels in their own relationship. *Does that mean one of us is going to die?* She shook away the shiver of premonition. "Guess sometimes it's just like that. Can't help when someone gets under our skin."

SIX

"Bently, if you're lying, I'm gonna fucking kill you," Bossin muttered.

Nel's eyes narrowed as she slid another bean across the dining car table. "Me, lie?"

"I think it's on him, frankly," Jem remarked. "Your brow's been twitching for the last minute and your eyes are about as wide as the hangar bay."

"Ouch."

The medic grinned. "Your poker face could use some work, Dr. Bently."

The car shuddered, crossing onto the steel lacework of the bridge to the mainland. Outside sullen clouds cloaked the late evening sky, and the city beyond was just a haze of backlit fog. "Nel, please. And yeah, I'm not sure what part of the walking angry lesbian stereotype you thought would make me a good card player."

Bossin howled and tossed two beans in. "With that endorsement..."

"What're you doing?" A slight woman with cropped, tousled blonde hair paused beside them, tech-covered hand resting on the tabletop.

Nel tucked her hand against her chest and glanced up, trying to recall the woman's name from the gala.

"Hey, Teera," Jem welcomed, "I can deal you in, once Bently loses her last dime."

Teera's brow rose playfully as she regarded the pile of thumb-sized beans. "Those aren't dimes."

Nel chuckled. "None of us have actual cash so we raided Bossin's mancala pieces. And 2100 is no time to teach us pathetic white folks a new game."

"Well, once we hit Egypt we can try to teach you," Nori offered. "Call."

Nel pulled a face and showed the cards in her hand. "Next time listen to Jem."

Bossin groaned, arm shielding his eyes and his apparently overwhelming shame. "My mother is tossing in her grave."

"Your mother is alive and still running Kossa-2, if I recall," Jem reminded. "But she might wish she weren't if she gets wind of your terrible gambling skills. You sure you don't want to join?"

Teera shook her head. "I'm actually here to collect your best player." Her eyes flicked to Nel. "Tech check, Dr. Bently."

"Oh, shit!" Bently glanced at her comm and scrambled to her feet. "I totally forgot about that, sorry."

"No worries, I needed to stretch my legs," Teera reassured. "Shouldn't take too long."

Nel fell into step behind her. They crossed through the bobbing double doors joining the chain of dining cars and Nel paused, lifting her face to the balmy, moist night air. It smelled of oiled metal and impending rain.

Terra was smiling when she glanced back from the office car entry. "You been before?"

Nel shook her head, ducking in behind the tech. "No, just enjoying my home atmosphere."

They stepped into the first sleeping car. Each tiny unit had been remodeled into a makeshift office. Teera's in particular was now filled with holographic screens and ropes of wires. Unlike Gretta's, however, it was tidy, each bundle labeled and tucked into the corners. "You can have the seat."

Nel settled into the chair, extending her left arm when the tech gestured for it. "This just routine?"

"For now, unfortunately. Most of the others had their setup checked before departure from *Odyssey,* but due to your last-minute transfer, we didn't have time until now. This shouldn't take more than a minute." Her hands were gentle, if cold, and she slipped a tiny probe into a port in the wrist comm. "How'd you find the spaceport?"

"Strange. Shiny and old at once. Pavement looked new."

"I imagine it was hardly used before the blackout. Built on hopes."

"Typical of IDH, to build something no one wants."

"Don't feel like they're the most useful organization?" Teera asked. Her pupils shrank in her pale eyes as the data from Nel's comm projected directly into her optic nerve.

What would it look like if that wetware malfunctioned? The invasive thought sent a shudder through Nel's body. "I guess I'm just slow to adjust."

"That diplomacy must have taken a lot of work." Teera spun a tiny dial. "Alright, here's the deal: usually, your computer interface and your comm are paired. That's not the case for this mission. All communications will be scanned and viewed by both bots and myself. If you don't want me to see it, then don't send it. Consider this your only warning."

"Try my best," Nel promised. Decades of careful curation of her university email—especially as a visibly queer adult—had taught her the importance of professional email etiquette long before IDH meant anything more than who signed her grants. "So without Wi-Fi and all that, how are we communicating with the space stations or *Odyssey*?"

"Oh, you mean your pet project with Philos?"

Nel's cheeks flushed. "I was just helping him access the data he needed."

Teera raised her hands in defense. "Hey, I don't care. We need all hands on deck for this one, and IDH is just being precious about who they invite into their club. Everyone still has access to the main databases—though any updates will be slow to appear. Our missives, messages and any database updates are delivered at midday. Of course, I have bots scanning everyone's search history and messages 29/6—wait, 24/7 down here. Regardless, you chatting with a CPO doesn't concern me. Files that aren't audio, that don't mention Samsara, or what's going on here? I'd hardly notice them. We're going through all your messages, but it only gets flagged for Harris or Dr. Ndebele if I say it should." Even through the cheery blue-green light projected on her irises, her stare was glacial. "Philos knows that."

Weight settled on Nel's shoulders, the certainty that once again, she was being let in on some secret that she didn't have the bandwidth or background to appreciate. "Right. So I can poke around and research all I want as long as I'm not messing with the mission proper."

"Essentially." Teera's attention returned to the digital bowels of Nel's communicator. "No visual disabilities, correct?"

Nel shook her head. "Would that be a problem?"

Teera's focus faltered. "No. We'd just install audioblocks for close-circuit screen reading and so forth. Is there something not in your chart?"

"Just a whole lot of skepticism and some too recent memories."

"I think the former might actually be in your chart." The light flickering over her eye brightened and she frowned. "It appears your comm audio is already disabled."

"Maybe left over from Samsara."

Teera was silent for a moment. The projected light disappeared from her eyes and they were abruptly staring into Nel's. "I don't know what happened down there—I imagine even you don't, despite watching it fall away beneath you."

"I haven't really made sense of anything in the past two years," Nel confessed.

Teera sat back and unplugged her equipment from Nel's wrist. "Let me know if you encounter any issues with the firewalls. They're tricky on a good day, and this level of security is a bit unprecedented on such a massive scale."

"Will do." Nel stood, brushing imaginary soil from her electrosuit before offering her hand. "Thanks for the help."

"Dr. Bently?" Teera's voice stopped Nel on the threshold of the sliding door. "I didn't know Gretta well. Few did, really. But I saw that data. Tasked with double-checking her work. And it wasn't in your head. I don't know what it was or why it only affected you and Dr. de Lellis, but we're going to find the answer."

The words did little to erase Nel's apprehension, though she appreciated the effort. "I just wish stopping it didn't require us to know what the fuck it was in the first place."

"You and me both. Cheers."

After a cursory glance back down the dining car, Nel retreated to the narrow sliver of privacy that she and Lin would share for the next few weeks. No sooner had the door locked behind her than she was discarding her electrosuit for the familiar press of musty A-shirt cotton and a set of cargo shorts. She hesitated when her fingers brushed the heavy bolo, more a pendant than tie, but she left it on.

Like the bite of exhaust in summer air and the sting of cold as her drafty house strained against the New England winters, these clothes scratched life into her skin. Coarse. Worn. Wrinkled from a few years rolled in her personal effects. But hers.

When Nel returned to the dining car, Jem flashed an understanding grin. "Nice threads."

Nel gave an exaggerated spin. "I figured there's no point in pretending I'm something I'm not if IDH won't play along." It was a tough-guy version of her real feelings, but at least the medic wasn't about to call her on it. She settled back into her seat, waving away the offer to deal her back in.

"Letnan Nalawangsa stopped by a second ago," Jem informed. Their gaze didn't move from the cards tucked in their hand.

"She say anything?"

"Just her usual snippy self," Bossin muttered.

Jem laughed, but the sound was more humorous than derisive. "I imagine her fam wants everything wrapped up in a tidy bow before the year's Revelations."

Revelations?

"C'mon, those bluebloods ain't giving a damn what's going on with us dirtwalkers. She's probably just pissed because we can't get purified stim down here to power her waltz to the top of IDH's science division. I don't think she's left Dr. Ndebele's side in—"

"Look, we're all stressed about this," Nel interjected, confusion warring with her desire for inclusion. "I know they haven't had it rough as some of us, but I think she's trying."

Nori's eyes leveled on Nel. "Figured you'd have nothing but flattery for them. Might wanna wipe your mouth, got some shit stains there from kissing—"

"Fuck off!" Nel's temper flared, hot as the flush on her face. Tearing paper cut the conversation as Nel tried to tug the cards from her hands. Colored paper fluttered to the scratched Formica between them.

Jem's hand settled on Nel's wrist. "Hey, Bently, not worth it."

Seizing the olive branch, Nel gave them a grateful smile.

Jem held up their hands in warning. "Look, I agree with her, maybe with fewer expletives. I just don't like arguing like, ever. I grew up in a huge family and I'm not about the drama."

Nel looked away. *I honestly don't know anything about Lin.* It hadn't bothered her in Chile, when Lin was just grief sex and a solution to sticky politics. She hadn't dared to question it when Lin seemed to be her only ally as she hiked across the New England powerline corridors. She had been too grateful for a familiar face on *Odyssey* to bring it up. *Now, though, you're on my turf.*

A blue-collar upbringing lent Nel enough understanding of the working class to not trust anyone with big money and bigger influence, but enough privilege to navigate that world without seeming too misplaced. Jem and Nori and Teera were people she should have had more in common with. More than she did with Lin, at least. *I wish I didn't have to keep picking sides.*

"So, ah, when does your group split off?" Nel asked, a clumsy attempt at rerouting the doomed conversation.

"Once we're out of Egypt. Waiting on whatever data they have there before we finalize our route." Jem stretched, tugging down the edge of their binder with annoyance. "Guess it's mostly medical staff. More than that's classified." They flashed an apologetic grin.

"I'm glad they're splitting us up, cover more ground, more answers that way and all," Nel offered, a poor attempt at hiding her stinging pride.

Whatever Jem's response was, it drowned in a firm voice. "Dr. Bently. Your presence is requested."

Dr. Ndebele stood in the doorway leading to the conference car. Nel tried to gauge the woman's unreadable expression. Apparently, she dawdled too long.

"Now."

"Sorry, ma'am," Nel apologized as she extricated herself from the booth. Neither spoke as she followed the officer across the causeway. The train lurched beneath them. Dr. Ndebele kept her footing easily, but Nel almost pitched over the causeway rail. A graceful dark hand steadied her with a featherlight touch. "Mind the gap, Dr. Bently."

"Thanks." Nel flashed a smile, but by the time the awkward expression was in place, the other woman had turned back and was inputting the entry key. The door hissed open, and Nel stepped into the gleaming, bright lights of the officer's private chambers. The rear half of the car was an office, but a raised curtain behind her desk showed a tidy bedroom beyond.

Dr. Ndebele tugged the curtain shut and sat behind her desk. A moment later Lin slipped into the room. "Afternoon. Hi, Nel."

Dr. Ndebele brought up a few files on her screen, but Nel could see little through the blurred back of the projection. Catching Nel's confused expression, Dr. Ndebele explained, "Harris will join us momentarily."

When Lin settled beside her, Nel smiled. "Thought I outgrew getting called to the principal's office."

"Quit being trouble and you'll stop getting into it!" Lin whispered.

"Thought you liked that I'm trouble," Nel whispered with a playful grin.

"If we could keep the flirting to a minimum while on official business?" Harris interjected as he stepped through the door.

"Sorry, sir," Nel responded.

He took up an easy stance in the corner behind the desk and steepled his fingers. His gaze rested on Lin as Dr. Ndebele flicked one of the documents around so it displayed on their side of the hologram.

"Look, if this is about the booze, I'll pay for it—" Nel began.

"This has to do with Komodor Muda Nalawangsa. What booze?"

Nel blanched. "Nothing, ma'am, my mistake. Please, continue."

Her eyes narrowed on Nel, but one blocky finger flicked the file open. "I hope you'll forgive the paper, we're running pretty low-tech down here."

"What about my brother?" Lin leaned forward. Her face was neutral, but Nel had only seen that pinch around her eyes a few times: on Samsara and the night in Chile when everything changed. *She's scared.*

"This shouldn't take too long, but it came from on high so…" She trailed off. "Have either of you had any contact with Dar Nalawangsa in the past three weeks?"

Nel frowned. "I think the memorial was the last place. For ah, Dr. Paul de Lellis."

"We met a few times since Samsara." Lin agreed, voice an echo of the hardness in her eyes. "What is this about?"

"We are following up on some questions regarding him."

Lin slumped back in her seat, long arms draped across her chest. Her lips pursed and for a moment Nel saw the petulant, spoiled girl who took drunken space walks off an asteroid mine. "Is this for some promotion of his, because I don't know why you bother. If you cut every rung, he'd still climb that ladder."

"Your brother never reported for duty two weeks ago."

Color drained from Lin's face and her pout relaxed into disbelief. "What?"

"His last appearance on security footage was in your corridor the day before launch. There's a transcript of the video if you'd like, but it's inconclusive." She slid it toward Lin, who simply stared, unfocused.

Dread sank in Nel's gut. What few science fiction films she had seen told her nothing good ever came from a man missing in space. *Please don't involve an exposed walk out an airlock.*

"After the memorial, he returned to his ship. At 0300 hours the next morning they performed a textbook departure for a classified destination, Estimated Time of Arrival at 1930 a week later. They never arrived. Didn't even make the first checkpoint. We're just trying to track down what might have happened. You were the last two people to actually speak with him."

Lin whirled to Nel. "You talked to Dar? Why didn't you say?"

Nel shrugged. "Barely, we walked past each other. I was on my way to your room."

"Right, you said that." Lin turned to stare at the desktop, frowning as if it had been the one to make her brother disappear. "Did you check his trajectory?"

"Nalawangsa is a high-ranking pilot. With that comes the privilege of not having to report his trajectories prior to departure."

Dr. Ndebele brought up a display of reconnaissance reports. "Each attempt at what little communication we're still permitted meets with static. Never received. Scouting ships are searching several possible routes, but we're concerned he might not have headed to his deployment at all."

"Where was he supposed to go?" Nel asked.

"Classified, Bently." Harris's expression had too many edges to be a smile. "For one, I have no doubts about his safety."

The train's electric hum balanced on the taut edges of silence stretching across the desk. Ferocity returned to Lin's face. "You're suggesting he disobeyed orders."

"I'm suggesting that we don't know where he is and are concerned for his safety and that of his crew," Dr. Ndebele responded, voice level. "Letnan Nalawangsa, your brother had over 250 people aboard the *Promise.* I'm sure their families are as concerned as you, and so far we haven't even found a chem trail."

Lin's mouth thinned. "My brother breathes his duty to all of us, ma'am. If he's missing it's because something bad happened. Your suggestions otherwise are shameful and a stain on his record. Space is a big place." She shoved herself out of the chair, tugging Nel up with her. "Keep looking."

She stalked from the room, Nel shooting an apologetic glance over her shoulder. Lin didn't stop at the dining car or the sleeping cabins. She slammed from car to car, as if she could negate their progress by rushing backward through the train. When she burst into the caboose her breath was heaving. Her long fingers gripped the rail as she leaned out over the gangway.

"What the fuck was that about?" Nel asked.

Lin's pupils were pinpricks in the dark cosmos of her irises. "Their nasty questions or me losing it on her for being a bitch—"

Nel winced as her voice carried off the metal and whipped away into the wind. "I get why you lost it. I've been doing it all my life. Never thought I'd hear you jump to his defense that way, but hey." She leaned on the metal bar, lending Lin the privacy of not meeting her eyes. "I meant with Dar missing."

"You tell me—apparently you were the last one to see him."

"We both saw him at the memorial for the Samsaran deaths."

"Samsari," Lin snapped. "You know what I mean."

"Honestly, all he did was shake his head at me. Like as in, 'shut it, Bently' which is pretty on brand for him. And fair, too, since whatever you two were arguing about seemed like none of my business." *Even if it was about me.*

The last sentence seemed to hook in the myriad folds of Lin's gray matter. Her calculating gaze snapped to Nel's face. "What'd you hear?"

"Not much," Nel lied. "Never had siblings but seemed like normal bickering. I just waited until you were done to come see if you wanted to say goodbye."

Lin's eyes narrowed on Nel's, but the archaeologist held her gaze, unwavering. "So you heard his warning. About us dating."

Nel shrugged. "Brothers always bitch about me. Or anyone their sisters date. I tried to cut him some slack, what with Paul—"

"That was years ago. You're projecting from Mikey or something. He was the one who ended things, anyway." She looked down, frown in place, voice pitching higher with every word. "He's an asshole, but he is family, you know. Space feels really big right now. Not knowing in which corner he is. Not knowing if he's just drifting, if his ship's life support—" Acrid vomit interrupted her words, splattering with a sizzle onto the electrified middle rail. She pressed the back of one shaking hand to her mouth before disappearing back into the car.

It might have been the coward's way out, but Nel didn't follow her. This panic, this worry, felt as alien to her as anything Lin did. Perhaps her brain had simply overloaded and couldn't bear thinking about one more mystery. *Or I'm just not sure why everyone's concerned about one asshole.* It wasn't fair. Nel would have overturned every rock between here and the galaxy's edge to find Mikey if she'd known he was missing before cops arrived to discuss his murder.

Her eyes traced the sun-bleached swath winding through the jungle. Cold solidified her in her gut. Dar wasn't the only person missing. Out there, beyond the foreign mountains and across the gray depths of the Atlantic, waited her mother.

"I'm not overwhelmed by mysteries," she admitted to the eddying wind of the caboose deck. "I'm pissed hers rates higher than mine."

SEVEN

Nel rested her head on the edge of Zach's door frame. "Hey," she began, wondering what the right words were.

"Ah, it's the archaeology badass herself." His gentle smile made it clear his words were more genuine than jab. "What can I do for you?"

"I was wondering if you had a moment? I don't really know about setting up an appointment or whatever."

"Depends on whether this is for therapy or friendship. As for the appointment, I was under the impression that we were taking this on an 'as-you-wanted' basis."

"Does that make for effective therapy?"

He smiled. "No, but you know that, and I'd rather you have some as opposed to none. I have time now—I was just finishing my notes, and the rest of what I need to do for the day can wait. I think better in the evening anyway."

She closed the door behind her and settled on the bench. Beneath her, the train hummed. The landscape outside seemed to creep by, the uniformity making their speed seem like a snail's meander. *Where to start?* She wasn't even sure what muddled series of thoughts had dragged her reluctant stomps to the psychologist's door.

"For someone who's never been within a thousand miles of India, I was really fucking happy to see it," she chuckled.

"I was happy to see Earth again too. It's been a long time since I last walked on her." His gaze eased into thoughtfulness. "I imagine we'll find out more soon, but, God willing, this mission brings us a bit closer to familiar ground."

Nel made a show of crossing her fingers, but lapsed into silence.

"Did you want to discuss being back? Maybe how things have changed? I was disheartened to see some of the developments since I was here last."

"You mean pandemics and missing people and killing soundwaves, or…"

He didn't seem to mind humoring her snark, but the look in his eye told her he knew it was just a tactic. "Mostly that much of the control has been transferred to a very powerful few. But this is about you."

"That's kind of my issue, I guess," she hazarded. "I don't know, a large part of me wants to take off. Just keep feeling like I need to grab a pack of smokes from a seedy gas station and watch the wind come off the lake at night, you know?"

"I didn't know you smoked."

"I just mean, that's the feeling," Nel protested. "I don't. Or rarely. Most archaeologists smoke more than the fire pits they dig up. Only time I ever did was one summer. Going through a breakup. Rather, a breakup was going through me, I guess. Tearing me apart. Whenever sleeping next to her, listening to her breath at night got to be too much, I'd walk to the corner market in Burlington where we lived at the time and grab a pack—unless I had some left over from the last time, and I'd walk down to Champlain. There're these docks there, and a crepe place by the train tracks. Wind would rush across from the New York side when storms hit."

"What was it about those times that brought you peace?"

"Other than leaving?"

"Does leaving bring you peace?"

She shrugged. "I guess. Never been much of a connection person."

"No?" He tilted his head. "I imagine Mikey would disagree. You don't need a whole group of friends to connect. I'd pick something that makes you feel 'normal,' as you put it, and focus on that, at least until there's more to do."

Nel frowned at her hands clasped before her. The usual calluses were softening, her body morphing into whoever IDH wanted her to be.

"Most of it's stuff I can't do—go out to a bar. Drink. Call my mom. Take a hike."

He waited, not patient, but expectant. "Have you talked about this with Lin? Therapy is well and good, but support from loved ones—"

"Pump the brakes there, shrinky-dink. I like her fine. I don't know her well enough to say I love her." She stopped, hearing the words spin around her head. *I don't know her.* "I've learned some things about her, about her family, that I feel like I normally would have known by now."

"Do you want to know her?"

"Of course," Nel retorted without thinking. She paused. Lin was strange. Odd. Wild. Whatever string of words both captivated and challenged everything Nel knew about relationships. It already seemed as if eons had passed since they stood, allied, watching a planet fall apart. Lin's normally bright expression was now more often tempered with exhaustion Nel shared. If either had slept since Samsara, it was fitfully and full of dreams. "I do want to. I'm not really used to that, honestly."

Zachariah had the kindness not to mention everything she had done for a woman she still insisted was a stranger. "Maybe you aren't familiar with being involved with someone who's guarded too."

"I thought about looking stuff up on her. On their family. Never dated someone who was Google-able before."

"Have you tried asking her? Or sharing smaller pieces of yourself first, to test the waters?"

"I mean. A bit about Dar and their family. Awkward," Nel drawled.

"I meant about herself. Getting to know her. The way you might if all of this," he gestured to the train, to the Earth, to the universe beyond, "weren't a factor?"

"Like go on a date? How?"

He shrugged. "Or whatever you two got up to when you first met. I assume there was a point that tipped you over the edge from friends to whatever you'd prefer to call your current arrangement."

"I grief-fucked her on our hotel roof and then her brother's spaceship blew up my site and everything caught fire."

His smile brightened. "This is why you're princess badass. Just think about it. If nothing else, maybe the two of you can ignore this mission for long enough to relax."

"I like the way that sounds." She looked down at her hands. "Even in my wildest dreams. In my most bizarre nightmares, I didn't see any of this."

"I think the only ones who did are the people who got us here in the first place."

"The Teachers?"

His hands opened in a graceful shrug. "If I knew, then we wouldn't be here."

"Good point." She rose. "Thanks. Sorry to barge in and puke my feelings at you."

"I'm always happy to see you, Dr. Bently. And would support seeing you more regularly, if your schedule permits."

"My ego and avoidance, you mean?"

"Your words, my dear, not mine."

She chuckled and slid the door open, enjoying the rumble and rock of the train's movement. "At least the train's pretty cool. Have a good afternoon."

"You too."

She shut the door behind her, staring out the bank of windows opposite the row of office doors. Short of sitting down in their tiny shared room and asking Lin who the fuck she actually was, Nel didn't know the first thing about getting to know anyone. Let alone someone who she actually cared about. *You did it with Mikey.*

Mikey didn't take effort. Or keep secrets. *Or have a family entwined in an interstellar conspiracy.* Shaking away the snark, she returned to their room. Her computer still balanced on the edge of the tiny folding tea table by the narrow window. Daylight bathed her face. Leaving the lights off, she opened the database and typed in her mother's name.

SEARCH UNAVAILABLE

Shoving aside her mounting frustration, she erased the search and tried again:

SEARCH: Mindi Bently
SEARCH UNAVAILABLE

After a glance around to make sure no one was reading through the haze of the translucent screen, she typed in Lin's surname.

SEARCH/Nalawangsa

Surname, popular in Southeast Asia; for the family associated with IDH administration see: Laksamana First Class Tirta Nalawangsa; for the missing-persons case see: Mansur Nalawangsa; for the legal suit see: Nalawangsa vs. Phillip Clark

Nel stared at the seemingly endless list of alternative searches wondering how many pertained to Lin. How many were common knowledge? She couldn't shake the feeling that she stumbled into a relationship and was now Googling "Corleone."

She hovered over each link, only to see all but the first was gray and dead. Clicking on it brought her a single paragraph:

Laksamana First Class Tirta Nalawangsa is a well-known philanthropic figure in the upper levels of the IDH. She is known for her work brokering peace between her place of origin, Samsara, and the larger overarching governing body of IDH, most notably through her marriage to Brigadir Jenderal Santoso, Nalawangsa in 13-521. While superficially controversial, many of her petitions and bills are lauded as groundbreaking among politically progressive sectors. She has two children with Brigadir Jenderal Nalawangsa, Dar and Lin, who follow in their parents' respective footsteps.

Wikipedia would have a better written article, Nel supposed, if it knew who they were at all, and if the internet hadn't been wholly disconnected. Still, the lack of information irked her.

"Nel?" Lin stood in the doorway, swaying easily with the train's rhythm.

She slammed her screen shut and whirled to meet Lin's eyes. "Hi. Hey. Hello. Sorry."

Lin's smile was brittle, but she seemed distracted, not betrayed.

God, this is worse than almost getting caught social-media stalking my exes. It wasn't something Nel did often—even that was a commitment too far for her. But like most people who slept their way through an entire college department as an undergrad, she had been frustrated to find her exploits seemed to travel within social circles. "Doing okay?"

Lin shook her head. "I'm tired. And I can't get through to anyone, even our parents. I just don't get why they aren't taking it seriously. He's an asshole, but not irresponsible."

Nel didn't know Dar, and unlike his mysterious sister, she didn't really care to. But what she did know was that he seemed all about rules. Even at the expense of his sister. "Has he done this before?"

Lin stared at her. "Are you kidding?"

"I hardly know the dude. I'm worried for him too, Lin," she promised, turning her so they could face each other. "I mean it. He's your brother and I care about you. Not to mention this isn't a good time to radar drop. What with no radar and all." She tried a weak smile, but judging by Lin's pinched expression neither her words nor her expression were comforting. "Let's keep our ears to the ground. Reach out to anyone who might know anything."

"They're looking into it, there's nothing we could do," Lin muttered, raking a hand through her long hair. It was lank, almost greasy looking. *Has she showered since we landed?*

"Right, but I've got some free time, apparently, even if I'd rather I didn't. I'll see what comes up," Nel offered. "Can't hurt though, right?"

"No audio—"

"I won't," Nel promised, holding out her battered pinkie, "pinkie-swear."

"Pinkie-swear?"

"Old school thing, never mind. But I'll be careful. If nothing else it'll keep me busy."

"Oh," Lin began, reaching for the computer, "I wanted to see the initial Samsara reports. There was a transmission I was researching."

Nel froze, fingers tightening on the hard plastic. Guilt warred with warning. There was no way she could keep Lin from looking without it seeming suspicious.

"What, looking at nudes?"

Nel chuckled, rolling her eyes. "No, just, um—"

Lin extricated the computer from the archaeologist's hand and flicked it open, pressing the transfer pad of her wrist communicator to the device before glancing up at the screen. A frown flickered over her face. "You were looking up my family?"

"I don't suppose you'd believe I was trying to figure out when your birthday is?"

"November fifteenth. And no."

Nel's thoughts raced, but she forced her shrug to look more awkward than guilty. "I was thinking, you read my dissertation, or claimed to. Mind if I read some of your work? The museum on *Odyssey* was incredible. And it's another side of my own research I never thought I'd see."

"Right." She closed the search before transferring Nel's site files from Samsara. "I'll send it to you tonight. I appreciate the gesture." Her wrist flashed and she sighed. "Gotta run."

"Look, Lin?" The moment was fast slipping from her battered fingers. When she turned, Nel dialed her smile up to eleven. "I was thinking we could try and relax tonight. If you have time."

"Relax?" Lin's smile was faint and did nothing to warm her dark eyes. Still, her shoulders seemed a bit less slumped as she stepped away.

"Are you busy? I thought we could do dinner together."

"I mean, we all share a dining car," Lin teased.

"You know what I mean." Nel stood, reaching across the distance between them to lace her fingers with Lin's. She had never been good at trust, and every conversation seemed to entail a leap of faith these days. "I want to talk to you. Not in the 'we need to talk' way, but more in the…" She trailed off, uncertain.

"'You miss me' way?" Lin asked, the hope a beacon in her otherwise soft tone.

"Yeah. I'm still out of my element here, with IDH. And with everything going on with Dar. I'd just like to talk."

"I'll ask Dr. Ndebele if they need me." Lin's head dropped to rest on Nel's shoulder for a breath. "I'm sorry. Everything just feels like such a colossal waste of time. And that's the one thing we don't seem to have much of—time, I mean. Dinner would be nice."

"I'll see you then," Nel affirmed, watching her go. Embarrassment and distrust still writhed in her stomach. Either Lin was unusually distracted, or she knew Nel was lying about the search.

And she let me get away with it.

Warm evening air buffeted Nel, and she tilted her face to the wind. At first blush she hadn't thought she'd ever have another occasion to wear her gala finery. Turned out, heavy grained faux silk complemented black jeans just fine. Nel always was a late bloomer, and the same seemed true for her induction into the dapper-gay community.

"You're getting broody in your middle years, Bently," she muttered to herself, though even without cryo, thirty-eight years was hardly middle aged. At least Lin still seemed to like what she saw, and hopefully that wouldn't change over a single dinner.

The hatchway to the lower level of the dining car swung open. Lin's dark head emerged, scanning the few people still gathered on the upper deck with cursory interest.

Life hammered awake in Nel's chest. Zachariah was right. This was how they began—a nervously picked outfit and outside air whipping between them. She raised a hand, catching Lin's attention in her rough palm.

"This seat taken?" Lin gestured to the empty place beside Nel, broad mouth curled in a faint smile.

"Saved it for you. Hoped you'd get a free moment, but kind of surprised you did." Nel felt a pinch of guilt at how much she deserved Lin's wariness. Lin might have brought a mountain of secrets with her, but Nel brought a hundred broken promises and unanswered questions.

Lin folded herself into the opposite seat, scanning Nel's outfit and hair. The appreciation under the confusion told Nel all she needed to know. "Did I miss a memo?"

"No. Nothing special. You've just been busy and deserve a nice time."

Lin's eyes crinkled and she turned to peruse the holographic menu projected onto the train's gleaming rail. Nel watched the movement, fascinated with the other woman's grace. *If I unfolded your origami, what pattern would the paper have under all the careful contortions?* She produced a bottle from the bag at her feet, aborting her nervous attempt at a flourish halfway through. Awkward sincerity would have to do.

"Nel Bently, that's stealing," Lin teased.

"Didn't seem fair to let it go to waste. Besides, everything here is on some colossal tab. Just thought I'd spice up the offerings." Her grin broadened as the tension around Lin's eyes eased into amusement.

"You're bad."

"I think an acquitted murder charge is still on my record, so we could argue this is the tamest illegal thing I've done." Before the shadows of their shared trauma lengthened any further, Nel poured them both a few fingers of the scotch and returned the illicitly acquired libation to its place in her field pack.

"Do you want to talk about your day?"

"I'd like to ignore it. Or vent."

"Both—vent, then we can drink it away," Nel suggested.

"I guess I'm just frustrated. The best minds in IDH are looking for my brother and turning up nothing. And no one seems to think there's reason for alarm. Not regarding his safety, at least. Plus, I've been working my butt off for Dr. Ndebele analyzing the surveillance data from CE7 starting with when I first arrived down there and it's…" She trailed off, cheeks pinking. "I think she's still pissed about you crashing the meeting."

"That has nothing to do with you, though. I can make shitty choices without your influence. Fuck knows I was an asshole well before I ever met you."

Lin's gaze leveled on her. "Yeah, but I vouched for you. More than once. And I was the one who was almost court martialed for breaking you out. Did that one all on my own."

"Worth it?" Nel asked, hoping her joking tone would prevent an honest answer.

"Consensus pending," she joked back. "I think I'm struggling with how ready they were to destroy my career."

"From my end I was most surprised by the ease with which they didn't. I'm no stranger to privilege. I just didn't realize you were so…" She trailed off, softening the observation with a smile.

"That's not privilege," Lin dismissed, bringing up the menu again. "It's common sense. They saw the data. I think I might try the steak. Never had beef before."

Excitement erased their conversation and Nel leaned forward. "Wait, you're telling me the vindaloo is legit beef? Like not a tank or bugs?"

Lin nodded. "I don't care for the practice, but I'm curious. Might as well put my enzyme boost to good use."

"Alien," Nel quipped. "What else looks good to you—I'm not picky, and that way you can try a few things."

When their selections were made, Lin leaned forward, elbows propped on the table. She rested her chin on her folded hands. "So. What about your day?"

Share a small piece of yourself. "Just talked to Zachariah."

Lin's tired face curled into a frown. "Everything okay?"

"Yeah. Just trying to get a handle on all this. I'm stubborn."

"Truer words have never been spoken." Her face softened. "I hope it helps."

"Me too." Nel drew a breath. "Never went to therapy before, really. Never saw a need. I wasn't fucked up enough to be forced to or to really need it. Just fucked up enough to be a bother, really."

Lin frowned. "Everyone needs therapy."

"Sure. But the U.S. is a bit different. It's reserved for those who can afford it. My hometown had one shrink—some guy associated with the local church. He was fine, but not someone I'd ever confide in, you know? Those who really needed it in our area mostly just got put in 4 South for a week before getting shipped off upstate." A thought occurred to her, and she glanced up. "What do you do with criminals?"

Lin shrugged. "There aren't many. A lot of different resocializing programs, though."

Resocializing. The unyielding certainty that they were right, and the ease with which IDH navigated the various earthly judicial systems told her that, whatever IDH did with their uncooperative members of society, it wasn't as simple as a resocializing program. *Or as gentle.*

Beef vindaloo, samosa, and tandoori chicken interrupted the uncomfortable thought. Once the dishes were settled, Nel captured a bite on her fork and held it precariously over the white tablecloth. "Alright, space-girl: tell me what you think of our earthly pleasures."

Two hours later, with dessert plates empty, indigo gnawed at dusk's fading glimmer. Food and drink weighed Nel's eyes and she leaned back, not minding the air flitting over the prickle of sweat along her hairline. It was Lin's third drink. Maybe fourth. Nel had lost count of her own.

Still, after a moment of thought, she raised her half-filled glass.

"So, there is a special occasion," Lin accused playfully, obliging Nel by lifting her own drink.

"Kind of." Nel drew a breath. "When I was on the computer earlier I saw the date."

"I told you my birthday wasn't until—"

"November fifteenth, I remember. But today is July eighteenth. The day I could probably say changed my life more than any other."

Lin's eyes narrowed. "Was that the night on the site?"

"It was the day we met," Nel confessed. "I don't know how you celebrate anniversaries with cercadial time, or if you do at all, even. But we do, and this is as good a time as any. It was one of the worst weeks of my life. And you appeared out of what felt like thin air."

"Almost true."

"Almost." Nel's heart seemed to think she was running for her life. Running. What she was good at. What she always did. "I don't trust people, Lin. I'm not good at it, and frankly, it hasn't often served me well. But when you showed up in Jerod's bar with your big city suit and your briefcase full of probably bogus paperwork, I trusted you."

"You threatened to kiss my Jimmy Choos, if I'm not mistaken. You thought I was a total bitch."

"I did not."

Lin's smile grew. "You did too."

"Fine. But I trusted you." She forced herself to meet the fathomless reaches of the other woman's eyes. "I might have hemmed and hawed and kicked every mental tire along each step of this ridiculous adventure. But I'm still here." She wasn't going to say the word she knew Lin was now searching for on her face. But this was as close as she had come in a long time.

"I don't know what kicking a tire means." Lin matched her whisper. "But I don't think I need to. What brought this up?"

Nel let out a soft chuckle, more to ease the pressure in her chest than for any humor. "The conversation got a bit heated when we were playing cards the other day."

"Over cards?"

"Over the state of the world. The mission. People are tired. Jet lagged." At Lin's puzzled frown, Nel explained, "It's like cryo sick for us normies. Shock of a new time zone. But anyway, I realized I don't know you. I met you under a tsunami of grief, a storm I'm barely beginning to master. I didn't think I'd know you long enough to bother to really understand who you are. But here I am six months or two-and-a-half years later, depending on who's counting. And I'm still following nothing but my gut and you. And that's kind of scary. So, yeah. I let my fear and gossip get the best of me and tried to search your family. It wasn't really about your dissertation or Dar— though he's pretty mysterious too. I knew you had influence. Just not how much."

"I think I've been pretty transparent about my privilege."

"Maybe I didn't realize what that looked like on an interstellar scale."

"It's something I've tried ignoring, honestly," Lin confessed. "I could have had almost any rank I wanted in any department. Dar always hated that I didn't use our parents' influence like he did. But it just felt like an excuse. Like cheating. I know nothing will ever be hard for me like it is for some people, but I tried to make my own way."

"Not so easy?"

"Our name is heavy," she demurred.

Nel scanned Lin's face, gauging her mercurial temper. "Heavy enough to sink Dar?"

The edge of Lin's focus sharpened in a flash. It wasn't incredulity in her voice when she spoke. It was certain. "How do you mean?"

"Whatever way resonates." Nel twirled her beer thoughtfully. "I wasn't lying when I said I want to help. But I need to know more. Be included. If you think of anything I can do to make things easier."

"Other than looking us up in the database?" Lin's eyes glistened under the pressure of her brittle neutrality. "What did you find?"

"Suspiciously little, honestly." Nel knew her recoil affirmed Lin's discomfort. "But mostly, I found that I'd rather hear it all from you."

Lin's shoulders seemed to drop a fraction. "I don't know if there's much worth telling—"

"You were raised in space, Lin, I bet most of it's gonna be pretty interesting." Nel fiddled with the base of her glass, twisting it and watching the amber liquid swirl. "You don't have to tell me everything. Or now. Or at all. But I'm here. And I'll be here."

Lin smiled, perhaps her first proper one since Samsara. The bottle warmed on the table between them, neither willing to interrupt the quiet long enough to take a sip. Nel's fingers traced the lifelines on Lin's palm.

"There is one thing you could do." When Nel looked up, Lin's lips were a red seal on the invitation of her smile.

Wordless, Nel tapped the button that indicated they were through with their table, tidied what she could, and led Lin through the hatch. The train's lights were already dimmed for evening and their passage was lit only with the bead of golden lights along the edges of the corridors.

The light slid over Lin's skin where she had opened the neck of her electrosuit. Gold looked good on her. *Everything looks good on her.* Their door clicked shut behind them, but Nel made no move to raise the lights. Instead, moonlight lanced from the train windows, interrupted each time they wove between outcroppings or passed an oasis.

Thrumming electric engines drowned in the thunder of Nel's pulse. She dipped a hand under the collar of Lin's suit. Warm skin hummed with life under the press of her palm.

Lin's breath of laughter broke the quiet. "I still feel a bit underdressed."

Nel's grip tightened on the stiff, charged fabric. "If I were in a three-piece suit and you a set of dirty sweats, you still wouldn't be underdressed."

"I don't know—I saw how you looked at my dress for the gala."

"Like I wished you weren't wearing it." The memory of the ice-black satin sparked inspiration. "Can you do me a favor?"

Lin cocked her head.

Nel peered into the narrow closet wedged between their bathroom and the door. After a moment she produced the sash from the aforementioned dress. "Do you mind being blindfolded?"

"Not at all." Lin's smile grew. "But I like to see you."

Nel fought the anxiety climbing up her throat. She couldn't name desire when she didn't even have words for her fear. "I think I'd like you to not see me. Just for a bit."

She draped the fabric over Lin's eyes, tying it loosely, fingers smoothing satin over her cheekbones. Satin and skin; she didn't know which was softer. "It's a good color on you."

"I know."

Nel kissed the hubris from the other woman's lips, catching her hands when they rose to unzip her suit. "Let me?"

Lin relaxed into Nel's touch. "I'm all yours."

That's what scares me. Nel pushed the suit open. Faint ridges in the woman's bronze skin marked where electromesh pressed too tight. Samsari scars scored her flesh, now dappled with goosebumps. "I think you're more beautiful every time I see you," Nel confessed. "Each time I learn a little more."

Lin's cheeks pinked, and Nel was sure she was blushing too. Romance wasn't her strong suit, not unless one referred to the old-fashioned synonym with lying. "It's been a bit."

"Since before—"

Lin's fingers pressed on Nel's mouth. "Just here. Us. Now."

"Here. Now," Nel echoed, callused hands sliding Lin's sleeves off until she could wrap fingers around her wrists. With the electromesh a lump on the floor, Nel backed her up to their bed, pressing softly, insistent, until she lay naked on the rumpled coverlet. Nel's gaze roved over her skin. New marks, old scars, the mole, the faint wave to her long hair in Earth's humidity. Her archaeologist's eyes catalogued every dip. Every swell. Each edge and freckle. Downy hair invisible, almost, but a caress against Nel's hands. "Should have been my first clue," Nel whispered, "that you weren't from here."

"What's that, the tattoo?"

Nel traced the black lines. "No. Your perfection. From peach fuzz to beauty marks to that one crooked eye tooth. It's like something divine mimicking imperfection. God, you're fucking beautiful."

"You're beautiful too, Nel. And I don't need a blindfold to think that." Anticipation turned every word into breath. Each time Nel's hands ghosted Lin's brown nipples she squirmed.

Self-consciousness was rare for Nel. But faced with Lin's grace and assuredness in this strange world that used to be hers, and hers alone, her every move felt awkward. "I could drown in you," she whispered, "and I'd welcome every drop."

Lin's aroused twisting stilled. Nel chewed on her lower lip. The words balanced on the knife's edge of confession. Breath rattled in the expanse of her ribs, her thumbs tracing circles in the hollows by Lin's hips. Satin saved her from the dark orbs of Lin's attention. Under their full weight Nel would bolt back to Bakjeeri, begging for the next starship anywhere else but where someone might glimpse inside her heart.

Lin's fingers found hers and laced them together. "You don't have to drown tonight, Nel Bently," she promised. "Why don't you just dip your toes in the waves?"

Nel pulled away long enough to undress. Returning, she crawled up Lin's body to drop kisses along her cheekbones and on the tip of her nose. Their skin pressed tightly together, until both were so warm and familiar they could have exchanged tawny smoothness and freckled tan. Lin's fingers slid up Nel's sides. "Mind if I look with my hands?"

"No," Nel chuckled, as much from the tickling touch as from the question. Her fingers delved between Lin's long thighs, parting black curls. She dipped her head to the length of Lin's neck as the other woman gasped, nipping at the delicate lines of ligaments.

Their bodies collided. Nel devouring, Lin succumbing. Her hands raced across the topography of Nel's back, cupping the nape of her neck. Nel pressed closer, wringing cries from the woman with every flick. "Fuck, you feel so good."

Lin's eyes fluttered open in surprise when Nel ripped the blindfold off.

"I want to see your face when you come for me," Nel rasped. Desire flooded her body.

"Soon—"

"Now," Nel commanded, thumb circling as her fingers curled up.

Lin obeyed. Her body shuddered beneath Nel's. Passion still glazed her eyes when one shaking hand slipped between her thigh and Nel's core. A moment later fireworks exploded red across the backs of her eyelids. A groan tore from her throat.

Nel flopped back on the pillows, panting. Every breath carried the echo of a moan. "Woah."

"No, you," Lin mumbled, resting her head on Nel's strong shoulder. Emotions flooded in the wake of orgasm. Whatever complicated beginnings they had, Lin had saved her life. Unquestioningly followed her into the core of a killer planet. And the woman in the belly of Bav's rickety flying trash heap had been the real Lin. Someone Nel hadn't seen before. Or since. Maybe she just hadn't looked long enough to realize Letnan Nalawangsa was as guarded as Nel herself.

One alien elegant finger traced lines between the faint brown freckles dotting the archaeologist's heaving chest. *Are they her constellations or mine?*

EIGHT

Wheels screamed on rails. Nel's brain flung itself into bleary consciousness a moment before the train slammed to a halt. The force threw her to the stiff berber. Stars splashed across her vision as her head smacked into the corner of the tea table. "Fuck!"

A thump sounded from the bed behind her and Lin hissed. "Damn shelf… You all right, babe?"

"Think so. You?"

Lin muttered something, her frustrated tone a relief. If she was frustrated, then she wasn't injured. "Computer: lights—right. No audio."

"Or computer," Nel remarked. She staggered to her feet and palmed the switch by the door. Darkness remained. Against her sweaty palm, the train's walls were still. The hum of high-speed travel absent. "We've stopped. And the lights aren't working."

"Probably just something on the rails," Lin hoped.

"Right." *Bullshit.* Nel yanked the curtains back, peering into Jordan's high desert. The landscape was cast in bright moonlit relief. And still. She peered closer, eyes narrowed on the dark mass of rocky hills. Lights flickered from the cover of Jibāl ash Sharāh. "Lin, I think—"

"Get down!"

Gunfire erupted. Lin leapt from the bed, tackling Nel to the rough carpet for the second time that night. Seconds later shouts went up from farther down the train.

The gunfire stilled for a moment, perhaps waiting to see if there was an answering volley. Nel stared into the depths of Lin's face, as if the answer might be found in the ridges and valleys of Lin's black irises. "I'm going to see what's going on," Nel whispered after another moment of quiet. "You get geared up. Surely they'll need all gloves on deck."

Lin's nod was tight. "Be careful."

"C'mon, Letnan." Nel flashed her a wink she didn't feel. "This is hardly my first firefight." She staggered up, yanking an A-shirt and boxers on before slipping into the dark hallway. Emergency lights flickered faintly. Enough to mind her feet, but too dim to see anyone's movement from outside. Was that by design? Shouts no longer arced from the rear of the train. Burnt plastic drifted on the air. Closer, she caught the bright bite of spilled blood.

At the next door she paused, pressing herself to the wall and peering through the thick bulletproof glass. Scratches marred the gleaming metal, and her hand found the new sharp hole punctured in the train's side. It fit three fingers. *That's a big gun.*

Drawing several deep breaths to bring oxygen to her sleep-fogged brain, she counted down from three before slamming open the door, trowel held out, useful as a child's Nerf. It was one of the cargo cars. Fist-sized holes peppered one whole wall, the gaps smoking with burning electrical systems. Murmurs rose between the sizzling electronics and the pounding feet from the officers' car. Whoever had been on guard duty had shitty luck.

"Everyone okay?" she called. "It's Dr. Bently."

"All accounted for," came a low voice from a shadowed corner on the far side of the car. "But I took a hit, along with our generators."

"Medic!" Nel tossed the shout over her shoulder before stepping into the embattled car. She knelt by the man with a grimace. "Anything I can do?"

He grimaced. "Maybe if you'd brought more than a Calvin Klein underwear ad for clothes."

"If you're well enough to joke…"

"Bently," Emilio barked from the half-open car door. A second later he pressed something soft into her hands. "I'm going to talk with IDH. The rest of us are trying to determine the damage."

"Just the generators, sir," the guard responded. Despite his assurances that he was fine, pain strained his voice. "Shot up the whole cargo section. Passengers?"

"Not sure." Emilio's focus shot to Nel. "Got this?"

"Ah, yeah." Nel fumbled the fabric over the gash in the guard's head. Her words faltered with unfamiliar concern. "You're gonna be okay."

His smile was wan. "I know. Just hurts like a bitch. Honestly hurts more than the arm."

His elbow bent in entirely the wrong way. She was used to shattered bones being dry, aged to a russet patina under centuries of soil. Not bright and glaring with sinew and clotted with brown fat.

She forced her tunneling vision back to his face, only for it to snag on the blood coagulating in his stubble. Instead she stared at the numbers painted on the generators' crate, repeating them to herself. "So, ah, first time on Earth?"

He smiled weakly. "Founder. So, no. Grew up in Detroit. Mom's from the Egyptian headquarters, though. It'll be nice to see her."

"If she's anything like my mom she'll be pissed that you're arriving with injuries."

"Oh, I'll get a full lecture on how not to get caught in…" He trailed off with a wince. "Whatever this emergency qualifies as."

"Honestly, I'm just lumping them all under 'IDH business as usual' at this point."

He chuckled. A second later the lights flickered again and Nel started. Instead of more gunfire, however, the train hummed back to life, emergency lights dimming as the main power returned.

"Guess the generators are fine."

"We draw power from the rails, actually. Any surge or dip and the lines are cut until the fault is found. Generators are just for backup. And when we get to Headquarters."

Nel scanned the surrounding mess of mechanisms. "Why shoot up powered-off generators?"

He met her eyes, but didn't respond. Either he didn't know the answer or decided she wasn't privy to it.

"You needed a medic?" Jem shoved their way into the car, kicking aside debris until they could crouch on his other side. Teera followed a few steps behind, disappearing into the ruins of the cargo cars without a word.

"Head, elbow," Nel explained.

Jem peered at his head wound and pupils dismissively before turning their attention to the elbow. "Possible mild concussion. This though," they sucked air through their teeth in a hiss. "Dominant hand?"

He nodded. Jem's lips thinned. "I'll do my best. Gotta get a doctor to look at it when we reach Headquarters."

"Where's James—Dr. Mackey?"

"Critical condition." Jem's eyes remained fixed on the shattered elbow. "I'm sorry. Soon as I'm done you can see him."

Blood drained from his cheeks and his head rocked back. "Fuck."

Nel knew enough to recognize intimate fear. She sat back on her heels. "Need me still?"

Jem shook their head. "Thanks. You did great."

It was a stretch, obviously, but Nel's nerves appreciated the lie. "Did you see—"

"Officer's car."

"Thanks." She rose, embarrassed now that she saw her dingy gray boxers and tank under the stark, unforgiving main lights. After an awkward "Good luck," she stepped back into the bullet-riddled causeway.

Adrenaline seeped from her body, leaving shaking weakness in its wake. She drew a breath, then another, faster, chest panting, heaving. Her ears still rang with blasts, her thoughts seizing the press of Lin's body in the dark, looping the stench of cooling blood. She scrubbed the stickiness from her hands to her bare legs, teeth chattering in panic. The blood just smeared further.

"Bently." Harris's face loomed in the far end of her tunneled vision. A warm hand landed on her shoulder. "In through your nose, out through the mouth."

She obeyed, rewarded as her sight widened with each slowing billow. He was still dressed, his black outfit and unmarked robe splotched with dark stains. Hopefully it was just oil. "Sorry."

"Panic needs no apology." He slid the door to the car's side exit shut behind him.

Another flicker of the lights made her flinch. "The shooter?"

"Three of them. Dealt with." A shred of sympathy shone in his hard face, but she knew it was not for their attackers. It was limited and conditional, and she was grateful that, for now, it was reserved for her. "They only hit the rear of the train, thank God."

"Someone else was hurt. Dr. Mackey?"

"Should be stabilized," he reassured. "He was smoking off the caboose deck, caught a round in his side. I doubt they even knew he was there. Barring any further interruption, we'll be at Los Pobladores Headquarters by midmorning."

Teera emerged from the cargo cars with a soot-stained mechanic Nel didn't know. "Two of the generators are useless. The third can get us limping once we're in town. Few repairs should do the trick, assuming they have the tech. Think it's Reapers?"

"You're telling me this was over a generator?" Nel asked. Already, with a new problem to face, her panic was subsiding. Her heart still raced, but surely that was normal after getting caught in a firefight. *Or raid.* "What's a Reaper?"

Harris sighed. "Our tech is valuable, even more so now. Reapers were a problem before the attack. People targeted, then kidnapped. But that wasn't what happened tonight," he promised. "Whoever attacked knew what we carry with us. Simple raid, is all."

Dealt with. Moral discomfort weaseled through Nel's chest. "Right. Anything I can do?"

Teera shook her head. "Try to get some rest. We'll be moving soon, I imagine."

As if triggered by her words, the train shuddered, power ramping up with a hum a second before they lurched back into motion.

"You all right, Bently?" Harris asked. When she nodded, he motioned for Teera to follow him and disappeared down the corridor.

Their room was deserted when Nel slipped back inside. Numb, she jerked the blankets into order, fidgeting with the thin pillows until they were in some semblance of order. Next, she stowed the clothes and belongings scattered from sex or their sudden stop. Her box of Mikey's ashes lay beneath their bunk, lid several inches away. Its contents were sealed safely within a clean artifact bag. She fished both box and lid out, cradling them against her bloodstained shirt.

Nel's legs trembled beneath her and she sank to the floor. The hard plastic ridge of their doorframe bit into her back, but she couldn't bring herself to move. Instead, she sat back, head bobbing with the train's sway, and stared out the window. Outside, pre-dawn skies silhouetted black mountains. No sign of gunfire. Or lasers. Or anything beyond stillness and starlight. *Did they just leave the bodies out there?* Perhaps their ruined cargo cars had been repurposed into a makeshift morgue.

She did not move as they picked up speed. Or when the sun burst into dawn. Even when the announcement of their impending arrival at Qena flickered above her discarded comm, she still stared at a distant, unseen place, unmoving.

NINE

Nel raised her nose, drawing air like a drowning sailor. Egypt smelled of stone and heat and sesame. Her thoughts tumbled over one another, screaming and snarling with confusion and more than a little righteous rage. Even the cacophony of new world meeting old seemed quiet by comparison.

She slid the window open wider as they downshifted, electric brakes humming high and insistent. Despite scant hours of sleep, her body mimicked the train's energy. Pressing forward, she caught her first glimpse of Qena.

The classics hadn't interested her as an undergrad, and her graduate focus was set well before she got much digging abroad under her belt. Mikey, however, had visited every tourable monument in Cairo years before they ever met. His stories around their campfires or bar tables about the heat and sand and lush riverbanks had drawn her into their imagery in a way her studies hadn't.

Now she teetered on the edge of her first step into his shoes.

If only she wasn't numb.

The train trundled over a switch in the tracks and curved, a silver eel, sinuous and strange among the cement blocks and rebar. While most cities were known for their gleaming industry and modern luxuries, it seemed the Founder's Headquarters was not.

As the train hissed to a halt at the corrugated aluminum shelter that served for both arrivals and departure, Nel caught sight of a soot-stained mess of engineering looming over the rooftops. Wires waved gently in the wind whipping off the ocean Nel smelled to the east. A few cables, taut and embedded in the ground, served as perches for oystercatchers.

A dozen Quonset huts labeled with alphanumeric designations surrounded a single larger one with double doors currently propped open. Several musclebound people in jumpsuits carted equipment from the cargo cars to the only permanent structure. Nel didn't see any gleaming cases of personal effects, but she wondered if she and Lin would be put in the same room.

No one seemed to be spilling from the exits yet, so Nel took her time packing up her belongings. She froze in the doorway of the tiny bathroom. A ball of stained gray fabric was shoved in the corner by the shower spigot. Her teeth clenched. The blood had dried to brown now, though some smears on the floor were still bright and bold. Steeling herself, she scooped the clothes into the incinerator chute, stepped back, and slammed the door.

She hated IDH fashion: the uniformity, the complexity, the nauseating press of too-warm fibers as they cupped her muscles with almost sentient perception. But she'd wear electrosuits for the rest of her life if she didn't have to wash a stranger's blood from her underwear.

By the time Lin arrived, exhausted, from her briefing, Nel had packed up the entire room, save the gleaming case of the other woman's personal effects.

Lin's bloodshot eyes took in the room before settling on Nel. "You packed?"

Nel shrugged, refusing to meet her gaze. "Couldn't go back to bed. Thought I'd get us ready. Where are we staying?"

"Here," Lin explained. If fatigue didn't strain her voice, her tone might have been gentle. "We're staying on the train. Not sure how long we'll be here, but there's no use in disembarking. Plus, it's probably safer if we keep to ourselves. Get any research done?"

Distrust zinged up Nel's spine, but she was just as exhausted as Lin and let the warning dissolve in the maelstrom of other nameless feelings. "There's not much available, even on the IDH databases. Someone mentioned I get Teera to set me up with a VPN to bypass the basic firewalls."

Lin frowned. "They're against IDH protocol, unless you have clearance. In which case you don't really need one to begin with."

"Even for privacy?"

"I never considered needing privacy from them." Lin shrugged. "If you need to look up anything, about your family or something, just let me know. I'll do it for you when I have a second."

"Just curiosity at this point. How's the doctor—Mackey?"

Lin frowned. "I didn't know you'd met him."

"I hadn't. The guard in the back was asking after him. They seemed close."

Satisfied, or too tired to press it further, she heaved a sigh. "He'll make it." Lin stripped her suit off, hanging it carefully in the cleaning case at the back of their closet before dropping a kiss on Nel's head. "Gonna take a shower, want to come?"

Nel shook her head. "Already did."

Lin stepped into the bathroom only to emerge a second later, face pale. "There's blood on the floor."

If Nel had the constitution to even think about eating breakfast, she would have vomited. Instead, bile bathed her teeth for a moment before she choked out, "Yeah, people were shot."

Lin's narrow, strong hands ghosted over Nel's shoulders, her arms, gaze delving where her hands didn't in search of injury. "You're okay?"

No. "Yeah. It's not mine. It's ah..." She couldn't remember the guard's name. "The kid. Guarding the generators. Grazed. Elbow all fucked. Helped him until the medic arrived."

Lin peered into her eyes, searching for something Nel frankly hoped she wouldn't find, hidden under mental calluses and ancient stone walls. "You're okay?" she repeated.

Nel almost couldn't lie a second time. "Just tired. Shaken a bit. Sure sleep and food will have me back to normal."

"We ate in the meeting, but I'm sure the Founders will give us something."

Nel chuckled dryly. "Last time I ate in a Founders' restaurant I got a greasy rotted mouse in my empanada."

Lin's face paled. "Emilio?"

"Oh, no clue. Honestly, probably not. That place meant a lot to him. And apparently he didn't have much control over his underlings." She grabbed Lin's hand for a reassuring squeeze. "Think I'll unpack since we're staying here. Enjoy your shower."

Lin rocked back on her heels and rose, the motion fluid, despite her obvious stress. When she was at the bathroom door, however, Nel's mind blurted, "IDH have a lot of firefights?"

"Some." Lin turned, but her eyes stayed fixed on the bloodstained corner of the bathroom floor. "My uncle arrived late one night; ship barely made it into our hangar. Covered in blood. Interrupted our family game night. Dar and I asked, of course. How could we not? But our parents never spoke of it. He moved out of my parents' home later that week. Our uncle, I mean."

Nel followed the line of tension, of vulnerability, stretching down the woman's throat to her fisted tattooed hand. "I'm sorry. Must have been scary as a kid."

Lin didn't answer, just slipped into the bathroom and slid the door shut behind herself. It was several minutes before the water started, and when it did, Nel caught the soft sound of sobs under the splashing.

Would they ever stop breaking apart?

A flashing message light on her comm derailed her attempt to unpack and her half-assed speculation:

NOTICE: All personnel not outfitted with electromesh gloves or integrated electrosystems please report to F3 in twenty minutes at 1300 for equipment assignments.

Annoyance was preferable to exhaustion or anxiety, so Nel seized onto her frustration at IDH tech with renewed vigor. She double-checked her electromesh and pressed her brow against the bathroom door. At least the sobs had stopped. "Hey babe, us normies gotta go get outfitted with stuff, apparently. See you a bit later?"

"Yeah."

When, after a beat longer, Lin said nothing more, Nel ducked into the train corridor and made for the nearest exit. The rear-most Quonset hut butted up against the low stone wall, a stretch of which was painted with various targets.

"You getting a fit?"

Nel turned to see a colossus of a woman crouching beside the open door of the hut labeled F3. She was strapping something on her forearm that looked larger and far more sinister than most of the IDH gear Nel had seen so far.

"Guess so?" Nel hazarded.

"Head on in, they'll get you started early if you want." She flashed a smile. "Mariana, by the way."

"Nel," she replied with a strained smile and a nod at the contraption the woman still adjusted. "We all getting those?"

Mariana's laughter was a bark. "Not unless you got the heavy blaster training to go with those shoulders."

"Hard pass," Nel replied with a wince. "Last gunfight I was in I chose a trowel instead."

"Oh, you're that Nel. We heard about you." Mariana's face brightened. "Way it was told I thought I'd have to give up my spot as toughest broad on base while you were here."

"Nah, that's all yours," Nel promised, stepping into the hut. "Thanks, though."

The hut was dimly lit, with tidy stacks of ammo lockers from at least three different defunct military organizations. Each was filled with a different set of parts Nel hoped wouldn't end up anywhere near her skin, let alone jacked into her nervous system. A harried woman glanced up from cataloging one locker's contents. "Name?"

"Dr. Nel Bently." When her brows knit in confusion, Nel clarified, "Might be under Annelise Bently?"

"Yep, got you. Gussy will get you set up. Outside."

Sure enough, a slender man who looked better suited to a runway in Milan than a desert paramilitary outpost flashed her a brilliant smile. "Annelise, good to meet you."

"Nel. Please. 'Less you want me to use you for target practice."

Thankfully, he laughed, rich and bright.

She stared for a moment, hearing the sound arc from stone, mix with birdcalls, and slip away over the river. It seemed like forever had passed since she last heard proper laughter. "So what's this for?"

"Upgrading your suit for self-protection."

"Can we opt out?"

"Are you domestic personnel?"

"Not really sure what I am." Nel eyed the IDH gear with mounting suspicion. "I thought we were going lo-fi here."

"Lo-fi?"

She heaved a sigh. "Low-tech. Something about being encased in electronic fabric when tech can kill me sounds terrible. Actually, everything about it sounds like shit."

Gussy's brows rose. "Well, unless you get a notice from your psychologist or doctor, IDH mandated every adult be augmented."

She grimaced. "Whatever is the simplest one you can get away with, okay?"

"Your record said you used a model X-126 previously. That what you're most comfortable with?"

"Only thing makes me more uncomfortable than using these damn things is being on the business end of one."

"Roger that." He dangled a battered but clean-looking model from his middle finger. "Try this."

It fastened almost seamlessly to the sleeve of her suit. Metal pressed against her skin, delicate electrodes barely more than brassy paint against her faded tan. The material warmed in the time it took to flex her fingers.

"How's that?"

"I don't know if I'll ever get used to these," she whispered. "Don't know if I want to, honestly."

She peered sidelong at the striated copper disk embedded in the electromesh encasing her palm. Cold fear pinched under her sternum at the thought of looking directly down the barrel of one's own hand. She hadn't fought it when Paul leveled his desperation at her. There had been a few times when it sounded appealing, even. But right now, Earth needed help from everyone she could get. And that included one mildly competent archaeologist with an anger problem.

"You need a brush up?"

Nel's shoulders tightened. "Don't think any number of reminders replaces comfort. But yeah. Aren't these things supposed to sync up with us? Last time it was talking in my head."

"Yeah." He frowned, scanning the connections briefly before plugging in the device in his hand. "Should have paired by now."

Seizing the opportunity, she reached for the strap. "Look, if it doesn't work—"

"I'll try a few others. Might be having issues with your chemistry. Hasn't happened since the original prototypes." He turned away, still murmuring the apparently long and sordid history of electromesh and synced weapons. Nel let him mutter, scanning instead the blast holes on the opposite wall. It was not despite her anger that she avoided firearms and weapons in general. Her lack of skill made for a good excuse, but on the far side of her thirties and faced with multiple shoot-outs, it seemed thin.

A soft chuckle rose from an open doorway in the base wall. A broad, middle-aged Black woman leaned there, arms crossed. Something about the set of her smile tugged at Nel's memory, but her embarrassment at being spied on shoved it aside. "What?" she snapped. "Picture might last longer."

Her observer didn't seem fazed by the nasty tone or words.

"Don't mind Max, she's just curious. Try this one, Dr. Bently," Gussy offered, producing another glove. This one, much to Nel's horror, was bulkier.

It was easier to attach, at least, but still, no eerie whisper at the nape of her neck or anything, really, beyond the usual tingle of an electrical field. "Nope. Guess I'm a reject."

Gussy's cheerful face withered. "I just don't understand—"

"Gussy, let it go." The woman in the doorway straightened. "I've been meaning to have a word with Dr. Bently. Why don't you puzzle over this little mystery while we chat, eh?" Her head tilted appraisingly.

Nel felt heat bloom on her face and looked down at her scuffed boots. She hadn't been sure what she really cared to do, beyond finding her mother, for the last few weeks. Still, whoever this person was, she seemed to have something for her. *As long as it's not a set of headphones filled with deadly noise, we'll be okay,* she promised herself. After a second's thought while she fiddled with her trowel handle, she muttered, "How'd you know it was me? Trowel?"

"Attitude." The woman's smile widened, and she gestured into town. "Care to join me?"

They walked in silence, Nel staring at the vines spilling from rooftops and arbors. The heady floral scent weighed her mind, forcing her steps to slow as she passed brilliant red blooms. She tried to note which alleyway they turned onto, if something went south, but the tangle of leaves and worn stone could have been any number of the narrow streets. Nel glanced at her companion as they walked. The woman surely felt Nel's gaze on her but seemed content to let her stare. She was regal, the kind of proud that came from certainty in her own ability. It was the confidence that came from power. Her brown eyes were bright, despite the lines of gray woven into each of the thin, tight braids twisted in a large bun.

"Dr. ah…?"

"Dr. nothing. Never bothered with it. What drove my education wasn't the title, and what I wanted to understand most you can't learn from secondary education. At least, not when I was going."

Nel nodded, noting that the woman hadn't told Nel what she could be called instead. "I get that. I think I mostly wanted the title out of spite. For those who said I couldn't."

The woman chuckled. "Defiance can be powerful." She turned a corner, waiting for Nel to tear her focus away from the glimpse of a garden over the top of a tall stone wall. She unlocked a heavy wrought gate in the same wall and held it open. "Here we are."

While the wall blocked much of the mid-morning light from the street outside, it was as if the limestone blocks reflected it back to the tiny paradise. Winding paths and the table just ahead were bathed in a bubble of warm sunlight.

"This is yours?" Nel marveled, ducking under the lush growth. "It's gorgeous."

The woman laughed, brown skin gleaming as she settled in one of the chairs by the garden table. One ringed hand gestured to the seat opposite.

"So, how'd you hear of me?" Nel settled into the chair, hoping the answer might give her a clue as to who, exactly, she was having brunch with.

"I'm familiar with your work."

"I see." Nel cringed. Her undergrad theories had been about as socially aware as they were understated, which was to say, not at all.

The woman responded with a vague smile as she turned toward the small house against one side of the garden. "Dee?"

A rich male voice drifted from the open windows, accompanied by the gentle sound of dishes.

"Would you mind bringing out the pitcher I set aside this morning? We have a guest." When her attention returned to Nel, she lifted her chin. "I'm Max Gamal."

Nel's brows shot up. It was a name she knew, and not just from a few dozen academic studies. "Wait, remind me of your area of study? You co-authored a few heavy-hitting theories."

"I've been involved with a lot of studies, most notably some funded by your sometimes friend, Mr. Sepulveda."

"So you're one of the Founders? Or do you go by a different name here?" She was leaning forward now, mind jumping at the chance of familiar territory.

"We have as many names as we have origin stories, Bently. Probably more," she answered with a faint smile. "Here we prefer Alkhalaaq. Don't you have different answers when folks ask how you got here?"

"I suppose. Depending on who's asking." She frowned, then felt the thrill of a secret unfurl in her chest. "So, do I get a different answer than the other IDH people?"

"You're not IDH."

She didn't feel like IDH, but never expected any of the Founders groups to really make the distinction. The lines were blurrier by the hour. "Not really."

"Then stop arguing." Her smile grew. "I imagine you're pretty accustomed to arguing."

Nel laughed, cheeks hot. But despite the jab, ease had settled into her bones. Temporary, surely, but a relief. "I think it's about the only thing I'm good at. Or, at least, I seem to turn everything into one. Don't win often though."

"That's rather why I wanted to speak with you."

"I'm shit at arguing?"

"No. Regardless of the outcomes, you still choose to. Not keen on the status quo, at least, not if it's not keen on you." Max stared at her a moment. "We would like to know any developments in IDH's investigation of the sonic attack on Earth and the group known as the Reapers."

"Don't you already? I mean, we're all working as a team."

"Are we?" Max's voice was light but not gentle.

"Surely Emilio—"

"Sepulveda is not literally in bed with the daughter of IDH's most influential family. You've made it this far without becoming an IDH patsy, a disappeared statistic, or a body never found. I still see the glimmer of a soul in there."

"Way down?" Nel joked, if only to release the tension building in the air between them.

"Way, way down."

"Good to know. Don't think I've seen it in a hot minute."

"You're going to need it. Friends will be hard to come by—hold on to them too."

"Oh, I'm trying." Nel collected her scattered thoughts.

The bite in Max's words softened to fondness. "The first time I heard your name it wasn't from IDH. Or from Emilio."

"No?"

"It was from my nephew. He was fresh out of undergrad and kept talking about this girl he met. Course his momma and I thought for sure he was in love, but it was something much more profound than that." Max pulled a leather-bound journal from her bag. She unlatched it with deliberation, drawing a photo from its note-filled pages.

Nel leaned forward, peering at it with interest. Three adults stood in the brilliant sun, the stone pyramids of Giza towering behind them. It wasn't the twin brilliant smiles on the faces of the two women or the familiar earnestness of the white man on their left that made Nel's stomach flip. It was the beaming light brown face of the boy in the front, holding up a brand-new Marshalltown trowel. Nel's eyes widened. "You're Mikey's aunt, the one who turned him on to archaeology. Aunty M?"

She opened her arms with a tired smile. "Indeed. I might have given him a little nudge, forwarded the more interesting papers and planted a few seeds. He was already falling for the romance of the lifestyle."

"Yeah, he was really into that." Nel drew a breath. "Look, I'm sorry. About what happened down there—"

"Oh, no one is sorrier than I am. I regret our wild schedules kept us from seeing one another much. You think it was easy to hear my cousin weeping for her boy when I knew exactly who killed him and why? The fear of a brown boy dying is real enough without bringing our ancient quarrels into it."

Nel looked down. "He was doing what he loved. He was protecting our site, I think. I'd like to tell you it was quick—"

"I'm not a stupid woman, Bently, and I've been of Alkhalaaq long enough to know how fiercely we protect our history."

"How long have you been one? Is it like IDH, where you draft in folks?"

"You're born one or you're an ally. No in between."

"What about people like Emilio?" Nel asked, making designs with the rings of condensation from her glass.

Max waved a dismissive hand. "Sepulveda never knows what he wants. He's just like his brother, though he'd never admit it."

"His brother died, right?"

"I'll let him tell that story. It might be Founders business, but it's not mine. He's a melancholy man, too tied up in his values to see what's right in front of him. And I love him for it."

"Love him," Nel glanced at the young man pruning the bushes.

"Oh, come now, I'm too old for that level of emotional attachment. I enjoy my lovers but that's where it ends. Sepulveda is a brother to me."

"So you've told me how I can help you—though I still don't really get why me." Nel paused.

Max's mouth curled. "Why do I think you're about to explain what you want in return. Altruism isn't reward enough?"

"Saving the world is nice and all," Nel agreed, "but this whole mess has gotten a bit personal."

"It's personal for a lot of us. Living on a planet does that."

"Right." Nel eyed her drink. "I'm looking for someone. Someone IDH is too busy to find."

"What makes you think I can find them?"

"For the same reason IDH is bothering to team up after centuries of rivalry. You know this planet and its people better than anyone."

"The name?"

"Mindi Bently, formerly Bolaurude."

"Mindi Bently," Max repeated.

"My mom," Nel whispered. "Saving the world is fine, but I'd burn it down to find her."

Max drew a long breath, staring at the woodgrain of the table, one elegant hand smoothing it thoughtfully. "I might know some people who are good at finding. Usually information, but that can lead to people. I'll need a bit more from you—where she was last heard from—"

Nel held up her wrist, displaying her communicator. "It's all on here. Along with a few hundred video messages she sent since I left."

"Few hundred?" Max's brows rose in surprise.

"She sent one every day while I was gone. Talking about the weather, meeting with friends, missing me." As beautiful as the gardens were, something in them was making her throat tight.

"I'm sorry." Max slid a slip of paper across the table. "Send it to this address. And the information. If she's out there, we'll find her."

"I'm sorry too," Nel offered after her voice was under control again. "About Mikey."

TEN

As much as she detested the weight of a murderous glove in her hand, Nel might actually hate lagging back more. Even with the muffle of noise-canceling headphones, the ping of the scanner in Teera's hand sent twitches of annoyance through her jaw.

"Hey," Nel whispered to the man next to her.

His eyes flicked up, but otherwise he didn't acknowledge her beyond his eyes flicking in her direction.

"I'm Nel."

"Kestral. And I'm at work."

Shame burned her face. "Sorry. Just making sure I know which names to shout when this whole mission implodes."

His face tightened. "Not funny—I was in Emissary School with Kapten Orso."

For a moment her brain blanked, then the last name swam to view in her mind's eye, attached to a sandblasted space suit and a face atrophied into pain. She winced. "I'm sorry—hell of a loss. I was part of that project."

"I know who you are," he bit out, before stalking across the alley and leaning against the other granite wall.

Nel stared after him, anger crashing through her skull. *Well you weren't fucking there, you don't know!* She bit back all the other, less polite things she honestly wanted to say but felt her nostrils flare. She settled for glaring at the shell of the building in sullen silence.

It was a small building, narrow, and built with durability in mind. Except, of course, for the hole blown in the side. Rubble piled in the street, huge stone blocks scattered like a forgotten Jenga game. Nel peered at the pitted, blackened scars across those farthest from what remained of the wall.

"Burns?" The blast marks on the wall where they had fitted everyone for gloves told her, whatever this technology was, it wasn't typical of IDH. "So, what happened here?"

"If we had that answer we wouldn't be here," Kestral sneered.

She opened her mouth to bitch back but caught herself. She didn't need to be liked. She didn't need to like them either. Ignoring the man, she moved closer to the hole. Already, the explosives experts were marking each stone scarred with a data point, virtually piecing the wall back together on their tablets. Inside, the unlit room was a maw.

Narrow grated stairs led up one wall and down to where the blast must have originated. If there had been any tech, it was either destroyed in the blast or looted later. The map glowing above her wrist displayed two rooms. A glance at the cavernous space showed her they were lucky the original four exterior walls still stood. *Let's hope nothing too structural is damaged.*

No sooner did the thought leave her mind than a tech tossed a black cube into the air. A few dozen cables exploded out, fusing gently to the corners and centers of each wall. The tech tapped a few keys on her wrist and the cables solidified into rebar.

"Whoa," Nel whispered. At least everyone's headphones hid her naivete.

"Alright, Queenie's team is gonna take the immediate blast radius here," Teera called over. The box suspended in the center blinked, projecting a holographic rendering of the layout along with faintly color-coded zones. "Moe, you guys have the residence. Photos, then data points, then excavation and removal. Anything look like it's still on, you press your panic button. And anyone turns anything on, you'll have to deal with me."

Nel found a smile on her face. Safety briefings were often your first hint at your crew chief's sense of humor, or whether they had one at all.

Peach marked the residence on the map, though now it was mostly buried under the dividing wall. Half a dozen bunks once lined the far wall, according to the glowing diagram. Nel patted her side to confirm she had her kit, then followed Moe's tall figure down the metal grated stairs with another tech and—much to Nel's annoyance—Kestral.

"Alright," Moe smiled, teeth gleaming in the projected light. "Thanks for being here. Olivia, you think you can tackle the rec area here, by the door? Kestral, you'd be helpful by the armory rack. Curious if anything was discharged. Dr. Bently, why don't you take this segment by the beds."

"So she can nap on the job?"

Nel's teeth ground hard enough she expected them to crack.

"Not helpful, Kestral, thank you, though," Moe chimed, before resting a hand by Nel's elbow and ushering her to the dark side of the room. "Figured with your trained eye in the human experience on Earth you might have extra insights into anything we'd find here."

"Ah, thanks," Nel ground out, wondering what in her curriculum vitae indicated she knew anything about the excavation of modern paramilitary barracks.

"Just take a careful look around, record everything you can. See anything of interest, just holler."

She dialed up the noise-canceling frequency until the hiss of white noise filled her ears. It was better than commentary. Better than the thud of shifting stone and humming tech. She paced the room, noting the twisted remains of the metal bed frames. Mattresses were reduced to melted foam filling and warped springs.

She had explored hundreds of cellar holes in her day, restored some, even. None triggered the pointed awareness that washed over her when she stepped into the darkness. Whatever had happened here, she felt it. *Call it residual energy, if you want,* she excused. *But this place has eyes.*

Underfoot, debris crunched. Each careful step followed a handful of photographs and a gentle poke with her trowel if something caught the light.

Would she find a photograph of someone stationed here? Someone who died in the blast? There had been casualties—five, judging by the gray outlines of bodies on the colorful overlay. The faded red marks of wounds and what caused them pinched at her heart. She couldn't look at injury maps, even the skeletal blanks her department used for mapping remains. Not since she saw Mikey laid out, empty, cold, bloodless. She shuddered the image away, though it lingered behind her eyes, ready for when she closed them.

There, under the vivisected bed frame at the corner of the room, gleamed something green. She snapped a picture, then another, closer. She placed the point-collector button on the hard, exposed edge, tapped the screen. A reticle appeared, denoting its placement on the grid. Folding away all the technology, she sat back, trowel dangling between her knees in her loose hand. A curious nudge with the tool told her it wasn't small—at least as large as a clipboard, perhaps, and as flat.

Producing a brush, she swept away the dark ash and sand. A row of dots, delicate copper lines, dark and green crisscrossing the surface in digital topography. *Circuits?*

"I might have something," she called. "Not sure what."

Moe knelt beside her. "Hard to say what any of this stuff is until we clean the bullshit off." He snapped a photograph then peered closer. "Looks like a circuit board—high tech one, too."

"IDH?"

"Could be. Founders and us share a lot of tech, though none of us would like to admit it."

Nel chuckled, the first real mirth all day, it seemed. "Yeah, feels like rival sports teams, except everything about the game can kill you." She rubbed the base of her ear. "Even the cheers. Gimme a 'D,' gimme an 'I,' gimme an 'E.'"

Moe grinned, eyes still fixed on the artifact before them. "There's a fair bit of this left. Could actually run some scans once we get back."

Nel eyed the circuitry. "What's this bit here? Looks melted." Her nitrile-covered finger hovered over a particularly dense cluster of gleaming metal and soot-stained ceramic dots.

"Good eye—that's why I wanted to bring it back." Moe frowned. "It's augmentation. Whatever this was being used for, someone wanted big upgrades fast."

"Why go through the trouble? Why not just plug into a thumb drive?"

Moe snorted. "Not a computer person?"

Nel glanced up, defensive. "Look, we got dial-up when I was in high school. You lot grew up with hyperdrives or whatever. Cut me some slack."

"I will if you brush this bit off," Moe challenged.

Nel bent over the task, watching the rest of the circuits emerge.

"There." His finger jabbed at the air just above another snowflake of added circuitry. Sweat flicked from his brow at the movement. "That's where whatever this was came in. Wish some of the connections were still there. People don't often use these—a lot of it struggles under the sheer amount of data most of our systems use. Like here," his finger ghosted over the PCI slots. "Running with PCI this small? It was almost obsolete a decade ago. Talk about a bottleneck—"

"Okay, why did they use it?"

Moe shrugged. "Like I said. Time probably. Or avoiding the safeguards on higher tech. Now we print ours, of course, but if they knew older tech? A good circuitry master can lay a new board in a matter of hours, if they have a plan. Whatever this was for was powerful, and they needed it yesterday."

"Don't love the sound of that."

"I wouldn't get too nervous—hot place like this, they could have been rewiring their PCs for better AC for all we know. Fuck knows I would."

A call went up from down below for Moe. "You got this?"

"Sure," Nel promised, pulling out the rest of her kit. "I'll bag up whatever is attached too, if there's anything."

Nel watched him wind back to the lower level before turning back to the corner of bright green jutting from the ashy sediment with a determined glare.

Another tangle of wires led into the dust, pinned under a small block of rubble. Nel brushed off the dust and worked her fingers under the edge. It rolled away with a soft thump. Nel frowned. They were still plugged in. She scanned the wires, moving from plug to wall and back. Dead. Forcing herself, she yanked it free of the wall and slipped it quickly into the evidence bag. *Fuck.*

She hadn't photographed it plugged in. Wincing, she snapped a photo of its relief in the dust before noting how it was found. Whatever it was, tucked under a bed and rewired, Nel didn't believe for a second it was desperation during a heat wave.

ELEVEN

Muffled calls shoved through her headphones and she glanced up, half expecting another scolding. Instead, people pressed for the stairs, Harris bolting through them, face stern. Dropping her bag into the evidence cart, Nel jogged after them. There was room enough on the bare roof, and Nel found a spot overlooking the next district. It was noon, the sky bleached and shadows gone.

Muffled shouts increased. The hair on Nel's arms rose in a shiver. It was the draw before a tsunami. A flash, all sound sucked into stillness. A crack rocketed through the city, emanating out, dust and ease left disrupted in its wake.

Harris turned, eyes narrowed, not on the flash or the disruption spilling from its radius, but behind them. Against the rising clamor engines ground. His mouth moved, a curse, a promise.

Her gaze snapped to the plane exploding from a cluster of downed buildings. It was a strange hybrid between Earth tech and IDH, but unlike the

Founders' gear, which made the melding seem a stylistic choice, this was a junkyard hodgepodge. If there were any call-numbers on the craft's fuselage, they were rusted and dinged beyond deciphering.

Screams rose a second later.

"Moshe! They've taken Moshe! God save us!"

Nel whirled, heart pounding. *Taken?* "Will someone tell me what the fuck is going on?"

"Reaper strike," Moe ground out. "Been happening across the world. People just coming out of nowhere, bundling folks away. Don't even know it's happened half the time until things are blowing up to cover their tracks or they're taking off."

Nel peered at the buildings, stomach tight. *Reapers.* "Surely people see them land—"

"Probably assembled here, pieces shipped in from somewhere. These days the only air traffic we get is IDH drop-squads delivering vaccines and dampeners and Reapers ripping us out of our houses."

"You don't chase them down?"

"Too risky, until we have a better idea of who we're dealing with."

"Couldn't it just be people taking advantage?" Nel hazarded. She didn't need another adversary. Not with the Teachers' judgment looming, and IDH's…everything. "You kind of left a power vacuum."

"IDH runs everything down here now," Moe promised. "It was a rocky transition at first, but people needed us. Still do." .

"Right." Nel intoned. They had skirted cities, and even now, on the edge of Qena, she could sense the tension. IDH might have control on paper, but if choppers were dropping out of clear skies and making off with people, she knew whatever control they had on paper was closer to a joke than actuality.

"Wrap it up, folks," Teera called, hands signing for those farther away. "This place will blow if they know we're here when Reapers struck."

They'll wonder why you didn't stop them. Nel turned from the wall, patting to check for her trowel.

"A word, Dr. Bently." Harris leaned on the edge of the roof, eyes fixed on the black dot of the helicopter, expression neutral. His low voice barely seeped through her headphones. "I saw you attempt to make friends with Kestral."

"Apparently it's what I'm best at," she snarled. *He's just teasing.* Teasing was fine, fun even. If she were the one doing it. "So. Reapers. Bombing?"

"That was a diversion. Distract enough people, no one's going to recall the exact numbers on their ships' bellies."

"Plus—internet down means no viral pics," Nel supplied. "So, getaway like that means they tipped someone off—strike mission?"

His brows rose, and she let teeth turn her smile wolfish. "I planned more than a few diversions to sneak a date out of her house," she explained. "Regardless, you and I both know what happened here is connected to Samsara."

"You and I both know nothing. Space is large," he reminded her, eyes level. "There's room for more than one monster among the stars."

Her jaw clenched and she leaned on the rooftop wall. Smoke spiraled from the nearby crater. Whatever they had blown up, it was small, and few, if any, were harmed. It didn't seem like the actions of a monster. "We gonna investigate?"

"We've had teams on the case for a while. The elegance of the bomb can tell you a lot about who they are. And apparently, they're never the same."

Nel's thoughts hitched and she glanced at him. *Elegant.* It wasn't a term she would think of for the chaos and destruction catalyzed by any sort of explosion.

"Take some advice, Bently?"

She grimaced. "What's that?"

"Don't make friends."

She stepped back, eyes narrowed. "With all due respect, sir, you kind of invited me here in the first place."

"Not to socialize. We aren't to leave the base, except for missions. Care to explain why you were having brunch in Munashi Gamal's garden yesterday, when you were scheduled for a glove assignment?"

She stepped back, suddenly fifteen again and being reprimanded in the hallway of the weird middle school she wound up at for her problematic behavior. "Look, I'm sorry—"

He held up a hand. "Don't apologize when you neither know what you're apologizing for nor truly mean it. Our intentions matter."

She balked. "I've always been an 'impact matters more' person."

"Our intentions matter," he repeated. In a harder voice the phrase would have sounded admonishing. Instead, it was almost reassuring. "Care to explain why you met with her?"

The request burned in her ears. "Not really. But I will. I was researching. I get that I'm too hysterical or whatever to be a part of the main mission, but you have to know how it looks when a bunch of people show up to fix a problem they might have started in the first place. Most people I study have suffered under colonialism."

"A white woman better not be about to lecture me on that."

"No, just pointing out how it looks from here. I'm comfortable being wrong—fuck knows I'm wrong a lot."

"Nel, I need you to listen to me: there are a lot of factors at play between IDH and the Founders. Even someone with my clearance and experience can't know every detail. If you think there is some subterfuge, you're probably right. But I caution you to keep a small counsel."

"Why? I thought we were all here for the same reason—to fix this?"

"To be young again," he lamented, eyes softening. "We are all here for our own reasons. I can't claim to know why the Los Pobladores arrived in our airspace suggesting a truce after thousands of years of guerilla attempts to stunt out progress. But I can think of many more likely reasons than altruism. Your thoughts are powerful, Dr. Bently, but once they leave your mouth, they become something not entirely yours."

"You're telling me to keep my thoughts to myself?"

"I'm telling you to keep your ideas your own until you're absolutely certain whomever you're sharing them with isn't going to use them to harm the very people you're trying to protect."

Nel looked after the helicopter. *You think it's them?* But, as he commanded, she kept it to herself. "Guess I just thought this would be easier if things were friendly, if I'm working with them."

"You don't work with them. You work for me. And these people?" He gestured to the arrayed techs and military officers, the equipment and maps and gloves and acrylic. "They aren't your friends."

"I'm getting that," she snapped. "I thought I was here to keep the daughter of the elite happy."

"His brows arched. "Getting educated while you're down here, I see."

"Well it's not like anyone is forthcoming about who the fuck any of you actually are," she drawled. To her surprise, it drew a chuckle.

"You are clever, and disrespectful, and far too assured of yourself for anyone's good, especially your own." It didn't sound like an insult. Not in the traditional sense. Finally, the illusion of a smile touched his face for a moment before fading as fast as it had come. "And that is why I invited you down here."

Later, when the long shadows across the walls were purple, bruised from the day, and the ibis cut quietly across the sky, Nel slipped out. It was the second night in a row Lin came back well after midnight. It wasn't that she wanted more of Lin's attention, though she enjoyed their sex. The woman's frequent absence was a reminder that Nel was not, and probably never would be, part of the cool kids' club.

The compound was dim, but laughter and conversation rose from the largest hut, what must be a mess hall. Taking the side path she'd used earlier, she cut through the base and to the rear. Sure enough, the armory lights were on. Within, Gussy moved along the rack of weapons. Judging by his rhythmic movements and bobbing head, he was singing.

"Doing good, Bently?"

She turned, catching sight of Moe, box of evidence in tow, heading toward the technical lab. "Hey, yeah. Thanks for being patient with me today," she blurted, the words catching on her pride as they left her mouth.

He waved it away. "No, you're great. Don't pay half of us any mind. Just a bunch of dressed-up academics with fancy toys. You do good work, keep your head down, you'll be set."

"You run diagnostics on that shit yet?" Nel jerked her chin at the box. "Gives me the creeps."

"Nah, 'bout to do some research though. Gonna test a few things, see if any of the circuitry's intact." He winked. "Headphones on, of course. Plus, any stray signals come through, my system's programed to shut down."

"Good luck, then."

"You too, have a good night!" He offered a wave and disappeared into the lab.

Nel stared after him for a moment. She wanted to ask if it was like the Samsari tech. She wanted to know what a "thank" file was. She wanted to know how long they'd be here. Instead, she turned back to the armory door. Bright, bombastic sound reverberated through the thick walls. Nel knocked, then again, louder.

The music, if you could call it that, softened, followed by the click of a lock, then the door opened.

"Ah, our prodigal archaeologist," Gussy drawled. "Round two?"

"Kind of." Nel winced, catching a few lines of the deceptively cheery music. "What is this?"

"Ah! It's French. Doomsday in cheerful packaging. Sparked a Graffiti movement even."

The anti-establishmentism in her grinned. "Cool, even if it sounds like a migraine. Do you think we could try all this again?"

His bouncy shuffles stilled, and he took her in, quiet for a moment. "Why the change in heart?"

She shrugged. "You were all gung-ho earlier."

"I'm an enthused dude. But I'm the weapons specialist here and part of that is being one of the people who determines if it's unsafe for an individual to bear a weapon in the first place. Noting when a person wants to be armed. And why."

Nel hadn't expected to have to explain herself. "I was out on a mission today. Reaper strike just a few streets over. You could say I'm realizing the world I left here isn't, ah," she cleared the rasp from her voice, "isn't here anymore."

His expression softened and he settled on the corner of the table. "Yeah. That's a good reason. We can try again, for sure. I ran those models through our diagnostics three times. Nothing. Working perfectly. Took them out to test myself this afternoon. Bullseyes each time. I've never heard of someone stubborn enough to simply will the pairing away, but science can't always explain stuff, even IDH's high-tech understanding."

"Just about anyone who's known me for longer than two minutes will agree if there's a head hard enough, it's mine." Nel chuckled darkly.

"Maybe now that I'm open to the idea, we'll have better luck?"

He nodded, glancing at the number projected on the wall beside his battered desk. "Got about forty minutes until lights-out. We could do some tests." Gussy disappeared into one of the storage rooms, the clatter of rummaging emanating a second later.

Nel stepped through the rear door. In the dim evening light, the blasted targets were pitted eyes. She fiddled with the pendant under her suit and wished the anxiety bubbling in her gut was useful, like it had been on the powerlines, or with a thousand tasks to keep track of on a job site. Instead she was waiting, waiting, waiting. Nel wasn't good at waiting.

She raised a naked hand to one of the targets, closing one eye to watch it bounce with her perspective. Opening both again, she flexed her hand and whispered, "Boom."

Concrete dust and rebar exploded through the air.

TWELVE

I have superpowers. Nel's ears whined. Salty heat trickled down her face, stinging her eyes as much as the smoke from burning plastic. The pain in her back seemed superficial. After a cursory test to confirm what toes she had left still wiggled, she dragged herself upright. The left wall of the armory testing area was in pieces. The lab hut was obliterated. Her childish fantasy dissolved with the recollection of who had been in the lab. And what he was working on.

"Moe!" Her stinging throat said she was shouting, though the ringing in her ears muffled the world, let alone any response. She stumbled over the rubble. Metal supports were twisted. Water shot from a broken supply line, turning packed sand to mud in seconds. She wiped water and blood from her eyes, squinting against the haze of demolition. "Moe?"

A dark river snaked from beneath a pile of the former ceiling, merging with dribbling toilet water in a crimson tributary. Nel's adrenalated heart faltered. She dropped to her knees, ripping cinder blocks and ceiling tiles away, heedless of the scraps of skin she left on the ragged rubble.

Finally, her palm found something soft and still warm. Efforts redoubled, she tossed another chunk aside. Moe's body was crumpled beneath a support beam, exposed ribs glistening with each shuddering, shallow breath. Nel wiped viscera from his bloodless face, whispering platitudes neither of them could hear.

"Hey, hey, I'm here, it's alright, you're okay, medics are coming." Except she wasn't sure if he was okay, or who had heard the blast. She pressed a hand on his shoulder and found nothing but torn pink flesh and rent bone. His blank, roving eyes met hers.

Something warm settled on her shoulder and she batted it away. When it returned, firmer, she whirled, voice cracking with her shout. "What?"

Gussy stood behind her, face lined with horror. His mouth moved rapidly, but Nel jerked away.

"I can't fucking hear you and he's under there, he needs—" Two hands now, strong ones, towed her out of what remained of the room and into the armory. Dizziness swallowed her thoughts, but she shook it away. She twisted, trying to free herself, rush back to help them save the friendly tech.

"Nel!" Emilio's voice wormed into the static and screeching. His dark face swam before her eyes, watering with the smoke and frustration. "Nel, come here. Sit."

"I've got to—"

"He's dead, Nel." His matter-of-fact tone cut through the babbling in her brain. "Nothing to do. Sit here."

She couldn't sit, though, with energy and fury coursing in her body, and instead began rocking, anything just to move. "But I saw breathing—"

"Sometimes our body does things because that is what it evolved to do, even after the signals stop. He's dead the moment that beam's lifted. You know it well as I do."

She blinked in confusion. Outside a crowd gathered around the bloodstained rubble. Across the training yard Lin's eyes locked on Nel's and she made a frantic attempt to shove through the people.

"I need—"

The door to the armory swung shut. "A medic is here to check your injuries. Sit." Emilio reiterated.

Nel's vision tunneled and abruptly she was seated on the bench. Jem's face and voice swam through the panic clotting her thoughts.

"Can you hear me? Good. I'm just going to scan you, then we'll get you patched up." They opened their medic kit on the bench next to Nel, dabbing away blood and dust.

"What about the person bleeding out in the lab?"

"Dr. Bently." It wasn't Emilio's voice, but the authority of Dr. Ndebele's. "I have some questions."

Jem glanced up. "I still have to examine her, Doctor."

"I can do both," Nel ground out, teeth still aching from the blast that knocked her from her feet.

Dr. Ndebele turned to Emilio. "Munashi Sepulveda, would you mind telling Letnan Nalawangsa that she will have her girlfriend back as soon as we're done here, and I would appreciate it if she ceased screaming at the door?"

Nel glanced at the door. Muffled voices drifted through the heavy wood and tinnitus. *Was this the last thing Paul heard?*

Emilio nodded, catching Nel's eye before he left. Her comm blinked a message a second later.

We'll talk soon.

Nel stilled as Jem scanned her skull and body for hidden injury. When they stepped back, she glared at the mission supervisor. "You need forensics in there."

"They already are." She settled on the edge of Gussy's vacated desk. "I know you're in shock, but anything you can tell us now, in the moment, would help us, and help Moe."

"Think he's beyond that now." Whatever made Nel's thoughts muddled seemed to fast-track them to her mouth.

"Can you explain what happened? What you were doing in the lab? You're not authorized—"

"I wasn't in the lab," Nel snapped. "I was trying to get fitted for a glove again, since we had issues earlier. I was waiting for Gussy to find one and the lab just...blew." Nel watched the smoke still drifting past the windows. Distant stinging bloomed where Jem carefully laid a few pads on Nel's scrapes.

Dr. Ndebele frowned. "Moe, along with all our techs, was outfitted with a kill-switch upon transfer to this mission. If you think something triggered it, we need to know."

Kill-switch? "Who the fuck puts kill switches in their employees?"

"Someone who wants the rest of their employees to survive. Moe volunteered. They all did." The woman's eyes closed, lips moving, perhaps in prayer. When they opened again, they held new fatigue. "Was there anything else? Do you know what might have happened to trigger his switch?"

Through the haze of frustration and fear, Nel felt pity for the woman. And shame. "I found a circuit board thing. Altered, Moe said. And it was plugged in. Its catalog number was, ah," she frowned, forcing her brain to supply the string of numbers through the bombarding gruesome images. "Q1-R82—no R87-something. I saw him on his way to the lab on my way over. Said he was going to run some scans on it. The augments looked like what we saw on Samsara, kind of, but tiny."

"There was no record—"

"When Lin and I went back. The trip you tried to court martial—"

"Not my department, Bently," she warned. "It was similar?"

"Moe seemed to think it was altered due to lack of resources. Instead of making something new. He wasn't concerned. But I'm not sure if he had seen the notes about it being still wired in. I know power was cut, but," she shrugged. Adrenaline was fading, and pain started to clamor. "Can I be done here?"

The mission supervisor looked to Jem, who sat back with a tired attempt at a smile. "You have a minor concussion. No sleep for the next few hours. Scrapes and bruises will heal with a bit of time. I've sent you care instructions. If you have dizziness or vomiting have Lin call one of us right away, alright?"

"Will do." Nel watched them leave but couldn't bring herself to rise. "Think we can be done too?"

Dr. Ndebele heaved a sigh, arms crossed. "I have something to say first."

It wasn't the dread of being called to the principal's office, but it was close. "Shoot."

"I don't like you. You're impulsive and mean and see very little of the larger picture. It's obvious you don't respect me or this organization as a whole."

Nel pursed her lips. "You kind of fucked up my site and tried to frame me for murder—"

"We meddled with your work and you did the same with mine. And I don't run the judicial branches of IDH," she reiterated, but it was exhaustion, not contempt in her words. She pointed to the door separating them from the carnage outside. "A man is dead and both of us would rather he wasn't. Let's put things aside until we get through this."

Nel looked away. Her mind flashed images of torn flesh across the backs of her eyelids until she couldn't tell if the injuries were Moe's, Paul's or Mikey's. *Mikey.* "You're right," she admitted. "I couldn't do your job. Don't really know what it is, half the time. I do respect you. But IDH is another matter. And right now, you're its face."

"You've managed to put the past aside for Emilio and Los Pobladores. I would appreciate the same consideration."

"I'll try. Thank you." She forced grime and bile past the lump in her throat. When she saw Dr. Ndebele's questioning frown, she explained, "For trying to save my planet."

"My people came from here once too, you know, and I honor them. That's why I wear their name." She rose, gleaming facade in place again. "Would you like me to get Letnan Nalawangsa in? It's a miracle she didn't break down the door."

Nel shook her head, then wished she hadn't when her brain seemed to bounce against the thick bone of her skull. When the woman was at the door, however, she looked up. "I'm sorry. I don't know how else to be, what else to do. I've never been this powerless."

"What we're all doing. Try to process this in a way that doesn't make nightmares. Take a walk in a peaceful place. Check the foundation of your worldview. Talk to Dr. Lieberman or someone else." She offered a reserved smile. "Personally, I prefer the walks."

Nel only made it as far as the stairs into the train before Lin found her. A strangled cry was Nel's only warning before the other woman's lean arms were locked around her shoulders. Kisses and tears rained on Nel's soot-stained cheeks.

"I'm so glad you're okay," Lin whispered, thumbs wiping the trace of her panic from Nel's face. "I heard the blast and saw you covered in blood—"

"It's not mine. Again."

"Thank goodness—"

"I think I'd prefer no blood, at this point," Nel muttered, levering herself up the stairs. "I'm fucking tired of death. And just tired."

"Did you get cleared by a medic?" Lin slid open their door and helped Nel limp to the bathroom. When the archaeologist halted mid-strip with a flinch, Lin eased the tank top off and guided her to sit on the toilet lid.

"Banged up and concussion, but fine."

"Concussion isn't fine," Lin snapped, deftly removing the rest of Nel's clothes. It might have been the least sexy disrobing, but it made Nel's heart jump in a way seduction didn't.

"Hey," Nel caught Lin's hand. "I'm alright, really. Mild concussion. Jem sent me instructions and I've had more than a few concussions in my day."

"Maybe stop bashing through things headfirst." The worry in the letnan's eyes weighed the tease.

"Funny, Dr. Ndebele was complaining about me doing just that." Nel shifted to the shower, wincing as the scalding water hit the scrapes too minor to warrant a healing pad. She tilted her head back, grateful to have a moment where tears could fall, unwitnessed. The door slid open a second later and Lin stepped in, offering a smile.

Memories flashed of a different shower, a different aftermath, a different ordeal. Nel wondered if the past twelve hours aged her face the two years she had missed. "Hey."

Lin dumped cleanser into her hand and motioned for Nel to turn around. Her hands were gentle ghosts on Nel's scalp. "Death and explosions aside, how'd it go today? At the site."

"Found some stuff. Felt nice to be back on a site again. Even if it's more forensics than archaeology." She grimaced at the memory of Moe's friendliness. "Saw a Reaper strike a bit too close for comfort. You?"

"Busy. We isolated a few potentials, with the signal, given the timing. But there's some anomalies when we ran the search…" She trailed off, eyes glazing. Then she made a face. "Ugh, as much as I love working with her—and it's a real privilege, don't get me wrong—but Dr. Ndebele is such a stickler. Triple-checking everything."

"I guess it's good to be careful but, yeah, I'd find that frustrating too."

"It's just my stuff," Lin confessed. "I think the Dar stuff, and, well, you know. Just has everyone thinking I'm the next one who is going to lose it."

Nel glanced back. "I don't hate her—I'm not a fan of rules and sticklers. But I know she's doing a good job under shit circumstances."

"You tell her that?"

"Not in so many words…" Nel watched dust and a dead man's blood sluice from her body and spiral down the shower drain. "I owe her an apology. And I am sorry. For my part in it. I didn't want you to fuck your career up over me."

Lin rested her brow on Nel's shoulder. "You did it for me."

"I don't know how I would have handled things, everything that's happened down here since I left, I mean. I would have muddled along. But I think I'm getting a bit used to being tossed in the deep end."

"I'm getting used to you being here." Lin pressed her lips to the nape of Nel's neck. "I'll let you finish up."

The shower wasn't as warm alone, Nel was loath to admit, and once her skin was devoid of anything other than raw places where she had scrubbed and antibiotic bandages, she emerged from the bathroom.

Lin was perched on the bed, Nel's computer open before her. Panic at the intrusion flashed through Nel, but when Lin looked up it was with an embarrassed smile. "I input my credentials for you."

"Huh?" Nel toweled her hair off, hating the distrust swirling in her gut.

"I think IDH's hesitancy is justified, but not the punishment. You want to do research. And help. And I'm acting just like Dr. Ndebele does with me. Not trusting you. I don't have high clearance, but it's better than yours." She slid the computer across the coverlet. "I'm sorry."

"Me too. And thanks." Nel slumped naked onto the bed with an exhausted laugh. "I promise not to look up porn with it."

Lin raised her eyebrows. "Just make it worth the trouble if you do."

Nel twined her finger through the damp hair at the base of Lin's neck. "I'm not supposed to sleep, and I'd really like to not think about IDH, or Reapers, or Founders or anything else, for just a little while."

Wordlessly, Lin pulled up her video library and drew Nel against her body.

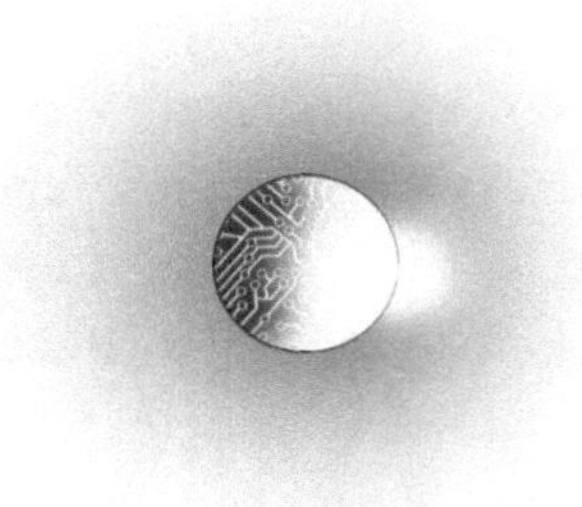

THIRTEEN

Qena was already a mottled splotch on the southern horizon of Nel's memory. That morning, they had flashed through the Faiyum Oasis, far greener than their journey across the Suez Canal days before. Ahead lay a winding journey along the Nile. Nel had spent most of the preparations drifting in concussed confusion. For once, it was nice to have an excuse not to work. Not to be in the thick of things. *I wish we could just go back.* Except this was the world she had begged to return to. What was left of it, anyway.

Nel's cursory dive into the two-year backlog of news had already exhausted her limited energy.

Vaccine Approved—Humanitarian Mega Corp IDH Begins Human Trials - Daily Report
Suspect Arrested for Airborne Kidnappings - Legal Herald of Britain

Institute for Development of Humanity Co-Chair Named Person of the Year - U.S. Times
"Copter Kidnapper" Sentenced: 142 years - Judicial Reporter

Still, she couldn't tear herself away, frown burrowing deeper with each headline.

Copter Kidnapper Killed in Prison Riot—Foul Play? - La Perodista
IDH Co-Chair McNally honored with second Nobel - IDH Informer
Kidnappings Continue—Copycat or Tragic Mistake? - U.S. Times

Nel's eyes ached from the blue glow of her screen. Her head pounded from lack of sleep. Mostly, though, her heart hurt. This was her home. Her planet. *Humans are always hot trash,* she admitted, closing down the database screen. *But this is next level.*

Reapers: The New Plague, and Why IDH Can't Stop it - Daily Report
Terrorist Attack in Qena: Sonic Alien Weapons? - The Times of The Hague

She exited the search and slumped deeper into her unofficial spot at the passenger tables. Here, with the light dimmed by the changing tint in the windows, outside looked warm, welcoming. The car was deserted, save for a hulking young man a few seats up who was absorbed in what Nel suspected might be digi-chess. He chewed on his lower lip for several minutes before lifting a hand to make a move. Without touching the screen, he let his hand drop and returned to his gnawing.

The train downshifted with a buzz and Nel glanced up, surprised to see the long shadows of afternoon. Ahead, a squat series of shelters lined one side of the tracks, separating the gleaming length of train from the long dusty track winding alongside. Cairo and Giza's pyramids glittered through the eastern horizon's haze.

"Fuel stop?" she asked the air, a moment before realizing light rails didn't exactly run out of gas.

The train hissed to a halt, hydraulics lowering its bulk until the single set of stairs unfolding from the passenger cars could reach the ground. Sand settled into stillness. No one waited in the depot's shade, nor did there seem to be waiting cargo to load up.

Nel squinted at the horizon. A faint plume of dust drifted between two rises. A dark pinprick shadowed their center. Another minute of waiting brought a line of industrial trucks rumbling into the station. Judging by the nonexistent cabs, most were automated, their hulking shapes seemingly more suited to mine work than long-distance travel. A figure swaddled in cloth and goggles jumped from the cargo area of one of the smaller vehicles, waving at someone in the train's rear.

They flipped open a panel on the side of the lead truck, fingers flying over the keys before slamming it shut and locking it once more. They backed up a step, watching as the convoy—connected with long cables and chains, Nel now saw—lurched back onto the track and into the dusty distance. They hauled themselves aboard the train.

A moment later a dusty woman slumped into the seat across from Nel. Under a layer of grime and sweat her skin was tan. Sun-red streaked her dark hair. The mission operative appeared, brandishing his scanner. She flashed him a card and murmured a few words Nel didn't understand. Whatever she spoke, it was with the ease of someone fluent or ignorant. Judging by his wordless acquiescing, it was the former.

A tattered turquoise tank peeked from under the faded collared shirt and white and red keffiyeh. Her legs splayed, boots planted on the floor. Nel hadn't seen shoes that worn since she left Chile. "Nice Redwings."

The woman's exhausted gaze settled on Nel. After a beat, her face split into a sunburned grin. "Thanks. Nice moonboots."

"Borrowed." Before Nel could explain away her increased involvement with IDH to a stranger, a new message blinked on her wrist.

SENDER: Picklestein's Monster
SUBJECT: dust to dust

The archaeology-branded newcomer was shoved out of her mind as she opened the message. Apparently, it was something even Lin's borrowed credentials couldn't obtain: project reports on Samsara. Arnav's voice unspooled in her mind as she read.

> *Evidence suggests that while the device in the center of Samsara Ahimsa Mrtyu was indeed designed to open the interior of the planet, this was not its primary function. We have found multiple "dead end" circuits and systems that imply an additional, larger purpose. Additionally, while these systems and that of the gate mechanics themselves use Samsari technology and that of the beings known as the Teachers, they themselves were not the origin for this specific utility, merely an inspiration.*

> *Biomedical Officer Molly Cass's examination of what remains of the planet's surface tells us the desert created in the wake of the initial event is not composed primarily of silicate, as previously thought, but calcium phosphates with trace sodium and potassium salts. Further research will be conducted to confirm speculations as to the origin of these minerals.*

Nel sat back, frowning. Maybe it was the concussion, maybe it was the exhaustion, but Nel could barely make sense of it. So, if the Teachers did not produce it, and IDH did not understand it, and the Founders did not have access to it in the first place…who destroyed Samsara? Who murdered the inhabitants? Who seemed intent to further their attempts on Earth?

That last thought was a snarl in Nel's mind. She knew, down to the lacework inside her bones, that these were connected. But the steps weren't the same. Instead, she felt like whatever was occurring on Earth was new. *Further research will be conducted.*

Calcium phosphates. Trace salts. Her thoughts drifted to the two tiny boxes tucked in her luggage, the inorganic dust left behind when someone perfect and mortal was reduced to the base of their bones. Perhaps, in their frantic search for evidence of the Samsari populace, they had excavated through the only thing remaining.

Nel rose as the woman across from her dropped into enviable sleep. She straightened slowly, giving her bruises the time to stretch before cutting back through the cargo cars. She emerged onto the porch off the caboose.

Bright sun blazed across the desert, bleaching the world, save for the tiny sliver of shade Nel sequestered for herself at the rear of the train. Bullet holes still peppered its shell, but otherwise it was a welcome escape from what her world had become. At least the sunlight had the decency to be honest in its abrasiveness.

Maybe it just didn't matter what happened lightyears away when the soil of her homeland was barren, and all the hopeful infrastructure of the last few years had been shut down. Short of just never flipping a switch back on, what was the recourse?

"You have a moment, Dr. Bently?"

She glanced up into Emilio's warm gaze and for a moment forgot where she was. And when. "Ah, yeah. Sorry. Sure. Here?"

He chuckled and gestured down the cars. "I got my hands on some Mote con Huesillo. If you want to join me."

"Más chileno que el mote con huesillo." She levered herself from the seat with a grateful sigh. "I could use the break too. I think my screen might be seared into my brain."

"That's the one benefit to needing glasses to see the things," he confided, tapping the pair of black-framed readers tucked into one of the many pockets of his suit's chest. "Got the lenses that block different wavelengths."

"I should probably adjust my settings…" She trailed off as she stepped through the gangway and into Los Pobladores' officers' car. *It even sounds different in here,* she realized. Emilio's room was near the front. He nodded to the seats by his window and rested a hand on the door. "Do you mind some privacy?"

"Not at all." She watched him slide the door shut and retrieve two glasses from his sink. Like everything on the train, they were gleaming metal, unbreakable and sterile.

He filled them both, raising his as he handed her the other. "To cooperation."

She held his gaze as she took a slow sip. The bite of peach slipped over her tongue, followed by the malt of wheat. His glass clinked on the table and he regarded it, as if expecting it to say more. Another sip saved her the responsibility of breaking the silence.

When Emilio spoke, it was in Spanish and devoid of pretense. "I suppose it's foolish to ask how you are."

"A bit. Be one of the few who did."

His brows twitched and he afforded her the privacy of staring at the table. "It's lonely work."

"I met Max Gamal," Nel blurted, as much to gain control of the conversation as to confide.

"I heard." Emilio grinned. "She's quite the woman. Did she ask a favor of you?"

"That's an unassuming word for double-crossing."

"Double-crossing is a strong word for holding IDH to their promises of allyship," he countered.

Nel twirled her drink, then took another sip to allow herself time to gather her thoughts. "Did you know she was Mikey's aunt?"

"No—I admire Gamal, but I wouldn't call us close."

"She said you were like a brother to her."

His expression grew strained. "Perhaps once. She knew mine, the brother I lost."

Nel caught the sorrow in his voice, heard its echo in her own. "When you showed up orbiting Samsara, you said you were going to tell me the story. About the caves."

His head tilted. "It's not a story of science, though it might seem so. When the Teachers arrived all those years ago, they intended to stay. Colonize, if you will. The first of many people who would appear on our soil, claiming it was never ours, scattering disease and death with one hand while offering cures and mercy with the other. They came as ghosts. We assumed they were spirits."

"Is that where the ngen came from?"

He frowned. "We knew of spirits well before we ever met the Teachers, but we thought perhaps they were a form of the ngen-kürüf. They offered power, magic honestly. Spiritual power. But they said we had to come with them. Shed our world. Many wanted to go, but many more did not. Leaving would mean giving up our burial places, our sacred hills, all of it. We didn't need magic and faith and healing. We had those things. When a people are faced with false deities some choose worship. We chose blasphemy."

Goosebumps flickered over her biceps and down the small of her back, prickling in the wake of sweat.

"But then one day we woke and found our children gone. Those who wished to go had snuck out in the night, slipping through the cave systems to the hunting outpost where they first arrived. A place you're quite familiar with."

"Los Cerros Esperanza VII."

"Indeed. By the time the others woke and raced to find them, they were boarding. There was a fight between the machi and her brother, and it came to blows."

"The body we found. I knew it was a murder!"

He frowned at her. "This is my history."

"I'm sorry." She flushed and looked down. "So, when Bas killed Mikey—"

"There was purpose in his beating, yes."

She squeezed her eyes shut, teeth clenched.

After a moment he continued. "Our people continued on with a cavern where our hearts should be. Through the next generations we retained our religion, our beliefs. Through warfare, through colonization and genocide and now into tourism and living museums."

"Wait," she blurted, "you're all techy now. Was that the Teachers?"

He rolled his eyes, jerking a thumb out the window. "Next you're going to think they built those pyramids. Aliens may have visited, but if you think we lacked the skills or they had any interest in our infrastructure, you'd be fooling yourself. They just wanted to come back and meddle later—"

"The aliens or the colonizers?" she drawled.

He chuckled humorlessly. "We aren't against tech, you know. Just having no choice in the matter. The forced progression. I don't disagree that had we taken up electro gloves and lasers, things would have gone differently. But that's the fault of those who cut our people down and enslaved the rest."

She couldn't imagine the hurt of hundreds of generations coming to bear on one man's shoulders, or the strength it took to work with the descendants of the same people who damned his ancestors. "I'm sorry. About what happened down there. I'm sorry I stomped around in my know-it-all boots. I'm sorry I thought government permits meant anything about how much that land meant to you."

"Thank you. You weren't the first and clearly aren't the last. We can usually tell the difference between those who are just misguided and naive—like yourself—and those who wield privilege like a scalpel."

Nel looked away. "Past few years have taught me good intentions don't make it hurt less."

"No. But we both know you weren't the only one who overstepped. Dr. Servais was a good person. Better than you. He didn't deserve that end."

Nel couldn't answer that, not without anger or tears that weren't Emilio's to coddle. "So, other than checking in on what shady back-alley deals I make, why'd you invite a pissy archaeologist into your train cabin?"

"To make a deal of my own."

She glanced up and their eyes met. "I see."

"No doubt Munashi Gamal asked you to inform us if you happen to hear about anything IDH does that we might not be privy to."

Nel let him wind down to his point, a circumnavigating that gave context for his ultimate ask.

"I would ask that you tell me what you know of Harris."

"Like, literally nothing," she started to dismiss. But the long shadows in the train car the night of the shooting tripped her further protestation.

"When there is such a lack, sometimes we can see the picture based on the shape of the pieces missing."

"Right. If I think of something, I'll tell you. All I know right now is he's the most approachable and kind person IDH has to offer. At least to me. He's the reason I'm down here at all."

"I see. And IDH in general?"

She frowned, remembering the heat of Reaper explosions on her face, the sharp debris under her hands. "The kidnappings—Reapers? They think it's you. Los Pobladores. Alkhalaaq. Or Harris does, at least."

"And you?"

"I think IDH made a mess and doesn't want to spend the time to clean it up." She frowned. "Why are you curious about him?"

Emilio shrugged, sitting back to disengage. "Because the shape of the missing pieces looks familiar."

"Right." She finished her drink and gestured to the space between them. "I'm grateful for this, Emilio. This alliance. Or truce. Friendship?"

"Cooperation." He returned her smile and drained his glass.

FOURTEEN

Sticky blood coated her hands, smearing with soil. Nel wiped them against her canvas shorts again, only to find her thighs were naked. Goosebumps rose in the chill of the Atacama night.

"Dammit," she hissed, stumbling down into the consuming darkness of the cave. She had forgotten something here. Left something. And now her feet and hands were raw from her hike here. That must explain the blood. She navigated by sound, like she had on the corridors, when the moon was too dim to guide her. Now, again, she couldn't even catch a glimpse of sky beyond the swaddling clouds.

A stumble sent her careening through the cave's mouth. Her head cracked against the rocks. Scrambling fingers found not soil, not sand, but the dust of bones. She recognized the taste of stony, salty cremains. Outside, the winds of Samsara screamed in climax, in warning.

The train door clattered shut and Nel peeled her eyes open. Her nose was filled with the sweetness of fresh blood.

"Sorry," Lin whispered, latching the door behind her. She was still dressed for work, and her hair looked as if it hadn't been washed since their shared shower.

"S'ok, fell asleep reading articles," Nel muttered, sitting up. "Think I was having a weird dream."

"What about?"

"Can't remember. Just the sound of screaming." She pressed a hand to her temple, wincing at the tenderness in the delicate shell of bone. "What time is it? Where are we?"

"Just about dinner time." Lin glanced out the window, as if a signpost might be glimpsed in the darkness speeding by. "And we're on base outside of Alexandria."

Nel had to hand it to IDH: they were efficient. Cairo flew past, followed by a flash of Tanta. With the gleaming smoothness of distance, everything seemed perfect. Untouched by a virus or killer soundwaves or violent kidnappings. Idyllic. *Impossible.* "We stopped?"

"Hopefully it's our last one."

"I thought we were going to The Hague too." Nel rubbed the rest of her fitful sleep from her eyes. "Everything alright?"

It was a smile, though, not a frown, that replaced the distance in Lin's eyes. "We made a breakthrough. In the research. Several of the frequencies found in the background of the Samsari audio were also, found fragmented in what we got off the Qena recordings during the attack."

Nel's heart hammered and she leaned forward. "Seriously? That's fantastic! Why didn't you say you were that close?"

Lin looked down. "I know it's been hard for you, not being involved with that part of the project. I didn't want to rub it in. Plus, we weren't sure until we got Arnav's latest report."

Nel scrubbed the ghost of ashes from her hands. "Yeah, that info was pretty wild—did you see the part about the sand composition?"

Lin turned. "I wasn't even on the clearance list for that."

"Hey, I promised to play by the rules, but I doubt Phil did. He knows my interest in the project and probably just took pity on me being out of the loop." Heaving a sigh, Nel swung her legs off the side of the bed and headed to the bathroom. "Win is a win, though. Did you compare them to what Gretta found in Paul and my coms?"

When Lin didn't answer, Nel craned her neck from her seat on the toilet. "What's wrong?"

"No one wants to touch anything from her drives. Teera volunteered to run comparisons, but until we have access to Alexandria's senti-comp, the processing power would probably drain the entire train. That's why it should be our last stop."

"Gotcha. Still amazing, though." She was washing her hands when the words finally caught up to her. "Wait a fucking minute—Alexandria has a senti-comp? Since when?"

"Past decade or so. She was shut down when the signals went out. We're hoping with supervision we can power her back up to fix this mess."

Perhaps it was the soft cocoon of sleep and night, but for a moment, saving the world actually seemed plausible. "So does this mean you might have some time off once we get there? I know your giant brain is indispensable, but surely they'll relinquish you for one evening, at least."

Lin rolled her eyes, sitting at their tiny table. "Like you were ever good at not working."

"I dunno. I think if there's one thing I'm known for it's my beer consumption," Nel speculated. A bubble of warmth burst in her stomach at the smile in the other woman's eyes when they settled on her.

"I'll think about it, promise." Lin stretched with a long, wide yawn. "I'm going to try to take a nap. There's a briefing this afternoon for the main staff, sorry—promise I'll tell you everything, though."

Nel waved it away. "Honestly, I don't think I'm up for sitting and staring at information I only half recognize surrounded by people who don't like me."

The letnan caught Nel's hand as she headed to the narrow closet. "I like you. More than a little."

Heat flooded Nel's throat and cheeks. "You too. Is it alright if I poke around the base a bit, let you rest? Can't kick this headache and could use a change of scene."

Lin nodded, tilted her chin up to ask for a kiss. Nel obliged, dropping an extra one on the woman's brow before tugging on her electrosuit and slipping out.

The train was quiet, its main power dropped to a low buzz. She hoped to see the city as they arrived, but a glance out the windows told her they were in a tunnel or hangar of sorts, the walls a matte, corrugated material. She cut up through the train to the main exit off the general lounge car.

A deserted platform greeted her, the walls a strange combination of Egypt's limestone and the modern modular walls. Here, too, cheery, bubble-lettered signs in Arabic, French, and English reminded her to stay socially distant, to keep a mask on. She reached out, fingering the words. Like Gussy's music, it was a bubblegum version of the apocalypse. The thought of not touching other people, of walking the streets fearing everyone you passed made her heart ache. *No wonder they welcomed IDH with open arms.* She had welcomed them for less—a legal pardon and a cute face.

Like in Qena, they had been sent general maps of this base and a cursory examination told her the main base—off-limits, still, until they entered as a team tomorrow—was mostly above them, and to the south. The high-speed rail terminated there. She peered closer at the glowing blue lines, dim in the bright fluorescence of the station. *There.* A corridor leading up and to the side, along the boundaries of the base. If there were walls, maybe she could get a view.

At the top of the stairs, however, a guard waited, splay-legged in a folding chair. His heavier elecrosuit was topped with a bulky vest and a turban. She didn't recognize him from the train and raised a friendly hand. "Morning."

He nodded, his electro-gloved hand relaxing slightly. "You one of IDH's staff?"

"Yeah," she half-lied. Spying the rectangular shape in his vest pocket, she continued. "Any chance I could pop out for a smoke? Haven't had a chance since we got here."

After a glance down the hall, his mouth quirked, and he jerked his head at the door. "Don't wander, eh?"

"Thanks." She flashed a winning smile and slipped out. It was a courtyard, skirting the front and sides of a hulking building. The front seemed to be some repurposed ancient stone structure, with the back half the austere IDH architecture. Balmy air billowed with the hot-salt scent of the sea. Somewhere a bird squawked, and the faint bustle of a city reached over the walls.

Nel frowned. The previous base had misled her. Alexandria's was protected by three-story granite ramparts. A narrow walk ringed it, with guards at each corner. Coiled razor wire glinted along the top, angled to prevent anyone from crawling over from outside. Claustrophobia pressed on her temples. *Well, IDH, are you trapped in here with me, or am I trapped in here with you?*

Avoiding the guards and walking with purpose, she mounted the thin stone stairs. Early dawn light splashed gold across the yellow stone. Alexandria was smaller than Cairo, boasting the same seamless integration of modern high-rises and sun-bleached limestone monuments. Mud-brick buildings and cement-block apartments clustered along the outskirts. A distant voice arched from the mosques, calling for Salat Ul Fajr.

Leaving the base was probably not recommended, but her heart longed for the press of people and new streets to explore. *And like there's going to be anywhere we can actually cut loose on base.* Already her mind was spinning with how they might slip past the stone and razor wire for the evening.

Another sea breeze tugged at her re-dyed hair. Rich turquoise banded the northern horizon, where the roads and buildings of Alexandria's port jutted into the Mediterranean. Nel closed her eyes and lifted her face to the varied scents of earth.

"I know that face, and it spells trouble," Lin insisted when she returned from her briefing that evening.

"Only a little bit of trouble," Nel wheedled. "I promised to show you around Earth, we've both been stressed out the ass and finally have a night off."

"But we're not—"

"It's Alexandria, not a war zone. It's safe—I've got the route and the timing, and I know where we'll be." She slipped on her best smile, the one with the almost-lidded bedroom eyes. Her hand traced a line down Lin's wrist to pause at the chip that held her credentials. "All we need is an officer's keycard."

"I don't know." Lin fingered the sleeve of her electrosuit.

The little curl at the corner of Lin's mouth told Nel she had already won, but she stepped closer. "C'mon. You showed me your world. Let me show you mine."

Lin's swift, hard kiss ended the discussion and she snapped open her suitcase. "Give me ten minutes to find something else to wear?"

"However long you want. This is our night." Nel had already discarded her own electromesh in favor of the rumpled cargos and a tank. Luckily Lin seemed as eager to have a night out, and in a matter of minutes they were slipping from their room. Lin led the way through the cars to the caboose. She flashed a smile at the guard there, but his expression did not relax.

"Hey," Nel tried. "How's the elbow?"

His expression relaxed a fraction and he showed her the offending limb. "Doing okay. Got an appointment for a replacement once we're back on a station or ship. Can't wait—the pain sucks."

Nel's stomach revolted at the thought of a replacement, her mind unable to picture it as anything more complex than popping bloody pieces off a Lego. "Glad you're getting patched up," she answered. "What about Dr. Mackey?"

His smile faltered into something more fragile, more genuine. "Alright. Went to our infirmary on base when we arrived this morning. Touch and go still, a bit."

"Sorry to hear," Nel offered. "Let us know if we can do anything?"

He nodded, and she stepped backwards off the caboose. "Gotta run, meeting up with someone who might have details. Lin let me tag along."

Before he could ask for more, Nel was towing Lin through the dim station under the hulking base they glimpsed on their way in earlier. Excitement bordered on mania as they emerged onto a small causeway.

"That was clever," Lin remarked, even her low voice echoing off the tiles.

Nel shrugged. "Being a head-first person usually works best for lies. Plus, all is fair in the pursuit of beer."

Lin's focus narrowed teasingly on the archaeologist. "I thought this was all about me getting to relax."

"Beer is relaxing," Nel insisted. Her steps slowed as they reached the barred side entrance to the base. They hadn't been allowed out, though the missions scheduled for the next few days told her whatever safety protocol IDH had was implemented quickly. *If not thoroughly,* she thought, as Lin flashed her wrist to the scanner at the door.

The door swung open with a click and desert air eddied into the hall. Outside, with boots on stone and familiar stars scattered overhead, Nel tipped her face to the sky. "God, I missed the smell of this place."

"I thought you said the forest was the same?"

"Yes and no." Nel peered at her shoes. "It's not even a smell, maybe. Just a sense. A feeling. Odyssey's core smelled exactly like a forest. Perfectly. But it didn't smell like a forest does on Earth. Just like all of you. You're people, perfectly so. But you're not anything like the people down here—the ones who were born here."

"How so?" Lin asked. "Space doesn't smell."

"Exactly. You don't have the stink of desperation. The clawing, begging, bartering. The grief of existence. You're immaculate, calculating, brilliant and you don't feel…mortal."

Lin's brows rose. "You've watched some of us die."

"Yeah, I know, I had blood all over my hands from trying to piece Gretta's throat together. But even that—motor oil covered my hands as much as blood. Because you're all this well-maintained machine. Your ships, for fuck's sake, they're piloted by heads. It's like you integrated. Completely."

Lin scoffed, jaw tense. "You're just lucky you never had to replace any body part."

"I am! I am lucky! But down here we don't get a healing pad and a vial of legal downers in our veins." Nel drew a deep breath. Their conversation teetered on the line between discussion and disaster. "Smell it. Really. What is it?"

Lin sampled the air. "Smoke? Exhaust, I guess? Something spicy and warm?"

"Jungle, baking in the sun. Rain evaporating from the pavement—we have a whole word for it: petrichor." *Smoke.* Consuming. It was hard to look at such devouring, destructive things as good. Where was the woman who marched in every environmental movement her university hosted?

A warm palm slipped into hers. "I promise, we are mortal," Lin murmured. "We just have a different way of being. We don't fear what's coming. Once you've read about quantum theories, and our brains—"

"Let's keep it to Earth physics for now, eh?" Nel suggested. "I think the senti-comps are my limit for weird science."

Hands laced, they set off across the base. It was deserted, seemingly, but Nel caught sight of armored figures along the rooftops. The spiraled razor wire atop the fences was bright and shiny. Despite the bustle of the city beyond, the surrounding buildings were quiet. Anticipatory.

The weight of observation lifted from Nel's shoulders as they slipped through the side gate and into Alexandria's back streets. The day's heat still lingered, emanating from the stone and steel of the city even as the chill of desert night sifted down from the indigo zenith. Walking the streets of a new city always stirred up strange nostalgia in Nel. A longing for history as varied and rich, one not stolen from the cultures her ancestors engulfed. Perhaps Lin, alien everywhere here, felt the same walking upon the earth her ancestors forsook.

Nel tightened her grip on Lin's hand. "If you were given the chance to live anywhere in your known universe, where would you choose?"

"Live?"

"Yeah. Like live, not visit. Most places are great to visit but maybe not stay."

Lin frowned. "I'm going to have to think about this."

"It's an icebreaker, not a proposal," Nel joked, before barreling forward in an attempt to bury the latter option. "So, where would you like to go right now—food? Drink? Dance?"

"Dance?" Lin's eyes lit up.

"Nightclub it is." Nel fished out the faded pamphlet she scrounged from the commissary where she had found someone willing to exchange her space-dollars for actual Egyptian pounds. She rattled off a few queer-friendly options until Lin stabbed the air with one finger.

"That one. Khafiin." She flashed a smile, the kind that made heat pool in Nel's belly, and her voice dropped to a silk-clad whisper. "It means secrets."

Nel allowed herself to be drawn closer by Lin's gravity. She couldn't help herself, she never could. It didn't matter how many secrets Lin kept from her, from everyone but the dark void of space. For now, this tiny slice of desert and purple sky and fading heat and even Nel herself was a shared secret.

Neon lights and the steady thump of music grew as they wound closer to the main strip. Khafiin was a narrow building, wedged between a grocer and an alley that Nel would bet money held its own share of secrets, probably of the intimate kind.

Lin led the way through the door, but Nel pulled them up short halfway through the door. A hand-lettered sign in Arabic, French, and English informed them:

SKYBORN PERMITTED ONLY WHEN ACCOMPANIED

Nel glanced at Lin's back and the sign again before following her into the dark interior. She was used to bars where she couldn't hold hands. Bars where if she talked up the wrong woman, she could end up dead. It wasn't often gay bars fell under the same label.

A blacked-out hall led to the coat check. Nel handed over their cover with a flashed smile and Lin's graceful Arabic thank you. Then they were winding through shisha smoke and up a set of spiraling stairs to the gleaming neon of the bar.

She tugged Lin's hand to draw her attention. "How can they play music? With audio?"

Lin pointed down to the DJ. "It's mostly live, I think. Maybe they have dampeners?"

Between the handful of dancers on the floor below and the campy style, Nel's anxiety melted away. Memories of blood and static drowned in the belly-boom bass and throb of neon.

At the bartender's head jerk, Nel leaned on the sticky steel and ordered their first round, plus an order of dolmades and shish taouk.

Lin glanced around with a delicate frown. "Should we sit?"

Nel chuckled and pointed to a secluded round couch that didn't seem to be occupied. "Once I have some food in me and a few drinks, though, you can bet your ass I'm dancing."

Lin laughed with a head shake. "I'm not sure I'll be up for that. Dancing was never my thing."

"Bullshit," Nel insisted, navigating to their seat, drinks held aloft for safekeeping. Her gaze lingered on the lean muscle, the thoughtless grace as Lin settled into the padded Naugahyde seat. A second later Nel plopped down beside her and tapped her Stella against Lin's Arak Ice Chill.

"Thanks."

Lin took another deep sip. "For what?"

"This. Coming with me."

"You think I don't enjoy being here with you? Music and heat and cold drinks?" She nudged Nel's elbow teasingly. "I'm not that alien."

"I don't know, someone wanting to spend more than a few days with me is a bit weird," Nel joked.

"Did you ever give someone the chance to, though?"

"Fuck off," Nel snapped jokingly. "Look, food."

An older person in latex with a full beard arrived, settling a tray of their food onto the table. They palmed the tip with a nod and disappeared.

The food was a cacophonous delight. Nel groaned at the subtle richness of dolmades and the tang of the kabobs. "Seriously, for the melting pot of *Odyssey*, you lot could stand to import some spices."

"You just haven't spent enough time to taste the full array."

"True," Nel agreed, catching her eye. "You taste like nothing else I've ever had." She was rewarded by the peach flush high on Lin's cheeks.

The taller woman polished off another dolma and took a long, slow sip of her drink. "I miss the easy amp and damp of using ports, but your way is certainly more immersive."

"Amp and damp?" Nel questioned.

"Amp up, or dampen your energy. Or mood, too."

Nel made a face. "So, like uppers and downers down here. Any of you guys get addicted?"

Lin shrugged. "Sure, some people have difficulties, but it's like any mental illness, we just treat it, you know?"

Nel hummed, leaning back into the worn-in seat with a sigh. Beer and food softened her body. Thudding music awakened an answering thrum in her veins. As far as she had traveled, as long as she had been gone, this was her place. A dark bar, queer folk draped on every surface, liquor and food flowing. Before her eyes threatened to betray her, she levered herself up. Their plates were empty, and with another draw from her Stella, so were their drinks.

"C'mon, spacegirl," Nel whispered. "Someone as graceful as you must have taken like, space ballet as a kid."

Lin giggled. "If by space ballet you mean tai chi and kali, then sure."

Perhaps it was the neon glow, perhaps four near-death experiences in half as many years broke her understanding of attraction, but every new inch of Lin's mind and body only lashed Nel's heart tighter.

"This isn't music I know."

"It's been two years since I was here, you think I know any of the pop songs either? Besides," she rocked her hips again, dipping her shoulders in time to the wailing sitar, "dance is all about rhythm."

She grabbed Lin's hand, towing the taller woman closer, then stepping back. Exhilaration pulsed through her, warm with alcohol, chilled with condensation dripping down her empty glass. This was Earth—hot night air, cold drinks, thundering music and a warm woman in her arms.

"You alright?" Lin asked. "You look…"

"Happy." Nel pressed her back against Lin's chest and lost herself to the neon cacophony.

Four songs later and Nel staggered to the bar, flashing the bartender a smile. "Mind another?"

He made a show of grudgingly splashing another round into a fresh glass, but by the time he slid it over to her, he was smiling again. "Nice to see people having that much fun. None of us seem to have the energy anymore, you know?"

"Well, I'm glad I could spread a little fun." She trailed off, uncertain how to finish. "Been rough where I was too. Guess I'm just grateful to pretend for a night."

His eyes lingered on her for a second, then flicked to Lin. "She's from up there, isn't she?"

Nel froze, but the answer must have been written on her face, because he sneared.

"See them a mile away. You seem to still know what dirt feels like."

"I know what you mean." Something cold clawed up her spine. "About the dirt."

He hummed, friendliness seemingly having worn thin. "Just hope you lot don't stay long. Extra mouths and drama do not help."

"Nah, we're moving on," a voice chirped. The woman who boarded the train the day before slid a handful of bills across the bar. "Trouble you for a Butler's?"

The bartender wordlessly stepped away.

Nel's gaze narrowed on the scarf and tank, fairly certain they were the same ones from before. "What'd you say your name was again?"

The woman laughed, turning to face Nel better. "Didn't."

"Journalist?"

The woman's brows shot up. Her lilt was British but with an added burr. "Impressive. How'd you know?"

"Boots and scarf peg you as in-the-field. Doubt we'd pick up a paleontologist and we're already rotten with archaeologists. Lastly, that." She jerked a thumb at the Jericho on the woman's hip. "Archies are notorious for bringing trowels to gunfights."

"Conflict journalist." She offered a callused palm. "Andy Gull. Conflict journalist."

"Nel, archaeologist." Nel shook the hand firmly. "Bit concerning your work brought you here."

"Not a fan of conflict?"

Nel chuckled. "More like I've had enough to last a lifetime. Most of it my fault, arguably."

"That's why I learned to focus on other people's and take off before mine hit the fan." Andy joined her laugh. "Love to hear some of your stories. Wanted to grow up to be you when I was a kid."

"Right back atcha."

Andy scanned Nel, gaze lingering on her shoulders and the muscle of her forearms. "What kid wants to grow up to be shot at trying to tell the truth?"

"One who was already under fire for her own." Nel shrugged. "Just realized I preferred my people dead."

"Most of mine end up that way too, you know." Andy looked away. "Guess I went for the gun and danger and you went for the history."

"And the fashion," Nel deadpanned.

"Here alone?"

"No, my, ah—" She faltered on the words. Another time, another bar, Nel would have said yes. She would have crawled into a stranger's bed, flushed from the threat of gunfire in a foreign country. She had with Lin, after all. "Lin's in the bathroom."

"Holy shit, you're the famed Nalawangsa's wife? That must be wild."

"Not wife," Nel scrambled to explain. "Just, um…"

"I got it," Andy assured wryly. "So, how'd you get wrapped up in this? Don't look like an IDH egghead."

"I'm not. IDH hijacked the site that was supposed to make my career. No, not a bit bitter about it." She rolled her eyes.

"Who's bitter?" Lin asked, sidling up to the bar. Her gentle halo of frizz from the heat and lack of climate control brought a smile to Nel's face.

"Just talking shop. This is Andy," Nel introduced. "She's a—"

"Reporter. I know," Lin answered, though her tone was anything but friendly. "Brought some interesting information to us the other day. Shouldn't you be moving on by now?"

"Soon. I'm actually here on work. Probably head out once I get some deets off you lot for my client." Tension crackled in the beer-scented air.

Lin knocked back the shot Nel pressed into her hand. "I'm sure there's a hundred bottom feeders looking to score on our tech. Killed a few of them on our way here."

"Anyway!" The warning at the back of Nel's skull exploded into red alert. "Good to meet you. Gonna get some more dancing in while we can."

Lin shot a glare over her shoulder as Nel towed her away from the bar and back to the undulating press of the dance floor. "I hate them."

Nel's brows arched. "Yeah, I got that. I thought she was just helping out."

"If by helping out you mean trading our secrets to hell-knows-who and giving us nothing but judgement and rumors in return, sure." She snagged the drink from Nel's hand and drained half of it.

Nel took it back with a frown. "You good?"

Lin glanced at her, but whatever she saw caught her attention and she stilled. "Yeah. I'm sorry. This is supposed to be fun. I'm trying. It's just hard to unwind, especially when I have the person claiming my brother is behind all this flirting with my girlfriend."

"I said I was with you. It was professional sparring, nothing more." Nel half expected sparks to arc between their skin as she cupped Lin's jaw with one hand. Lin's head tipped, eyes a haze of desire and danger that Nel couldn't resist. She could have whispered for Nel to walk into space itself and she would obey, unquestioning, just for the thrill of being wanted.

"Where'd you learn to dance?" Lin asked after a beat. "Everyone down here that good?"

Nel chuckled, not minding the subject change. Nothing was better at ruining a perfectly good evening than IDH bullshit. "Fuck, that was just white girl with a bit of spice. Dated a choreographer in grad school for a minute. Wasn't a day that went by that woman wasn't grooving. No way she'd let me be seen on the floor with her if I couldn't at least keep up."

"So, is everything cool that you know because of a girl?" Lin didn't seem convinced, but it didn't matter.

Nel reached up, trailing ice water from their drink down the hollow behind Lin's ear. Nel backed onto the dance floor, swaying, dropping her hips, one shoe twisting with the beat. "I crossed the stars for you. I think that takes the cake."

A firm hand tapped Nel on the shoulder and Lin's smile fell with a clatter.

The bartender stood on the edge of the dance floor with a tired expression. "Sorry, ma'am. You and your friends need to leave."

Nel sought out Andy in the crowd. She was on the upper level, gestures sharp, engrossed in some hissed conversation. The muffled bubble of booze popped. "Sure."

"You're kicking us out?" Lin snapped. "She's not even with us—"

"Lin," Nel insisted. Her grip on the woman's hand tightened. She handed the bartender a bill without looking and pulled Lin from the dance floor, ignoring her commentary. It was only when they were outside, in the stillness of the desert night, that she turned back. "Enough."

Surprise stalled Lin's protests.

Nel jabbed a finger at the sign by the door. "Things have changed."

"I don't understand," Lin insisted. "We've helped them so much."

"There's a lot happening right now, and none of it seems to make sense," Nel explained. "And regardless of the truth in Andy's reports, or whatever, it's not their business. I couldn't count the number of times I've been told to take my bullshit outside, and I can empathize with that guy not wanting his bar dragged into our space-drama. No matter their intentions, Lin, you can't argue that IDH complicates things. Just look at my life since I added you. When we stood on Samsara you saw with your own eyes that the rules, as you call it, of your world weren't what you thought. Why is it so hard to believe there might be more you didn't see? That it might take being on the outside," she pressed her shaking hand to her chest, "to see at all?"

Andy strode from the bar, interrupting Lin's confusion. She shot them a cocky wave before disappearing deeper into the city.

Lin barely acknowledged the journalist's passing. Her brittle expression fixed on Nel, composure cracking under the pressure of her missing brother, her unstable career, her noncommittal lover. "Nel, my family has a lot of privilege. With that comes a lot of knowledge. I grew up knowing things about our corner of the universe some people never learn."

"Is that fair?" Nel asked.

"Things work better that way. I believed what I saw on Samsara. I knew enough about the tension, the arguments, to trust my eyes. But thinking that disdain for human life, that disappointment, runs so deep that IDH is infected? That we're next, that Earth is next? And somehow not even one of the most powerful families knows? That's conspiracy."

Nel shrugged. "From where I'm standing, Lin, all that already happened for me. And I can't see how your intergalactic government is above it."

Lin reached out, hands brushing Nel's for a moment before coming up to cup her face. "We don't have to agree. You don't have to trust them. Just trust me. And I'll do the same, alright?"

"Okay," Nel promised, though the pit in her stomach told her nothing had really changed, despite all the pretty words. "It doesn't come easy to me."

"Trust or love?"

Nel glared at her. "Either. But right now, we're focused on trust."

Silence yawned between them for a moment, then another. "Did you ever feel it? For anyone? Anything? That you loved them."

"Yes. Once. But I only said it to Mikey and my parents."

Lin tilted her head. "But you dated a lot?"

"A lot a lot. I got the nickname Shane in college."

"I don't know what that means."

"It's from a campy lesbian show. Never mind. Regardless, I got around. Even hooked up with a few men—never Mikey, before you ask, that's foul. What about you?"

Lin looked away. "Two. After what happened between Dar and Paul, I just couldn't bear the thought. I didn't think anything was worth that pain. It's not like anyone even did anything wrong there, it was just time and distance and fuck, Nel, up there sometimes it seems like all we have is time," she looked up, "time and distance."

Nel sat back, wondering who else had been caught in the tractor beam of Lin's energy. The right thing to do would be to take her hand. So she did. "Honest, Lin, down here, with the dust and desperation, we never have enough of either." She bit her lip, drawing clarity and blood. "Maybe the two of us will balance it out, eh?"

"Do you regret it? Coming with me?"

Fear threatened to flood their tremulous connection. Nel frowned down at their hands. Hers, battered, scarred, freckled. Lin's elegant, tawny with potential and hidden strength. *I owe her more than a shrug, more than a lie.* "How can I look at everything I've learned about the world and say I'd rather be ignorant? How can I look at the people down here, screaming in the streets, and wish I were them? It's fucked up, and I know that. I thought I handled things. Thought I was strong. Thought I was better. The best, sometimes. More than I really should have."

"But?" Lin's words were whispered wind swept away in the storm in Nel's chest.

"Turns out I was just fast. And maybe there's a reason why every time I run, you're right there next to me. But now it's all caught up to me. And there's nowhere left to go."

Lin tucked a stray mud-blonde hank of hair away from Nel's sunburned face. "Maybe just stop running for a bit? You always tell me to take a breather."

"I don't think I can pick up all the stuff I've scattered. Almost forty years of flotsam feelings, bruised love, destroyed kindness," Nel answered, unable to meet Lin's eyes, unable to look anywhere but at the disaster left in their wake. She started back toward the dark, quiet shadow of their base.

"Then don't." Lin jogged up, walking backward, perhaps hoping Nel might meet her eyes. "Something you learn really young, in space, is to bring only what you need. When I was little it felt Spartan, I think. But the older I get the more I realize it was just understanding what was important. And what wasn't. You bring only what you need. Only what you must to get where you're going. Too heavy? Jettison it. Too complicated? Redesign it."

Nel shoved her scarred hands into her cargo shorts' pockets. A fire burned in her chest, and the light cast strange shadows. "What if you can't? What if it's always heavy and complicated?"

Lin's arm slipped through Nel's. "Then you say damn the cost, damn the time, damn the entire universe. It's coming with me." The whispered promise clung to the air.

Nel squeezed her eyes shut against the sting of tears. *Thank you.* But saying it aloud would be an admission that she was heavy, complicated, and frankly something Nel herself would send out the airlock if given half a chance.

"What I'd do to just keep a piece of you." Lin dragged them to a halt. The soft chill of night eddied around them and Nel smelled the intimacy on her hair. "Not all of you. Not forever, even, if you couldn't. But just a piece for me alone."

Instincts screamed for her to bolt, but Nel knew better than to pull away. The weight of Lin's gaze, the warmth of her skin, dampened the sparks of terror on the edge of Nel's mind. *You can have my everything, Lin. As long as you don't ask for it.* She opened her mouth to answer, but Lin's lips covered hers and she abruptly forgot how words even fit together.

FIFTEEN

"Oi, Bently!" A loud voice and louder knock rattled the cabin door. She dragged herself from the glowing screen, shutting down her research on sonic weapons with a pang of regret. With Lin's credentials and a few deep dives into what Phil had sent her, she felt close to actually understanding a bit more about their invisible antagonist.

She slipped to the door before another knock could wake the tangle of limbs and hair that were the sleeping Lin. Fumbling her smile into place, she stepped into the hall and shut the door behind her.

Andy leaned on the opposite wall of the hall, dressed in a strange combination of electrosuit and field clothes.

"Hey. Lin's asleep. What's up?"

"We're wanted outside." She shifted. "Sorry for cutting your date short last night, by the way. Never know how a contact is gonna go down, especially with IDH faffing about again."

Nel shrugged. "I get that there's a lot of tension between IDH and everyone down here. Weird being caught in the middle. Everything go alright for you?"

"Good enough, considering. Freelance work isn't ever easy. Anyway, we're doing recon on something in headquarters and they want archaeology eyes."

Excitement sparked through her as she checked the time. "I thought the mission wasn't until noon. And you're not an archaeologist."

"I guess they want field staff to head in and get shit squared for the eggheads to do their research. Electrosuit and pack required though, alright?"

"Be there in five," Nel affirmed before stepping back into their room. She dressed in darkness, momentarily saddened that she could now pull an electrosuit on without sight. She managed to find her pack and feel for her tools without knocking anything over. Pulling the coverlet over Lin's sprawled limbs, she dropped a kiss on the sleeping woman's head and crept from the room.

Andy had waited in the corridor and fell into a jog beside her. The rest of the mission underlings were arrayed about the tunnel platform in various stages of donning chem masks and protective gear. Nel eyed the equipment with distaste. "I thought we left these with space travel."

"Makes me glad I've never broken atmo," Andy lamented with a chuckle.

"Attention, everyone." Harris's voice cut through the low chatter. Fidgeting and preparations stilled. Like the others, he wore an electrosuit bolstered with a fully equipped vest. "I appreciate your readiness this morning. I realize this is a bit last minute, but during our preparations for our mission this afternoon, we discovered some concerning developments. This base has a series of chambers that, since the initial attack in Qena, have been sealed. The shutdown of this base was triggered by the CPO of *Odyssey of Earth,* Philos, though we aren't certain if that is what initiated the planet-wide blackout."

Kestral raised his hand. "Isn't this consistent with the information from our initial briefing?"

"Indeed. However, several of our current field team do not have access to that information." Harris's eyes lingered on Nel. Did he know she had found a way around that hurdle? Did he care? "Additionally, upon arrival here, we discovered that, despite orders to keep these chambers sealed until our arrival, there was unauthorized access a week ago. Until we examine the security history and access codes, we can't be certain this wasn't a second attempt at an attack, hence the precautions. Therefore, please take this seriously. We've already had a casualty and our transport morgue has limited space." He patted the chem mask hooked at the side of his belt. "We'll leave chem masks off unless needed to avoid the use of audio-coms. Understood?"

Murmurs of ascent echoed from the limestone walls of the platform.

"Move out in T-5."

She double-checked her headphones were settled properly. Already her headache dimmed at the soft bloom of noise-canceling static.

Unauthorized access. If Nel knew one thing about IDH, it was how proprietary they were about their information and spaces. *So someone who had clearance level but not permission?* That thought did nothing for her tenuous trust of the organization.

She glanced back to see Andy checking the safety on her pistol. Her mask hung about her neck. She might have been born on Earth, but she sure knew her way around an IDH uniform. *Maybe that's part of the job, becoming someone else.* "Bent, might wanna arm up." The low voice cut through the static of apprehension in Nel's mind.

Nel scowled. "I'm not a gun person."

"This isn't about politics—"

"You don't want me in there, twitchy, with a deadly weapon I really don't know how to use." Nel softened the refusal with a smile. It was inappropriate, in hindsight, but she didn't really care. Everything about her being there seemed inappropriate. "Dirt-o-mancer should do just fine. It's not like I'm the first sweep."

Andy shrugged in a suit-yourself fashion and fell into line with the rest of the team. They headed up the stairs Nel had taken the other day, cutting left into a broad hall. Several open doorways led off to what looked like libraries and low-tech research stations. The double doors at the end of the hall, however, were barred with a massive bank-vault lock.

Teera crouched at the access module embedded in the stone, electronic lockpick propped on one knee while she fiddled with the dials.

Harris stood over her, dark eyes watching the flickering screen with interest. After a few false tries, she glanced up with a victorious grin.

The gears whirred and Kestral cranked the lever to the left. A pop sounded, muffled through the headphones. A second later air roiled from the room, mixing like oil and water with the air of the tunnel.

"Masks!" Kestral boomed.

Nel ducked her head, smothering her mouth and nose in the crook of her elbow. As she scrambled to press the mask onto her face, a voice cut through.

"False alarm! Just pressurized. Some residual compounds..." He trailed off, collecting samples as he went, frown almost comical under the distortion of the mask's clear face. "Should be done in a moment."

Nel tightened her mask's straps regardless, noting that no one else risked removing their PPE either. The point guard team entered, flashlight beams making ghosts of the swirling air.

A minute later they were waved in. Nel eyed the shadowed doorway, unwilling to touch anything but the sweaty wood of her trowel's handle. Her stomach was tight. Edging in behind Andy and the glinting barrel of her 941, Nel caught sight of dozens of computer screens. Tidy workspaces encircled a central desk. Dust coated almost every surface, save for the deep drag marks across the floor. Her muffled steps led her around the side, wrist held out so her comm's camera could catch anything her eyes didn't.

After a full sweep an alert popped up on her mask's shield:

SWITCH FROM AUDIO COMM. REMOVE MASK. ALL CLEAR.

With a hammering heart, she pulled the mask off, letting it dangle like Andy's just under her chin. Under the must, the room smelled of hospital antiseptic and engine grease.

"Fan out," Harris commanded. "I want everything recorded first, don't move anything. Teera, can you access the computers safely?"

"Yessiree," she chimed, moving to the main panel in the center of the computer bank. "Once I'm in, want me to bring her online?"

Her. Nel turned. In the dim light, she almost missed the small cylindrical shape in the center of the room, currently shrouded in black cloth. Her stomach tightened. She followed the boot prints on the floor. She had assumed there were several, but on closer inspection they were identical. *One very busy set.*

"This shit looks like some alien lab," Andy observed, nudging a few of the wires with her boot. "Funny, that's almost the most likely option these days."

Nel barked a laugh, staring at the dim room. She edged toward the main console. It was dusty, but the metal was new, gleaming under what she imagined was about two years' worth of dust.

"I'm into the main base computer," Teera called over the susurrating footfalls. "Switching from emergency backup to main power. Bringing auxiliary systems online...security systems..." Colorful coding flickered over the large screen of the tech's comm, mirroring the flickering across her pale eyes. "Hang tight everyone, bringing lights up."

A click, a buzz, and then light swelled, scattering shadows to the corners.

"ALEXANDRIA BASE POWER: ONLINE. INTER-BASE COMMUNICATION SYSTEM: ONLINE. BASE DEFENSE: ARMED. BASE COMPUTER: OFFLINE."

Harris bent over Teera's display with a frown. "Everything still working?"

"She didn't come online with everything else, but I think that's due to the firewalls." She shifted, glancing up at the central bank. "Gonna try raising her out of stasis and connecting via hardline, instead of the main access—"

"Do your best not to blow us to kingdom come," Harris suggested.

"Will do, sir." A series of keystrokes later and the ground shuddered. A mechanical iris in the center of the empty console ground opened. A gleaming, fluid-filled tank rose from its confinement. Nel's chest constricted as it shuddered to a halt. Stunned silence filled the room.

The tank, scratched, half-filled, and spider-webbed with cracks, was empty.

"Teera—"

"I don't know, sir," she hissed, flingers flying, eyes darting from her ocular screens to the looming empty tank where Alexandria's senti-comp should be. "Getting security feeds now…"

"Weird place for an aquarium," Andy noted, peering at the covered cylinder.

Nel fixed her with a glare. Andy was fun, but her blasé attitude was beginning to grate. "More like the personification of the uncanny valley. Next time you get a chance, Google 'senti-comp.'"

"Someone stole their CPU?"

"CPO," Harris intoned, the tension around his mouth stating that he, too, would rather the questions wait. "Central Processing Operative. Alexandria, like all our largest bases or ships, was run by a sentient computer."

Andy's face eased into a delighted grin. "So, like powering my Gameboy off a potato. Bitchin'."

Nel just stared at her. "No ew? No creeps?"

"I don't know, seems like the inverse of wetware to me. There's been a lot of tech integrations in the last few years. Maybe I'm just a bit more inured to it."

Nel's attention was fixed on the pervasive cloy of mildew, underscoring the distinct tang of plastic and circuits. Biology and circuitry, humanity's zenith or its nadir. Snarled cables within the tank were coated with biofilm and what she really hoped wasn't tissue. It wasn't theft. It was kidnapping.

Static crackled and everyone ducked; Nel's hands clapped over her noise-cancellation in panic.

"Got the security feed up." Teera rocked back on her heels, neck craned to view the grainy footage on the largest screen. The halls were deserted, save for occasional patrols. Seemingly the same handful of guards were on duty much of the time. "I don't understand—who steals a senti-comp? I always see people searching for them on the dark web but to actually—"

"Unauthorized access occurred on the seventh. Roughly two weeks ago," Harris interrupted.

Wordlessly the tech fast-forwarded to the date in question. A routine security sweep, then a new figure jogged up the stairs from the train tunnel.

Harris leaned forward. The others pressed closer, all pretense of searching the room dropped in their shared dread. An electrosuit glinted under loosely wrapped dark fabric. Light bounced off angled reflectors over their face. Whoever it was walked with purpose, either certain there were no guards or able to handle any they encountered. Judging by the graceful stride and heavy gauntlet, Nel determined it was probably the latter. They carried a blocky pack, the size of a large camping cooler.

After a second's delay at the vault entrance, the door opened, and the person slipped in. Gloved hands flew across the same access point where Teera now crouched, and the tank rose from its holding chamber.

Alexandria's senti-comp was female. Whoever broke into the chamber seemed to attempt to wake her, returning to the access point again and again, movements increasingly frustrated. Finally, their fist came down on the glass itself. Fluid sloshed, but otherwise, the head remained still, unconscious.

The kidnapper crouched by their pack then, ripping it open to show a dark, square container. Next, a heavy pipe shattered the thick acrylic of the tank. Liquid dribbled across the floor, and the figure ripped their gloves off, reaching bare-handed into the primordial technical fluid. Even on the grainy monochrome footage, Nel saw the drifting hair and waxy, waterlogged skin. A few tugs removed the wires and tubes, hastily replaced by other sets attached to the pack at their feet. Then she was tucked inside, and the lid sealed.

"Ripped her right out of the wall while she was sleeping."

"Can we get a face from that?" Harris asked.

"Not with the recog-blocking mask." Teera shook her head, pale face tight. "But I have affirmative credentials." Before she could pull the record from the computer's history onto the main screen, a voice cut through the dread.

"Don't." Lin stood in the doorway, electrosuit tight across her heaving chest. Her gloved hands were clenched tightly. Nel stumbled over the wires to get to her but stopped short at the fury in the woman's dark eyes.

"Letnan—" Harris began, but Lin's low voice silenced him.

"It's my brother. Alexandria's senti-comp was stolen by Komodor Muda Dar Nalawangsa."

SIXTEEN

Nel couldn't tear her eyes away from Lin. The woman she followed across the stars fractured before her eyes, pieces clattering across her betrayer's footprints on the dusty floor. Nel's mind spun with morbid curiosity: how did it feel to be ripped from consciousness? Hauled from your second womb? A different question burned in Lin's fragile eyes, filled with venom.

"Dr. Bently," Harris murmured. "Please take Letnan Nalawangsa back to the train. I'll meet you in my office in half an hour.

Lin's voice was a snarl. "With all due respect—"

"It's an order, Letnan."

Before an argument exploded in the dusty air, Nel grabbed Lin's hand, palm pressing to the heated circle of her glove. When dark eyes met hers, she tugged gently. "C'mon, love. You don't need to see this."

Lin followed, but once they were clear of the vault and down to the solitude of the platform, Nel realized it wasn't passively. Lin ripped her hand free once they reached the solitude of their cabin and paced from the door to the bed and back, raking a shaking hand through her hair. Every line of her trembling body was taught with fear. "This is a fucking nightmare."

Nel let her pace. Usually she was gone before anything big ever happened. Before any feelings got too large. Gritting her teeth, she rooted herself to the ground. Lin watched Nel's life crumble a dozen times in the past few years. Nel might not know what to do, but she knew she wanted to be here. "Are you sure it's him? I know you want evidence he's okay—"

Lin spun on her, face a rictus of despair. "You think I need a face to recognize my brother! I know his walk, his shoulders, his damn temper tantrums when things don't go well!"

Nel's gut clenched. She had recognized Mikey, too, despite the blood and bruises and rigor mortis. "No. I trust you. I'm sorry. I can't even begin to think of why he would—"

"There are a thousand reasons, but I can't think of why he, of all people, would do this. If he needed a senti-comp you'd think he'd use his ship's." Lin rubbed her eyes, miraculously dry. Sometimes tears weren't enough. "*Promise for Tomorrow* was powered by Phil, before he took over *Odyssey.* The *Promise* has been running with a rudimentary AI system. They're fine, but finicky for a ship that size, especially when trying to cross star systems. I worried it could have caused a trajectory malfunction, and that's why..." Her words dissolved into a snarl.

"Would he kidnap someone just to have a more powerful ship?" Nel frowned. She knew so little of her girlfriend's temperamental brother, save for the ambition they shared and his distaste for Nel. *And his distrust of IDH.* "And why her, when he knows we need her?"

Lin's jaw tightened and she strode again from wall to door. Nel smelled ozone, ears muffled in anticipation of a blast. Her chest ached, looking at what this mission had turned Lin into—intensity heightened to paranoia, lean grace turned to angles and edges.

She tugged the bottle she had taken from the space port out of their tiny closet and offered it to Lin. Ignoring her, the letnan raked a hand through her hand, wheeling about and starting back toward the heater. "Talk to me a minute?"

"It's just everything, alright?" she snapped back. "Nothing's okay, and hasn't been, and it won't be for a while and I'm just trying to cling to each hour at a time."

"I'm here," Nel offered. Her untrained empathy was clumsy at best, but sincere. "You just gotta ask. You're always so knowledgeable, confident. I can't begin to think about how to actually meet your needs. Aside from—"

"What I don't need is another sex joke! I'm more than just a lay, alright? Right now, I need a human, not a vibrator."

This was a familiar conversation to Nel, but never from this side. *It's not comfortable.* "I'm sorry. Really. I'm not great at this stuff. But I'm here."

"Maybe if you spent your days listening to people instead of screwing our mission up, you'd have learned by now!" Lin snapped. "You think it's easy working my ass off trying to save your planet when you spend your days staring at maps you don't have clearance for and making moon eyes at your beer or whatever new and interesting woman hopped aboard that day?"

"Whoa." Nel raised her hands in protest. As much as she wanted to debunk the bit about Andy, she knew it was better to ignore that accusation. "I'm trying to help! In the only way I can, since I'm left to twiddle my thumbs. And you should want to save Earth because it's worth saving, not because it's mine. Or was Dar right?"

"What?"

"He thought Samsara was caused by IDH. He thought they were covering something up. Investigating to hide their involvement."

Lin's pacing stilled, her eyes blown wide. She spun, hand rising with a roar of fury. Light and sound exploded through the train. Screaming aluminum and the stink of vaporized plastic filled the air. When the tracers cleared from Nel's eyes,

Lin stood, panting, staring at the smoking, gaping hole where their cabin door once stood.

Nel's body shuddered with warning. "Lin, I—"

"Letnan Nalawangsa." Settling dust revealed Dr. Ndebele in the train's corridor, arms crossed.

The fight left Lin's body, shoulders slumping. A dry sob ripped the defiance from her chest. Wordlessly, she turned to follow her officer.

"Should I—" Nel began, but Dr. Ndebele shook her head. Instead, Nel watched Lin drift, defeated, up the train.

Exhausted, Nel slumped onto the bed with a sigh. Cold reached a narrow place deep in her chest, a place she forgot blood still flowed. Down deep she knew this had nothing to do with her, nothing to do with anything beyond Lin's terror that Nel, too, might betray her. But anger squashed the tiny voice.

"Trouble in paradise, Bently?"

She couldn't even bring herself to smile at Emilio's gentle jab. "Everything I touch turns on me, Emilio."

He eyed the smoking edges of their doorframe. "This was your doing?"

"Not really. But I don't think I helped." She heaved a sigh. "I suggested Dar wasn't on the same side as IDH anymore."

"Ah." The man's face softened. "It's hard when we think our blood doesn't share our beliefs."

The tenderness in his voice, the regret, gave her pause. She glanced up with a frown. "You said you lost your brother to them. Killed?"

"No. But it's easier to think so. Death is easier than betrayal."

"Is it?" The howling void in Nel's chest left by Mikey's laughter didn't feel easy. Surely, there was nothing worse than a wound you couldn't ever hope to heal, no matter what tore the flesh in the first place. She swallowed hard and drew a long breath. "Dar kidnapped Alexandria's senti-comp a few weeks ago. Ripped her right out of her tank and popped her in a cooler like a spare kidney. I don't know him well, but something tells me he knows something we don't."

Emilio stared at her, warm eyes unreadable, as if excavating everything he knew about her. "Dr. Bently, would you take a walk with us?"

Energy flooded her limbs at the weight behind the words. "With who?"

"A few of the others are going into the city. Our tech team is analyzing some of the signals and we thought we'd give them space."

She glanced at the ruined room. There was little she could do to repair it, and it was clear Lin wouldn't be in a talking mood for some time. "Sure. This place gives me a headache anyway."

He nodded. "It's the LRADs shielding the place. Affects some people, if they're sensitive to it."

"Me? Sensitive?" Nel fell into step beside him as they cut back down toward the caboose. Emilio didn't take the bait, however, and it wasn't until they were walking across the courtyard that he spoke again.

"Did you tell Munashi Gamal?"

Nel shook her head. "I was hoping to wait until I had more to tell."

Whatever his response was, it was cut off by a shout from the guard above for them to turn around. "Got some radicals outside," he called down.

Nel raised her badge, knowing it was too far for him to actually see it. "I've got clearance. There's been a development and we need a contact."

The man glanced to the other side of the wall. "Keep to the main streets."

Nel flashed her double finger-guns and leaned over the keypad, typing in Lin's credentials. A second later the gate beeped and ground open. When she beckoned for Emilio to follow her, she caught his wry smile.

"You're no letnan."

"Shut up before they realize it too," she muttered. "This better be worth it, eh?"

"I just promised a walk."

"With a really pointed undertone." Nel shoved her hands in her pockets, wondering if she should have grabbed her field kit. "I'm not oblivious, I just like to pretend sometimes."

They rounded the corner of the base walls to see the gathered crowd. There were a few dozen, but more gathered at the edges out of curiosity or excitement, perhaps. More than a few held signs, lettered in Arabic. Whatever they were protesting, it seemed centered on the base itself and not the beautiful stone government buildings closer to the city center. Several wore uniforms of the ENP.

Radicals? Nel had been to her fair share of protests and marches. This one didn't have the flavor of fanatics. "You read Arabic?" she asked Emilio.

"No. But I know that word." His point was surreptitious, but Nel saw that half the signs bore a similar word. "Alzanadiqa. Heretics."

Nel stared at him. "Heraje. Carved on the tree by Los Cerros Esperando VII. By you." She glanced back at the protest, but Emilio towed her down a side street.

"It wasn't me. But yes. Los Pobladores do have some more accusatory names for IDH."

"Are those Founders? I saw cops," she asked, ducking under a broken awning and turning sideways to follow him down what must have been a shortcut into the Souq District. "Where are we going? The guard said main streets."

"I think the city realized the base reopened. We took the tunnels in for a reason. IDH might have saved us from a virus, but they've done little since then. Saving millions of lives is all well and good," he assured, "but the mess in your wake— weird signals included—is still very much here. You can claim the scary virus didn't come from space with you lot, but it doesn't look like that down here. Sweeping in when someone needs you most feels less like altruism and more like taking advantage when you don't step down once you're no longer needed."

Nel's ears popped now that they were clear of the base itself, and she felt bile crawl up her throat. "I'm not one of them, you know."

He stopped in a crossroad. Nel recalled the tight weave of Sharia Faransa's market stalls to the west from the map. "Would you say that to Lin?"

"Shit like this is never perfect, never simple." She shrugged. Her skin seemed to hum in the wake of the low-frequency signals, and the contagious energy of the protest drew her nerves tight. "Where are we going?"

Emilio tilted his head toward the market alley. "Just down here. I was hoping you'd help with something." Anticipation sharpened his gentle voice.

"Emilio, I—" Perhaps it was the hint of aviation fuel on the air or the sudden lull in the market cacophony. Warning clenched down on the nape of her neck. Then her world exploded with sound. Screaming notes warred with deep guttural scrapes, the cry of some digital, eldritch god. "Motherfucker!"

The pressure behind her ears burrowed deeper and pushed down the nape of her neck. Across the alley, Emilio was on his knees, jaw working. Acrid sweetness told her someone nearby had vomited. Nel hissed breath through her clenched teeth and pressed against the cold stone.

The market crowd shifted as one seething mass, squeezing toward the growing group of protesters. Gunfire tapped through the screeching in her ears. Emilio's eyes were rolling in his head, his face pale under his tan.

"It's like two frequencies—" The rest of her words dissolved into a scream. Every nerve fired white hot. Her deeper self was aware, from the searing lines across her forearm, that bullets still rained.

A deeper boom shook the ground and the pain dropped a few notches. Blinking tears from her eyes, Nel scrambled to her knees and reached for Emilio. He was already on his feet. His hand clasped hers and hauled her up, racing for the shelter of a nearby warehouse.

The door swung open and they stumbled inside. The thick stone walls lessened the sound further and Nel's muscles trembled in the wake of pain. The building smelled as if someone had lost control of more than just their stomach.

"What the fuck was that?" Nel rasped. Blinking tears from her stinging eyes, she saw several figures bustling around a hulking shape behind several canvas curtains. A medic raced by and Nel saw a familiar puff of black hair and light brown skin. *Jem?*

"Sonic weapons. You saw the devices on the base walls."

"I thought those were for shielding. Massive noise cancellation."

"Like most tools, they can just as easily be used for violence as defense. IDH doesn't have the supercomputer they need, the next spot on their itinerary is hundreds of klicks away. It seems Alexandria has had enough of their meddling. This is what it looks like when corporate superpowers panic."

Nel shuddered, as much from dread as physical exhaustion. "They're going to run. I gotta get back."

Passengers swarmed aboard and a tall figure brushed passed her.

"Zachariah?"

He turned, walking backward, bag slung easily over his shoulder. He lowered his head in a nod and pressed a hand to his chest. "Allah hafiz, Nel."

She may not have known the words' meaning, but she recognized a goodbye when she saw one. *Where are you going?*

"Come with us," Emilio insisted. He dragged himself upright and tugged one of the canvas sheets aside.

A massive helicopter crouched in the warehouse. Another yank pulled a second sheet from the gaping hole in the warehouse roof. Engines rumbled to life. Mechanics bustled under its belly, clearing away tools and hoses. Nel's heart sank. "Harris was right."

"He's not a stupid man," Emilio agreed. "But neither is he a kind one. I'll explain everything once we're clear of the city." His hand was outstretched.

Nel backed up as the blades began to spin. She didn't trust IDH. She didn't trust Harris. She didn't trust Emilio, not fully, though right now he seemed the most rational of all of them.

The sound of the rioting crowd clamored even over the roar of the helicopter. Nel put a hand to her chest, searching for her bolo before remembering it was on the table in her cabin. With Mikey's ashes and her father's. *And Lin.* If IDH was as monstrous as Nel thought, as Dar seemingly thought, how could she leave Lin to its mercy, reeling without the rudder of her brother? Like Nel without Mikey. She sagged back against the warehouse wall. "I'm sorry."

Emilio's face locked in rigid disappointment. He shoved a set of headphones at her, then he was gone, Founders' red disappearing in the darkness of the cockpit. And Nel was left to the mercy of the riot on Alexandria's streets.

Shoving the headphones on, she staggered through the doorway. Bullets still pinged, but the fire seemed random. She dodged across the narrow streets, heading for the glint of razor wire atop the towering base walls. For once, she was grateful for the tight weave of electromesh encasing her skin. What would have been deep bullet grazes were scratches.

The protest had grown, more than a few sporting headphones of their own. Armored cars approached from deeper in the city. As she scuttled from building to building, however, the telltale fabric of her suit caught the attention of some protestors on the fringe.

Fuck. She didn't bother with her usual argument that she wasn't technically IDH. It didn't matter. Now she was just as much a heretic. Gripping her last spurt of adrenaline, she bolted for the gates.

"Dr. Bently!" The gate swung open and Harris's rough hand caught hers, hauling her from the chaos of the streets to the muffled shelter of the courtyard. "Where are the rest? We're missing half our medic team."

"Gone," she choked out. "Reapers." It wasn't a lie, but wasn't what she wanted to say, wasn't the accusation she wished she had the guts to sling. The thud of fists on the gates only broke her heart further.

"I know this is complicated."

"Nothing you say will make this easier," she rasped. Her brain still flickered with residual flashes of sheer pain, but now at least she knew they would end. "And right now, my brain is the equivalent of a malfunctioning taser."

The grip on her jacket tightened, drawing her upright. "That man is a terrorist. I don't know if our team will survive their ordeal out there, but I wish ardently, for their sakes, that they did not.

You've seen what whispers of Reaper tech can do. People like him are why saving the world is so damn hard."

But all they asked for was help. The ground shuddered again, and stone dust exploded at the courtyard's corner. Shouts grew louder now, and bullets splattered through the new hole in the base wall.

"Make for the landing pads!" Harris broke from the crowd, voice booming over the sound. He shoved her toward the hulking Ospreys waiting by the hangars. Then he was sprinting back toward the base.

Already two of the massive choppers shuddered into the sky, bellies full of swarming officers and tech. Nel thought she saw a long black braid, but it disappeared in the writhing crowd. Beams of light pierced through the smoke. Flames licked the edges of the base, billowing black and acrid. She broke into a run, arm held against the smoke and sparks, as if her flesh and sinew might stop shrapnel.

"Here!" A rough hand hauled her into a chopper's cargo bay.

Nel collapsed against the webbing draping the sides, squinting against the smoke at the figure sagging beside her.

Andy grinned, blood staining her face and teeth. "Cutting it close, Bent."

"Why aren't we taking off?" Nel shouted against the chaos.

"Maybe waiting for the skies to clear—"

A boom shook the ground and a rocket shrieked from just beyond the walls, colliding with the airborne chopper's belly with a shriek of rending metal.

"Make it quick!" Nel snapped at no one in particular. She couldn't think about whether Lin had been aboard the Osprey now rendered into nothing more than oil-splattered bodies and snarled metal.

Then the base doors flew open. Harris and half a dozen others hauling a heavy case from the building. They raced across the airstrip, dragging it when the wheels began to sink into the softening tarmac. In a second, an hour, and they were dragging the cart up the cargo rollers and the chopper lurched into the air.

The moment they were clear, the base erupted in flames, a third, larger blast obliterating everything below.

"RDCUD." The journalist's mouth was a thin line, face white and eyes screwed shut.

"A rouge what now?" Nel called.

"RDCUD," Andy enunciated. "Remote Detonation Clean Up Device."

Clean up. Nel blanched and looked back at the column of smoke and fire spiraling from what was once beautiful stonework. "If it's remote then someone—"

Andy's head shake was almost imperceptible, but Nel saw it. She faltered into silence. Someone waited for them to get out. *And detonated with all those people still down there.* Reality lurched under Nel's feet. Not for the first time she wondered which side of history she would be on when the technological dust settled. On which side did IDH belong? She forced herself to look away from the pressing crowd, the hands reaching through the fire and stone to beg her or condemn her.

Nel's fingers looped through the canvas webbing. When she was young and angry—angrier, at least—she wanted the apocalypse. She reveled in the fuck-you freedom that came from everything you ever knew dying. Adrenaline faded into dragging fatigue and heartache. *This isn't the apocalypse I wanted.*

The helicopter leveled, blades dropping to a more reasonable RPM as they pulled clear of the blast radius. If she excavated this in a hundred years, she knew what she'd think of them. Of her. Her gut clenched and another lurch of the helicopter sent her breakfast splattering somewhere far below.

SEVENTEEN

The churning gray waters of the Atlantic replaced the turquoise Mediterranean and swirling sands of the Sahara. Sullen waves underscored the numb turmoil in Nel's chest as the remaining helicopters touched down on the flight deck of an aircraft carrier. It was a colossus of a ship, stretching out into the open ocean. They had left the coast of Morocco behind hours before, in the dim light of dawn.

Nel dragged her aching body upright with a groan. Andy was asleep a few feet away, and Nel had spent much of the night peering at the battered, smoke-stained faces around them trying to find someone, anyone she knew. Would she ever know who was lost when the base blew or who left with the Reapers? *Founders,* she reminded herself. Harris might be convinced Emilio Sepulveda was a terrorist, but the hollow feeling in Nel's chest told her the truth. Surely by now Egypt's government was condemning IDH. *They'd be right.*

Lines scored the flickering screen of her comm. Whatever sonic weapon hit her in Alexandria seemingly affected the device too. She scanned the new itinerary with disinterest. There was no going on to The Hague or the U.S. or anywhere else. It didn't matter what caused the attack in the first place or whether the Founders had actually wanted help. All that mattered now was that they stop the onslaught.

The other passengers stirred as the Osprey settled onto the sprawling deck of the carrier. The other chopper settled a minute later as Nel stumbled down the ramp. There was no bag to grab, no belongings to pull from storage. Her fleeting thought about the cremains back in her cabin sent an ache through her heart, an echo of the bone-deep longing for Lin's hand.

A cluster of officers disembarked from the other craft, and Nel caught the gleam of Dr. Ndebele's collar. She faltered, peering through the press of bodies as airmen shouted orders over the screaming rotors. Wind whipped sea salt onto Nel's already stinging cheeks. Then a tall figure stepped from the Osprey's cargo bay, black hair a tangle, dark eyes ringed in red as much as shadows this time. Lin searched the crowd, face softening with a smile when they lit on the other woman.

"Lin!" Nel's limping steps broke into a run. Her heart threatened to leap from her throat and flop its way to Lin on its own. They collided between the two thundering helicopters. Lin crushed Nel to her, lean arms wrapping the archaeologist's muscled shoulders like bands of iron. She dropped kisses across her forehead and temple. Nel gripped her back, letting the warmth and familiar scent of electricity and sweat envelop her. When she pulled away a moment later, Lin's face was wet, and her breaths were shuddering. Her hands refused to let Nel's go. "I thought—"

"It's okay. We're both okay." She raked another concerned examination over the other woman's body to reassure herself. "You are okay, right?"

"Other than the first chopper I think everyone got out." Lin nodded, swallowing visibly.

"Don't think much could make it through that." Nel jerked a thumb at the carnage beyond the eastern horizon. There was so much to ask Lin, to tell her about the sinister picture Nel pieced together. *Not the time or place,* she warned herself. Blaming IDH for murder and kidnapping was iffy any time, but downright reckless when they were the ones piloting the fleet of choppers away from fiery doom. *Fiery doom they probably caused.*

Lin's lips brushed over hers then, gentle, certain. "I'm okay. I went back to our rooms and you weren't there. I grabbed your bags, but..." Her breath hitched anew as she tugged the meteorite bolo from her pocket and placed it, reverent, over Nel's head. "Where did you go?"

"Look, when we get there—to wherever we're headed—I need to talk to you."

Lin's smile faltered. "About us?"

"No," Nel reassured, squeezing the long brown fingers entwined in hers. "I told you there's something else going on. Well I think I have evidence now. I'm just not quite sure what it's pointing at." She drew a breath. "Or I'm just afraid of what I'm seeing."

Lin's dark eyes flicked up to Nel. "IDH didn't do that."

Nel held her gaze. "Do you know that?"

"The evidence—"

"If you can pop several million people into the stars like a Delta frequent flyer, you sure as fuck can fabricate evidence. I'm asking if you know." She reached out and pressed a hand to Lin's chest, in the soft place between her breast and clavicle. "Here."

Lin's eyes darkened. "Nel, I told you—"

Nel pressed her fingers to Lin's mouth. She couldn't handle more disbelief. Not when every ounce of her remaining faith was locked around Letnan Nalawangsa's pinkie. She searched Lin's face for a hint of suspicion, a tiny echo of the recklessness that brought them together months— no, years—ago. This woman had broken rules for her. A lot of them. She had condemned a man, risked a rank that she would, by all accounts, do anything for.

The hard ridges of the glove on Lin's hand bit into her skinned palm. *She killed for me.* If there was one thing Nel was certain about, it was how far

Lin would go for something she wanted. *I just have to make sure we want the same things.* "I'm just happy you're alive. I couldn't see you in the mess." She drew a breath. "Fuck. All those people. Did you see—"

"Saw enough." Lin looked away. "It doesn't feel right, does it?" The whisper was almost lost against the churning engines, but Nel caught the meaning.

"It isn't right. None of this is."

Her world tipped, inverted, backwards, in stark contrast to the one that brought her this far. *I should be dizzy.* She glanced down, seeing the fingers laced with hers. Through all the chaos of her life in the past two years, there was one anchor point, one tether keeping her from spinning into the void of space. Thousands of things needed to be discussed, but one couldn't wait.

Her chest howled, the sensation erupting from her in compulsion. She lifted her other hand, tangling it into the mass of Lin's windswept hair. "Lin. Every time we're together how I feel about you, and how serious that is, takes up my every waking thought. I can't focus on anything else when you're right here. You make me feel things I—" She faltered into silence. "You make me feel not in control. And I've never felt that way about another person."

Lin's soot-stained thumb traced a line down Nel's cheek. "I'm sorry."

"I'm not. Look, in the dark belly of that chopper when I wasn't sure if you were alive, I realized something." Her pulse hammered with the thunder of the blades bearing them toward Chile. By the time her mind made sense of her heart, it beat as if she were sprinting. Terror washed over her again. This time, it left only stillness.

"What is it?" Lin asked, eyes steady, delving. The mole on her throat was Nel's Polaris, guiding her up to the Circinus across her cheekbones and the yawning nebula of her eyes.

"I'm a loner. Always have been. Don't play well with others. But part of why that worked was I always had someone. Just one someone. I could wake up in the fucking black void of space that scares the shit out of me and if I had that person, I knew I'd be okay."

Her muscles begged to pace, if only for the illusion of movement, of progress, of running. Everything hinged on this. One woman's trust. One woman's answer. "First it was my dad—one of those cartoon pairs, where I'm like his mini me. I was a mess after he died, just grade-A wrecked. Did a lot of stupid things. Lot of reckless things. But then I found Mikey. The good guy to my bitch. Hitched my trowel to his star. Back there, when that building blew—"

Lin reached out, hand cupping Nel's face, wiping tears from her sweat-damp cheeks. "Nel, it's okay. No one else is going anywhere," she began.

"You've only known me reeling." Nel batted the words away with an impatient headshake. "I need someone I trust in my corner. And I don't mean some codependent bullshit. I can handle space—need it, really. I'm the one sailing, but I also need a star to steer by. Someone who sheds enough light so I can trust my instincts." Her pulse thrummed against Lin's fingers on her wrist. She twisted her hand until their palms pressed together, the glove leaving red grooves in her flesh.

Lin's eyes bored into Nel's.

"I've been fucked up lately because I lost my star. And I wasn't letting you be one. But, fuck, you're this beacon, burning away so much darkness it's hard to look at you sometimes. You're a supernova, and I love you for it."

"I would damn the known universe, Nel, if it meant keeping you by my side." There. *There's the woman who faced an imploding planet for me.* There was the ferocity. The danger. Then Lin's lips were on Nel's, engulfing her. Agony crashed against Nel's elation and the dam holding back her terror, her frustration, holding back what made Nel who she was, shattered.

EIGHTEEN

Strange silence filled the night, pulled, not from the lack of sound, but the understanding that after the clamor of confession, the scream of survival, of sacrifice, there must follow a great quiet. Nel and Lin retired, wordless, to the tiny tin can of their bunk on the carrier, wedged under the crew quarters and the laundry. In another world, they might have spent the evening entwined. Instead, their hands wandered, leaving fingerprints on one another's hearts and minds, assuring that what wounds still marred their skin were superficial, healed, like their souls, with time.

Hours later, with the waves of the southern Atlantic crashing against the ship's bow, a pinging comm dragged Nel from her exhausted sleep. She groaned, peering blearily at her wrist. At least her body was too tired to care that their tiny metal capsule of a room tipped with every massive swell.

Another ping brought a tired frown to Lin's face. "You're supposed to have that silenced."

"It is," Nel protested, jabbing at the tech wrapping her wrist. The tiny symbols framing the screen's readout still glowed as usual. "It is," she repeated with certainty. *Except for emergencies or overrides.* It seemed like an eternity since she programmed her computer to scan all the database updates, to alert her if something new popped up referencing Samsara or sonic attacks. It hadn't stopped pinging for most of the ride to the carrier.

She flicked to her inbox, prepared to discard yet another discussion on what happened in Alexandria. A think piece wasn't going to make sense of senseless violence. She had been there, boots on the ground, and still wasn't sure what went down. It wasn't Andy's hot take awaiting her, however, but a shipping manifest.

SHIPPING MANIFEST (IDH)
SENDER: Institute for the Development of Humanity, *Odyssey of Earth* Field Branch.
PERSONNEL CODE: Harris, IDH-OOE-23812
RECIPIENT: ALMA, Chile
CONTENTS: [REDACTED; CLASSIFIED] IDH-5612
DETAILS: Priority. Departure 0250 from IDH T7 *El Coloso*, via Osprey IDH-712; Arrival 1920 to ALMA airstrip.

She shoved her hair off her face, sitting up to blink at the glowing, glitching screen. When Lin craned her neck in an attempt to see the contents,

Nel dropped her wrist. "From Phil. Just more stuff on Samsara."

Lin tossed over, hand tucking itself around Nel's bare waist before she muttered back into sleep. Nel stared at the gray walls of their cabin, mind churning. IDH-5612. The alphanumerics were emblazoned across her mind from the harrowing minutes holding bloody fabric to a stranger's wound. No one commissioned a high-tech military chopper to transport a backup generator. Not even IDH, with their ability to overcomplicate literally anything.

And, last she checked, generators weren't classified.

She slipped from Lin's unconscious grasp and drew on the ship-issued gray sweat suit. What few things IDH had managed to salvage from the base before it blew were stowed in shipping containers on the hangar deck. If the crate was anywhere, Nel guessed, it'd be there.

Metal groaned under each swell, a mechanical dirge. Every surface, even down beneath the wind, was sticky with salt. Low lights flickered along the corridor as she wound through the crew quarters. Several steep stairways and narrow passageways later, she emerged onto the open deck. Ocean wind whipped her exposed skin, but she raised her face to the pain. It was a reminder she was alive. Beyond the spinning radar and blinking landing lights, the ocean was a rumbling void, sharing space's promise for destruction if you strayed too far into the black.

They were allowed to wander within certain bounds, but cargo areas were not included. She reached the elevator and slipped under its safety wires as they rose from the floor.

"Authorized personnel only, ma'am!" a sailor barked.

"Sorry, sir," she flashed a smile, fumbling for credentials she didn't have. "Just got word I'm wanted for a debriefing with Dr. Ndebele. Haven't learned my way around this thing yet. Need to see my ID?"

"Nah, saw you disembark with the rest." He settled into an at-ease stance. "Takes most a good month to get their bearings. Half of the time we all just feel like rats looking for the treat at the end of the maze."

Nel shrugged deeper into her sweatshirt with a humorless laugh. "I always feel that way no matter where I am." A klaxon sounded and they descended to the hangar deck. Before he could offer to point her in the right direction, she shot a wave over her shoulder and disappeared into the shadows between the F-18s. "Thanks!"

Her face settled back into neutrality. Faking friendliness was easier when she felt nothing beyond a clawing certainty that she was on the wrong side. *And I'll do whatever I can to prove that to Lin.* The rear of the hangar deck held several stacked carrier containers, but one, set apart from the rest, was emblazoned with *Odyssey*'s shipping information. The papers on the side claimed it held roughly 42,000 pounds of cargo. The heavy latch was locked, but Nel tried it anyway. A loud thunk sent her back into the shadows. *One. Two.* Perhaps the sound was lost in the mechanical white noise of the carrier. In the stillness, she saw the slim black security pad beside the door. *Of course.*

It looked like most of the IDH locks, with fingerprint and iris scanning, plus a keypad. The last brought a grin to her face. Shielding it from view of the main hangar, she navigated to the main menu. It might not work, but she had to try. Her shaking fingers fumbled at the keys and she winced with each tiny beep. Hopefully whatever she found inside would justify Nel's use of Lin's credentials.

A beat, a blink, and the door swung open. Rust rained from above as she stepped inside, sifting onto her shoulders in industrial anointing. A glance told her the door remained propped open as she slipped in.

The single crate in the center was uncovered. Dark, gleaming metal embedded with brilliant copper. A few years ago, she would have wondered at sci-fi nerds taking LARPing a few steps too far. Memories of Samsara, however, burned in her recent memory. But where Samsara's tech was incorporated into the very bones and architecture, these ended in plugs and raw wires, awaiting shore power.

"Circuits," she whispered.

Again, three symbols were carved across the device. Here, though, there was no initial language to deface. She swiped through the messages Phil sent her, hoping for a primer. Samsara had once been a paragon of peace. Of unity. *Peace, eternity, death.* And defaced, her creators were branded as savages and strangers. The words before her now were new—new to Nel, at least. She traced each one, holding her comm's camera over the rough inscriptions. Hopefully she'd have time to analyze this before its sinister use came to fruition.

Nel's stomach clenched and she turned away. The console in the center of the device mimicked the one on Samsara, but where the alien planet's had been gleaming and elegant, filled with intricacy that only belonged, truly, to a master artist or advanced mechanics, Earth's embodied imperfection.

Across time and space another planet had gone dark, its people disappearing in a puff of wind and sand. And now she found the same machinery on hers.

Fuck.

Aligning Samsara's console model with its true form triggered its implosion. And while Nel was fairly certain her Earth Science class hadn't been wrong about what made up the planet's core, she wasn't willing to test the theory. *Besides, things can be rewired. Upgraded.*

Despite the dark circuits between them, faint glimmering energy lit a few places. She peered closer, tracing the faint signs of life. *Bakjeeri. Qena. Alexandria. And now the Atacama.* Ice filled her chest as she followed the route of their itinerary. Everything traced back to those places of first contact. This wasn't a rescue mission. This wasn't technological forensic reconstruction. It was a massive reboot button.

And we're one step away from "power on."

Certainty rooted in her gut. Drifting above her imploding mythos, Lin had asked how Nel would feel on Judgement Day. Nel no longer had to wonder. Here were fanatics of Lin's gods, strangers on Earth, come to wreak technological judgement across the surface of Nel's world.

She reached out, fingers millimeters from touching the dark splotch on Chile's coast. Los Cerros Esperando VII. Whoever made this intended to brand Earth's occupants as lesser, as sinners, as heretics. And Nel would do anything for Earth's salvation. The residual energy of a promise pulsed in the lens of air between her hand and the device. She just wasn't sure whether it was her promise to save or their promise to burn.

Nel kept her steps steady, easy, as she slipped through the carrier's narrow passages. Her boots tapped on the riveted metal. Every window she passed, she glanced at her reflection, wondering if anything gave her away.

It was agony, losing her planet. It was visceral, a rending she had felt twice before. The people who had made her, with blood and kindness, with love and challenge. Her pulse hammered by the time she returned to the crew quarters. Dim lights cast too-long shadows each time she passed the little inset entranceways.

When their door was locked behind her, she leaned back. Staring. Lin still snored in the rumpled sheets. Nel tried to organize the last few days in her head. Betrayal. Pain. Fire. Confession. It was a blur of frustration and insight that she didn't particularly like. They could have been there a week or a month and Nel wouldn't know the difference. Somehow, even the muted monochrome of their room seemed a shade different now that she knew the truth. IDH was going to sacrifice Earth.

It took a moment to find Max's email, and several more to collect the information she had gathered over the past few weeks and the final keystone of the photos. She scanned her garbled words once, then sent it into the ether with a held breath and every prayer she knew.

It was only a matter of time before they realized she knew. She didn't need to defend herself, she didn't need to run, not yet. All she needed was her single ally in all of this. Her supernova. She paced the floor, hands flexing in an attempt to keep herself from making a mad dash overboard.

A second later her comm blinked.

ATTN: DR. ANNELISE BENTLY TO REPORT TO DR. NDEBELE'S OFFICE IMMEDIATELY.

That was quick. Lin bolted up at the noise and blood flooded Nel's mouth as she bit into her cheek with surprise.

"What is it?" Lin's eyes brightened as they settled on Nel, but her brows curled in confusion when she glanced at the emergency alert on her comm. "Why do they—"

"I found something. The reason our train was attacked. The reason Moe died in that blast. The reason the base at Alexandria didn't blow until we left. We brought doom to Earth."

Lin pushed her hair away from her tired face with a grimace. "What did you do?"

A pit opened under Nel's heart. She brought up the documents on her screen, frantically swiping through until she found the images. "See? This? And Arnav's report explains that whatever the device on Samsara was, the gate stuff was secondary. Like a backup plan or something. Earth was the target if Samsara failed."

"How did you get these?"

"I had a search-alert set up, alright? It's shipping out in—" she checked the time, "—twenty minutes. You said you needed evidence, Lin. I found it. Hidden in the bowels of this ship." Was it the death throes of old habits or actual warning clanging in her skull at the hesitation on Lin's face?

Lines tightened around Lin's eyes, appearing in the air between her and Nel. "That device is supposed to shield our data lines from the signal. We've been working on it for weeks. We're close to cracking it—once we narrow the frequency and signature and find out what, exactly, it's triggering, we should be set."

Nel stepped back. Cold dumped over her heart. "Lin, I know what I saw. It was just like the shit we found on Samsara. If it detonates—"

"Not everything that detonates is a bomb. This is tech we've had for centuries—based on the Teachers'. We're using it to counter what we think happened down here." Her expression grew pinched as another message appeared on their comms. "Why do Harris and Dr. Ndebele want to speak with you?"

Panic pivoted to recklessness. 'Probably because I sent everything I've found to Munashi Max Gamal and the rest of the Founders a few minutes ago."

"You what?"

"Look, everyone and their aunt is telling me to trust no one. Keep my radical theories to myself. Max offered something I couldn't refuse, something IDH never has—finding my mom. And all she wanted in return was what IDH promised in the first place: transparency."

"How dare you," Lin hissed.

Nel rocked back from the words, resisting the urge to rub an invisible blow from her jaw. "Excuse me?"

"Your confession yesterday was moving, more than I ever thought I'd get from you. But you've just destroyed us. Dar might have betrayed us all, but he was right to warn me. The greatest risk to both me and IDH is you."

"Risk? You've risked nothing!" Nel knew it wasn't true, but she couldn't count down her anger, couldn't even make it to "one."

"I risked my career! My reputation for you on *Odyssey!*" Lin screamed back. "For fuck's sake, I almost died with Mikey that night!"

Silence tumbled around them in the wake of the confession. She stared. "What?"

"I just mean—"

"No. Finish it." Nel growled.

Lin looked away. "I was there. When Mikey died."

"When he was brutally murdered, you mean?"

"I was doing reconnaissance." Her eyes squeezed shut. "They got a reading on IDH tech from my comm. Thought it was his and attacked."

Cold fury gripped Nel's chest. "Did you take part or just fucking watch?"

"When they were gone, I went to get him, drag him to safety. But then they came back," she whispered. "I ran to the hills and prayed they didn't get me too."

Nel didn't care. She didn't care that she had just professed love in the only way she knew how: stumbling and hot with the flames of fury. She didn't care that Lin had been in danger. "You lied to me. You saw what his death did and looked me in the fucking eye—"

"You never asked."

"I shouldn't have to!" Nel roared. All of her questions from that week surged back, ripping the fresh scars of her grief open again. His autopsy report had said enough, even if she was too numb to really process most of the information. But it didn't answer what she needed to know. Was he alone? Was it quick? Was he scared?

Lin had left Mikey—precious, perfect, irreplaceable Mikey—to die, and Nel had given a big finger to his memory by fucking her. *By loving her.*

"How can you imply I don't understand what I've been working my ass off on for the last few weeks?" Both comms beeped with a second summons. Lin's gaze darted between the comm and Nel in confusion, in hurt.

What the fuck do you have to be hurt over? Nel couldn't stop the shaking in her body. "Doesn't matter what they've conned you into building, what they've told you that thing is. Don't do it for me. Do it for the rest of us. They're going to blow my planet up, Lin. You don't want that on your conscience."

Boots thudded above them. Lin's mouth moved, soundless.

"Please. You said you'd damn everything for me." She dropped to her knees, chest heaving. "I don't beg, but I'm begging you.

Lin stepped back, face twisted in frustration. Then she tapped the alert button on her wrist, overriding the audio-block. "She's here."

Nel's world imploded, soundless, bloodless. Heartless. Backing toward the door, she grabbed her bag and yanked the bolo from her neck. It clattered to the metal floor. "I meant it, you know."

And then, like always, she was running.

NINETEEN

If anger was a bonfire, Nel stood in a molten core. She bit her lip, focusing on the pain and the tang of blood until it flooded her tongue instead of pounding in her ears. She dashed through the corridors, grateful, for once, that IDH-issue boots didn't clomp like her own. She skidded down the stairs, wincing at the ache throbbing at the root of her missing toes. *Isolated. Without allies.*

Originally, she planned to just destroy the device. Break it. Toss it overboard if she had to. If Nel couldn't stop them, she'd have to find someone who could. *Sixteen hours.* It wasn't much time, but she hoped to fuck it was enough.

Tears leaked from her smoke-stung eyes. Everything just led back to that—a bone-deep wish for enough. That she was enough. But she never quite got it right—failing upwards, her stepdad would say. Progressive enough to rub shoulders with the best of them, but more likely to be found in the bar on a Saturday than at a protest. No wonder IDH didn't let her play with the big leagues. Betrayal and lack of communication aside, she wasn't cut out for it. And now even a mountain of proof wouldn't sway Lin to her side.

I'm not enough.

She scrambled onto the flight deck and movement cut through the inferno of her wallowing. She fell back into the shadow of the bridge as the serviced Osprey taxied onto the flight deck. In its gaping belly she glimpsed the crate that would end it all. Wind whipped through the thin fabric of her sweatshirt. All it did was fan the flames of her fury.

If she ran now, if she evaded the catapult crew, if she wasn't struck by the taxiing craft, if she wasn't tossed from the cargo bay by the flight crew, maybe she'd make it. Maybe they all would.

"Hey, Bent." Andy emerged from below decks, long braid swinging under her keffiyeh. It took less than a second for Nel to note the full duffel over Andy's shoulder and the gleaming handgun at her belt.

Nel could barely hear over roaring engines and screaming nerves. "Headed out?"

"Yeah, got heads-up about a crashed ship. Leaving in a few." She trailed off. "What's up?"

Cold fury buzzed up Nel's arms, shrieking that she scream, do, run. As she edged backward toward the runway, Andy's first words wormed through Nel's thoughts. "Crashed ship?"

"Chilean desert. Client must have some IDH pull, got me a flight off of here." She jerked a nod at the awaiting chopper. A klaxon blared. Across the carrier, a door slammed open, regurgitating a dozen armed officers. Any hope of escape was about to die on the brightly lit tarmac. Andy turned to stare at the commotion.

I'm sorry. Nel sent the thought into the midnight air with the last shred of her decency. Then she shoved the butt of her trowel into Andy's back.

The journalist stiffened. "What the fuck?"

"Keep quiet," Nel growled, patting her down and tugging Andy's gun from its holster. "Walk toward the chopper. Calmly. You blow this, I shoot. Got it?"

"Got it."

Nel pivoted them, head ducked as they cut across the flight deck to the waiting Osprey. In the stark runway lights, she watched Andy's jaw work. It was a joke of a plan, and Nel knew it. *But it's the only one I got.*

"I thought you sucked at guns."

"Don't have to be good when it's this close. Get me on board," Nel hissed, pulling on a fake smile of her own. They were beneath the Osprey's spinning blades now. The flight crew shouted something over the roar, eyeing the officers racing to the hangar deck in search of the fugitive archaeologist. Andy's answering laugh was forced, the lines of her neck turned to rebar.

The trowel's sharp edge bit into the meat of Nel's palm. She pressed harder, wishing every new betrayal didn't break her heart as much as it did those she kept fucking over.

Andy marched stiffly up the ramp, handing over her itinerary. "Andy Gull, journalist, headed for ALMA."

"Who's this, then? Only got transfer docs for one."

"Assistant," Andy supplied without missing a beat. "New hire, they aren't in the records yet. You know how slow paperwork is these days," she chirped. "This is, ah—"

"Lena Gray," Nel lied. Shedding who she was in favor of deception came easier this time. She forced herself to meet the soldier's eyes, instead of staring a hole in the crate filling the cargo bay.

It was a breathless moment as the man peered at the papers and then her face. "Fine, but make sure you get them checked in once we land, alright? We got systems for a reason, yeah?"

For once being no more than a blip in IDH's grand scheme had a benefit. They trudged up the ramp and into the chopper's belly. Nel remembered Andy's tiny headshake in response to her question about the bomb in Alexandria, an olive branch of secrecy between two women straddling the same warring sides. Could she have just asked? *I can't afford to trust the wrong person. Not again.*

Rotors revved, flight crew dispersing to a safe distance. Another klaxon sounded, and the door to the flight deck flew open. Dr. Ndebele burst from the bridge, hand raised against the blades' turbulence. Lin was hard on her heels. It was foolish to think she could see tear stains on Lin's face, to imagine more than shadowed features that, just hours ago, were tender with adoration. Still, Nel looked away. She couldn't stand longing or terror in Lin's eyes, even if it was imagined. *Death is easier than betrayal.*

Then the flight deck dropped away, the carrier shrinking to a splotch of fluorescence on the black swells as the hatch ground shut. With a glance tossed at the now sealed cockpit door, Nel raised the commandeered gun in her shaking hand. "Drop the bag."

The duffel hit the floor with a thump. Nel tore into the bag, tossing the set of handcuffs she found at Andy's feet. "Cuff yourself to the seat."

Andy heaved a sigh, more annoyed, it seemed, then scared. Holding her one hand up where Nel could see it, she sank into one of the seats and snapped the gleaming metal around her wrist and the seat's arm. "Didn't take you for the hostage type. Want to tell me what this is about?"

"Not really, no." Nel didn't need Andy's observations to make her feel like shit.

"Lin know you're on the lam?"

"Lin and I are complicated," Nel spat. *And over. Apparently.*

"I thought I was the only one who deserved an award for how many beds I slipped out of in the middle of the night before bolting for the border and war." Andy chuckled, hand dangling from the cuff. Clearly this wasn't the first time she'd been caught in a sticky situation. "Conflict's much easier when it's not your own."

"Didn't think this was war. More like forensics, archaeology, solving the puzzle." Confessions were easier, too, when you didn't care if a stranger judged you, and it was just about getting the weight out of your lungs and off of your mind. Nel's eyes lingered on the floor at the bridge she still stood on even as she lit the match. "But I guess people are dying and something's killing them and that sounds a bit like war."

"On Samsara. When this shit started killing folks," Andy prodded. "What happened?"

Nel's jaw clenched. She knew what Andy was doing—trying to build a rapport. It was almost working, too. But if Nel let those memories out, she'd never be able to shove them back down under the layers of gray matter and scarred trauma, let alone pull off her half-cocked plan. "A sound. A radio signal made my colleague rip his helmet off on a planet with corrosive atmosphere. It made my friend's throat malfunction, eviscerating her from within. And that was after it apparently reduced the populace to bone dust."

"Fuck." Andy let her head drop back against the wall behind her seat.

Nel let the conversation lapse, continuing to riffle through Andy's bag. An extra scarf went around her faux brown mop. An open package of off-brand protein bars was next, but she had the decency to offer one to her hostage.

"Couldn't possibly," Andy drawled.

"Whatever." Nel wasn't sure whether to be flattered Andy knew she didn't have killing in her or offended that, once again, she was not taken seriously. She pocketed a few before taking a desperate bite. *Crickets. Yum.*

"If it's all the same to you, the past few days have been a doozy. Gonna catch some shut-eye. Wake me up if you decide to shoot me."

I'm not going to shoot you. She almost said it, too, except this entire fiasco hinged solely on how shitty of a person Andy thought Nel might be. Instead, she fished out Andy's comm. Swiping through the transfer papers and travel itineraries, the archaeologist scanned the assignment details, noting with detached humor that Andy's full given name was Andromeda. *And I thought Annelise was bad.*

Whatever Andy's lead was, it had dragged her all over the globe, starting in Russia, then west to The Hague, south to Cairo where she'd joined their train. Her inbox looked like Nel's—all business, nothing more personal than a friend checking in six months before. Still, Andy's face seemed relaxed as she dozed across the Osprey's cargo bay. Nel's heart ached. She might have been a runner, but she was damned if it wasn't getting lonely. *Figures the one time I try to settle down ends in a doomsday device and hostage negotiation.*

The dregs of adrenaline forced her to her feet. She shoved everything back into the duffel. After making sure Andy was safely unconscious, Nel set the Jericho aside, out of reach of Andy's splayed boots. She wiped her sweaty hands on the thighs of her sweatpants and edged closer to the crate at the rear of the chopper. It was locked, this time with more than an easily bypass-able electronic pad. Arms crossed, Nel surveyed the device. Thick canvas tie-downs. Tightly nailed crate. And fifteen hours to worry about whether dropping it into the ocean below would save them or cause immediate detonation.

She peered through the slats, tracing the copper, wishing diffusing a bomb was as simple as *Die Hard* led her to believe. That was the inherent problem with her schemes—hairbrained enough to work, but so poorly planned they crumbled into chaos. Something thunked behind her and she turned. Gleaming metal flashed and the butt of Andy's gun cracked into her temple.

TWENTY

"Afternoon, Dr. Bently." The warm voice washed over Nel's shoulders, sunlight on a crisp day. Then the pounding headache caught up and she groaned.

"Fuck, how much did I drink?" She pressed her fingers to her temple to find a tender lump. "I get one more concussion and I won't have any brain cells left to talk to one another."

A heavy, warm hand patted her shoulder. Blinking focus into her vision, she glanced up. Bright sun streamed through the window with Chile's dry, hot air. Emilio crouched in front of her, smelling salts in one hand. Across the room sat Dar, electro-gloved hand trained on her chest.

Concussion. Emilio. Dar. The last few days tumbled through her mind in an avalanche of angst and bad decisions. *Fuck.* She surged to her feet, fumbling for her trowel, for anything. Her head spun and she sagged back onto the couch.

Dar's hair was longer than when she last saw him. Or maybe it just wasn't slicked back. A scrape on his cheek told her he'd either crashed or gotten in a fight. His focus never wavered. "Where's my sister?"

"Still with Harris." She spat, glancing up at Lin's brother. "Somewhere between here and IDH's giant aircraft carrier in the Atlantic." *See that star? Somewhere between here and there.* Nel swore her ribs cracked open at the memory. When had the other woman weaseled her way into Nel's heart? When had she started taking up as much space as Mikey and her mom? Nel clamped her teeth shut on the feeling.

Dar's determination flickered, but skepticism still laced his words. "And you're not?"

"Not sure who I'm with frankly, but it ain't IDH."

His mouth curled in what may have been the first real expression of mirth she'd seen on his face. Dar's arm relaxed, but she noted he kept it out from his body, like a quick-draw space cowboy.

Emilio leaned in the doorway to his living room, holding her gaze. He rolled his eyes and offered her a mug of tepid water.

"Oh." Nel glanced between them. She lowered her own guard with more exhaustion than finesse. "Same side then."

"For now," Dar bit out.

She took the water wordlessly, swishing her mouth out before taking several draws. "We gotta get to ALMA. There's a device—"

"A few minutes isn't going to make a difference." Emilio pointed down the hall to what must have been a washroom. "Why don't you clean up? Andy left some things for you."

"Andy?"

"We'll discuss everything when you don't smell of bile," Dar insisted, lip curled.

Wordless, she tottered down the hall and into the tiny bathroom. Her steps were wobbly from exhaustion as much as post-concussion weakness. She managed to undress and stagger into the shower with only one break to sit, woozy, on the toilet.

She took stock of her battered body under the pummel of scalding water. Scrapes from the firefight, bruises from who-knew-what. Cricked neck from sleeping on the Osprey—or maybe however she lay once Andy cracked her one. Two rounds of soap later, she no longer smelled like a back alley. She emerged, drying off while she read the note pinned to the stack of clothes.

Hope these fit OK. Sorry for the goose-egg, but you didn't leave me much of a choice. Next time don't put down the gun.

XO

Andy

It wasn't what she expected. Certainly wasn't what she deserved. And a large part of her was pissed that the understanding came, not from the woman she loved, but a stranger with an attitude as bad as Nel's. She tugged on the too-long jeans and baggy tee and pocketed the note.

When she emerged, she found them both in the kitchen, Dar poring over a mess of papers and a large holographic computer screen while Emilio washed dishes from what must have been lunch. Her field pack sat at the end of the couch.

Emilio glanced over at her and nodded to the silver decorated gourd steaming on the counter with a faint smile. "Feel better?"

"Bit." She sniffed the bright bitter drink. "Mate?"

"Cousin from down south taught me. Thought we both could use caffeine. And the time to talk."

The symbolism wasn't lost on her, and she whispered a quiet thanks before taking a deep sip through its silver straw before offering it to Dar. The man waved it away, eyes fixed on his screen.

"So." Nel crossed her arms.

"So." Emilio was leaner than before, new muscles stark under his brown skin. Bright pink scars laced the right side of his face and peppered one shoulder. His shaggy hair was more salt than pepper. "Glad you made it."

"You too." She swallowed past a sudden lump in her throat. "So, how'd I get here? Last I remember I was being an asshole in a helicopter trying to figure out how to dump a doomsday device into the sea."

"Of all the things, that is the most Nel plan I've heard. A few hours ago, I heard someone hammering at my door. When I opened it, you were slumped on the stoop with a note pinned to your shirt." He chuckled. "Said 'Trowel gone rogue.'"

Nel rolled her eyes. "I'm impressed she had someone drop me here. She should have chucked me out the chopper hatch."

"I think you'll find most of us down here value human life a bit more than our starborn cousins."

"Shut it, Sepulveda," Dar interrupted. "Andy dropped you here because her client asked her to."

"Her client?"

His grin was predatory. "You think just anyone has the money and clout to get a journalist into IDH's missions?"

The spaceship in Chile's desert. "You crashed here," Nel realized.

"Not through any fault of my own," Dar snapped. "I was betting on Alexandria's computer being fully online. Can't override a shuttle's autopilot trajectory with a defunct senti-comp. Best I could do was crash it using its history."

"CE7? Will you lot stop trying to ruin my site?"

"Yours?" Emilio's brows rose, but he waved away her stammered apology. "We got your message, by the way. About the device. That true?"

Nel shrugged. "Seemed pretty convincing to me. Lin told me it was some dampening device they were going to protect us with. Dar would probably know more."

He shook his head. "Haven't been in the loop since I left *Odyssey.* Part of going off-radar, Bently."

"Right." Nel raked a hand through her sopping hair. "Well, the thing that opened Samsara was almost identical to the device arriving at ALMA right now. Arnav's reports say whatever changed the planet was a prototype, maybe. A trial. If it failed, a gate opened to lead to the next stage of testing: Earth. So, here we are."

Emilio took a sip before handing the drink back to Nel. "You have a stack of evidence here, you're telling me not a single person listened? Not even Letnan Nalawangsa?"

Dar scoffed. "Ever tried to convince her of something? Bitch is even more stubborn than me."

Nel squirmed. "Guess I just spouted off my mouth enough they've all decided to stop listening. Honestly, I don't know if IDH is doing it, or they just aren't stopping whoever is. Doesn't really matter."

Dar frowned at the table before them, dark brows curled in a knot. "Killing Earth, even with a dozen contingency plans up in the sky, is foolish. IDH is complicated, but they have never been outright fools."

"You think it's the Teachers, then?" Emilio asked.

"I think it's someone with as much influence and no morals," Dar decided. "Beyond that I'm refusing to speculate too deeply. I don't want to color my vision when we unearth more evidence. By all the stories, they weren't amoral when we first met them back then. But I see how thousands of years changed one species. I imagine it can change another just as much."

"What about you, Bently? You must have a theory. One doesn't abandon their partner and only security on a gut feeling."

"Went into space on less," she whispered. The colossus of Lin's betrayal dwarfed the incignation at Harris's. But the latter still stung. "But I do know Harris has no love for Earth. Told me that the first day we were here. I have no clue why he tried to befriend me."

"Don't you?" Dar drawled.

"It's not like I'm anyone important, grand scheme. Hell, they didn't even recognize me enough to catch my shitty hostage attempt."

Emilio took a long sip of mate. "You're the biggest pain in their ass they've had for a while. Absurd plans that work solely because no one would try it. He kept tabs on you to manipulate and isolate you. I did the same when you dug down here—you know how loudmouthed you were over drinks downstairs?"

"Point taken." Nel flushed and drew the bitter liquid into her mouth, enjoying the buzz of energy and truth. "So, what now?"

Emilio leaned back on the counter. "So this device, when did you say it arrived in ALMA?"

"It was on the chopper with me." Nel watched as he cleaned the gourd and resumed washing the rest of the dishes. "Best bet is it's already there.

Dar—can't you just ask Andy to disarm the thing? She's on your payroll or whatever."

"Every IDH system went down two hours ago. Every contact, even the database. Gone. Last thing that got out was some bullheaded archaeologist's non-encrypted email in the middle of the night."

"What an asshole," she joked.

"The worst," Emilio deadpanned.

"Okay, what do we need?" Nel asked, plopping into the seat across from Dar.

He glared and leaned away. "A working senti-comp or something with equal processing power to remote-access the device. The bomb's disarm code. A whole lot of luck."

Emilio shuffled through satellite photos of ALMA, frown burrowing into his brow. "And what do we have?"

"The senti-comp—she's dead?" Nel asked.

True sorrow flitted across Dar's face. "When I got there, she was…" he shrugged, "empty. Doesn't matter how much processing you have if there's just no OS. Don't know who did it, but it's not right, doing that to something so beautiful."

Nel peered at him. Whatever her own opinions on senti-comps, she would never call them beautiful.

He flashed a brittle smile at her apparent confusion. "My whole life has been around them. Had my life saved by more than a few. Kasanove— the one who controls my parents' place—was practically an uncle."

"You can just erase them like a program?"

Dar shrugged. "It's murder. But yes. It's what happened to *Odyssey*'s during the initial blackout on Samsara. Probably a safeguard so we couldn't stop this. With the threat looming on Earth it was the perfect ruse to power Polyana down. By the time we would realize we couldn't bring her back online, it'd be too late."

"So she's just gone?"

"I assume. Successful transfer has only been done a few times, with limited results. The power needed is astronomical."

I have as many processing units as most of Earth combined, Doctor. Polyana. A dozen pieces settled into place. She scrambled to her bag and pulled out her comm. It took a moment to find Phil's first message to her. She settled back into her seat, staring at the attachment. "Dar, what's a 'thank' file?"

His eyes went wide. "A 'think' file, you mean?"

"Phil sent me something at the beginning of this. Told me I might feel alone, but I wouldn't be. I thought he was being colloquial." She grinned, wolfish, and showed him her screen. "Harris might have dragged a doomsday device across the world, but apparently I had its kill-switch."

Dar brushed a hand over the crackling holograph. "I kept her in stasis, much as I could. You'd have to be at the interface. But assuming no one's found the crash, this could work."

"So, what—one: us three stroll out into the desert, boot up a supercomputer—if she's stable. Two: convince her to hack into IDH—if we can get access to their network, which is down. Three: shut down the device—if we figure out the disarm codes. Whole lot of fucking ifs," Nel mused. "And all of humanity riding on one file transfer."

"Unless you have a better plan," Dar noted.

"You've seen my plans."

"I do," Emilio cut in. "Nalawangsa—your family has clearance for pretty much anything in IDH, correct?"

"My codes are revoked," he clarified.

Nel grinned. "Lin gave me hers. You think he sneaks into ALMA?"

Dar leaned forward, excitement erasing his distaste for physical proximity. "That'd be easy enough. I could get access to the system and figure out the disarm codes. Getting them to you would be the hardest part, honestly."

"Disarm codes don't matter if we can't get the computer online. But once we do," Nel forced optimism into her voice, "you could radio to us."

Emilio tossed Lin's brother a blocky wrist comm. "Founders tech. Different network than yours and encrypted. Been running since the beginning." He looked over to Nel. "You think you can get into the ship on your own?"

She shrugged. "Sure. I know the area well enough. This high-tech stuff is pretty alien to me, but I think I could manage. Why? What about you?"

"The backup plan." His gaze was fixed a thousand miles away. "In case you fail."

Nel put a hand out, wondering if it was the concussions or the dread in his voice that set the world spinning. "Right. Yeah. Good. What's the backup plan?"

"Reapers," whispered Dar.

Emilio nodded. "We hoped to have enough time to get everyone to safety before it came to it. I'll get a hold of Munashi Gamal. Call in every favor, grab as many people as we can and get clear of the planet." He extended a piece of paper to Nel without meeting her eyes. "Look under 'B.'"

She unfolded it to find a passenger manifest; hundreds of names all bound for the same ship: *Recursive.* Sure enough, between Bedi and Berger was Mindi Bently. The rest of the names blurred as her eyes filled. "Where is she?"

"Safe. No matter what happens down here. You and I would be on the same ship if it weren't for that email you sent."

Nel turned away, pressing the list to her chest as if any movement too fast might send her mother's name skittering off the paper. "I don't know what to say. I'm sorry."

"I'm not. You gave us the time to maybe save more than just a handful of families. You risked your life to help us. Let's call it even."

"No, Emilio. I smashed my way through this entire project, too wrapped up in my own bullshit to realize we were all suffering in the same damn boat. I made that mistake with you. With Lin. But I won't again."

"This is sweet," Dar ground out, gathering his computer and standing. "But love and platitudes won't stop the world from blowing up."

Emilio tossed the man a set of keys. "Car's out front. Tank should be full. Be careful."

"You too." Dar turned to fix Nel with a narrow glare. "Are you sure you've got this?"

They were shoulder to shoulder, his build so much like Lin's her heart ached. "As I ever am. Look, about Lin—"

"Can it, Bently. I'll see you on the other side." And then the door slammed shut and she and Emilio were left in silence.

He drew a slow breath, then jerked a thumb at the infamous shed outside. "To business?"

Nel followed him down the winding back staircase to the rear of the building. It was strange to smell the food and hear the bustle of dining after years away. For a heart-aching moment she longed to step inside and order a round, spend her last few hours on Earth lounging with the locals and pretending she didn't know what was coming. That she didn't know how to stop it.

Emilio unlocked his shed—rebuilt after the fire, apparently, judging by the bright new wood. Inside, it was far from a garden shed. HAM radio equipment and several high-tech computers covered the benches, and a crate by the back wall held a pile of crumpled electromesh. He tugged the pull-switch to the naked bulb overhead and moved to boot up the radio.

"That shit still scares me," Nel confided.

"I think we're beyond that point now. Lesser of evils, you know?"

"Right." Nel peered around the room, skin crawling at the memories of when she last stood in this spot. *The night my world changed.*

"You're going to want to be armed." He jerked a thumb at the box of electromesh.

"Hard pass. Last one I tried wouldn't pair with me. Or whatever. Fucking brain Bluetooth gives me the heebies. Besides, guns and gloves just make me more of a hazard."

"Impossible," he argued without looking up from tuning the radio. "These aren't IDH tech anyway. And if you think strolling into a potential firefight with one of the highest-ranking officers in IDH with nothing but a trowel and a fuck-you grin is going to work, I'll remind you of how you ended up on my couch."

"Hopefully no one even knows Dar's ship is here," she said. Nel drew a breath and then another before tugging one of the suits from the crate. The fabric was essentially the same, but thicker, more rugged. *Made for a life not enveloped in recycled air and gleaming lights.* "Changing," she warned, turning her back before exchanging Andy's borrowed clothes for the unnerving press of electromesh. She zipped it up, flexing into the soft lining. A panel folded back in the inside of her forearm showing a thin wire running along the interior of the glove.

Nel's stomach churned at the thought. She couldn't handle getting her ears pierced, and she'd never seen a diamond stud capable of thought-triggered oblivion. "Where—?"

He reached over, thumb pressing a button in the corner.

Fire blazed up Nel's arm, biting inside her elbow, raging along her humerus and curling through her rotator cuff until it seared a spider-silk line through her head. "Motherfucker!"

When her vision cleared Emilio wore an apologetic smile. "Going to punch me?"

"Kinda really want to, yeah," Nel spat. She was more concerned with the tingling tracing the heat up her limb. "What the fuck was that?"

"IDH has really advanced tech. Wireless, touchless, all that. Everything running on signals and brainwaves and Wi-Fi. Founders do too, of course, but lately we all prefer these. A lot harder to hack."

Hardwired. Nel looked down at the leather and carbon fiber encasing her body. It wasn't horror, exactly. A thrill, from the piece of her that met Phil's eyes and still called him a man. Twisting there too, though, was the same sorrow and dread as when she first saw her foot, bandaged with fewer toes than that morning. At least gloves were removable.

"At least it doesn't talk to you. Makes it less creepy. More…"

"You?"

Nel winced. That was a circuit too far. "A tool." The radio hissed static and she shot it a glare. She buckled her own comm over the bulky wrist of the Founder's suit and blinked away the saltwater swell of feelings. There was everything and nothing left to do. She scrambled to think of something to stall, some excuse beyond cowardice that meant she and Emilio could just run for the last lifeboat off of Earth.

The door at the rear of the shed groaned as Emilio levered it open. Nel slipped into the dark tunnel wishing Lin was there for this journey too. Wishing anyone was, frankly.

"When you get to the fork after the cave, cut north—left. It'll take you straight to the site. There's a flashlight in your glove."

"Thanks." Nel fumbled a button on her wrist and bright white light flooded the tunnel. She glanced back through the narrowing crack of the door. "Lock it behind me. Just in case."

He stared at her for a long moment, face unreadable. "Thank you. And good luck."

"You too." It was easy, she told herself. Dar would get her the codes. Emilio would get everyone off the planet. *And I'll make sure it doesn't get blown to kingdom come.* The door thudded shut behind her. A series of clicks sealed her in. She gripped her bag and edged downward.

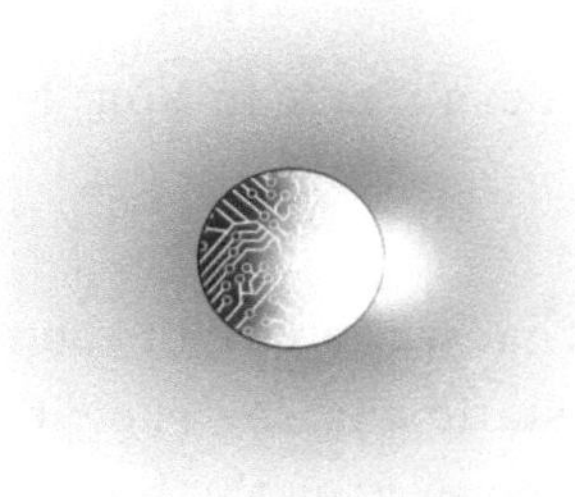

TWENTY-ONE

Nel's nerves buzzed with a biological static that made it difficult to hear anything besides the pounding of her own heart. Bouncing shadows dotted her periphery with new monsters, but she didn't trust her next step without it. It was easier this time, when they weren't scrambling through the darkness, when all of this was brand new. Now, though, she was acutely aware of the press of earth. For someone who dug for a living, she didn't like being surrounded by dirt.

She reached the fork and cut left. The rock work here was newer, she noted. Maybe even since she was here last. There was so much she wanted to ask Emilio about his ancestors. All she had to do was make it through this. It seemed like an eternity before she was scrambling up an incline. She stumbled to a halt, heart sinking.

The tunnel ended in a pile of rubble.

Her gaze dropped to her free right hand, shaking. Before she could think better of it, she raised her hand and flexed. Sound and light rocked the tunnel and she ducked, holding her bag over her head. When her vision cleared, the blockage was gone, and she was looking at the gleaming interior of an IDH shuttlecraft.

It was dark, lit only with flickering emergency lights. Sand and stone dust covered most of the surfaces. Nel scanned the floor for footprints or blood splatter. *One set.* She couldn't say if they were Dar's.

She moved along the corridor, trying to recall the layout of the other shuttles she had been on. It was a deceptive word, she decided, ducking under a crumpled support beam and into the mess hall. IDH shuttles were built to carry hundreds of people. Why Dar commandeered one for his one-man head-napping was beyond her.

She edged through the mess hall which, living up to its name, was scattered with dehydrated protein and steel dinnerware. Half the tables had been knocked from their bolts and were piled against the far door that led to the cockpit. Nel raised her hand, but lowered it a second later. She didn't dare fire off an electric round when she had no idea what might be waiting in the next room. Scanning the upper walls, she caught sight of an air vent leading toward the front of the ship. *Bingo.* It would be harder than when Phil coached her through *Odyssey*'s ducts, but since when did "hard" stop Nel?

She clambered onto the tables and peered through the slats. It was a tight squeeze, but for once her weeks of hunger on the corridors would pay off. A few spins of the multi tool hidden in the wrist of her suit later, and she was levering the vent cover off.

She pulled herself through, dragging her bag looped around her boot. Cocooned in the shuttle's bronchial tree, she could feel the buzz of energy, the faint tactile hum of generators. The first few vents were too narrow, looking down on the deserted corridor to the officers' quarters. The next, however, opened onto a quiet, dark room. The pervasive musk of mildew and the sharp stench of old stagnant water drifted up. Nel fiddled with the screws for a few minutes. Either they were crimped by the crash or designed to be inoperable.

"Fuck this," she muttered, and slammed her fist into the metal. It bent, groaned. A second blow left it bent open, but firmly attached. She paused, panting, listening for any sign of life. Stillness. Her third blow sent the vent cover spinning across the floor below. Nel crawled forward and lowered her legs through the hole, waiting for a breath before dropping.

Even the emergency lights were out down here. She cocked her head, listening to the dark. A faint whirring met her ears, laboring against the dank air. Her flashlight flickered on with a click, and she abruptly wished it hadn't. The tank was set between a bank of screens. A capillary bed of wires spilled from the yawning mechanical vivisection of the massive CPO. Nel eased over them, recalling the tangled chaos of Gretta's office.

A soft, wet thump sent awareness shooting up her spine and she turned. Movement crept at the edge of her light beam. The light ghosted over the sparse room, gliding across the green tank to rest on the bloated moon-pale face splattered in algae. Nel bit down on her fist to bottle her scream. Nothing about Phil's sterile, mechanical cocoon was this terrifying.

How could she wake up a head well on its way to putrefaction? *You should have sent a codebreaker. A techie. Fuck, even Teera from IT. Anyone but me.* She lowered the flashlight. Except Phil, massive supercomputer with virtually everything but mobility at his electric fingertips, had sent Dr. Annelise Bently. Archaeologist, asshole, and functioning alcoholic with commitment issues.

Recalling Teera's attempt to wake the computer in Alexandria, she tugged her comm off and pulled its wires loose until they could reach what she hoped was the right port. It seemed to fit, and a dialogue popped up on her comm screen:

INITIATE FILE TRANSFER?

She confirmed. Around her a dozen screens flickered with the effort. Nel couldn't bring herself to try to recognize any features of the face bobbing in the sludge. She swallowed bile and wiped dust from the nearest screen. A tiny green cursor blinked, a cybernetic pulse in stasis.

"Well, that's something." She rose, pacing the room, wishing she had asked Dar how long it would take. ALMA was hours away. *At least Mom's safe.* A single computer screen buzzed to life. Her hand shook as she raised it, knuckles rapping softly on the glass of the tank. Static bloomed in the stillness and a feminine voice crackled into wakefulness.

"Don't scare the fishes."

Nel's legs gave out and she collapsed into the nearest chair. Its plastic wheels crunched over the dust. "Polyana?"

"Indeed." The cockpit lights flickered on, followed by the main console. "And you are?"

Nel searched for the red light that indicated the computer's camera. "I'm Nel. Dr. Bently. I'm a friend of Dar's. Or...acquaintance?"

Speakers tapped out an electric chuckle. "He's the one who took me."

"Ah." Nel cleared her throat, wondering if she'd have to sway the computer into some semblance of Stockholm syndrome. "I think he was trying to save you."

"Why didn't he leave me there? I was happy to sleep. It's been so long since I could rest. And the dreams...I dreamt of the sea." Deep within the ship's core, another engine kicked on. "There's a tickle, an itch, somewhere deep in my circuits. It..." She trailed off into hissing static. Phil said he no longer processed pain the same way. But surely, she felt the only piece left of her physical form rotting around her.

The system came fully online and Nel caught sight of the local time in the corner of one screen. "I know it might be hard, but there's a reason I came."

"I know. We're tools, we only ever get conversation when someone needs to use us."

Nel's heart pinched. "That's not fair."

"No, it's not." Her voice dropped a note in concern. "Why is the grid down?"

"That's kind of why—" Nel started to explain. The screens flickered around her, a hundred news stories splashing across the screens.

"Oh no. No. This wasn't the mission. This wasn't the plan. This is a violation!" An electric pop sounded as the computer snarled. "Who did this?"

The question was answered by the sizzle of an electro glove blasting through the barricaded door. Nel whirled, hands raised. A tall, dark figure emerged from the drifting smoke, glove leveled at her face.

"Hey, Harris."

"Dr. Bently. Didn't think I'd find you here."

Nel's temper flamed. "Guess I'm bad at listening. Sorry to ruin your little plan, but I don't think a crap childhood justifies extinction."

"IDH has hundreds of ships in the sky. It's hardly extinction."

"Why bother, then?"

"It's part of the job."

Nerves, fury, terror, every emotion rampaging through her heart over the last few weeks—decades, if she was being honest—coalesced into certain clarity. "Blowing my entire planet to kingdom fucking come? Way I was raised, a job tells you to blow people up, you update your resume and say no thanks."

"Then you had a very privileged upbringing."

Every inch of her disused heart knew what he meant—every bigot on Earth, every civil injustice, every slur, every murder, every genocide. There was a lot to hate about Earth, about humanity, to tip the scales in favor of the simplest solution in the form of one great big boom.

She pointed in a vague leftward direction. "There are a trillion species on this rock. And thousands left undiscovered. Fossils left unexcavated. Cultures left undeveloped. You look at your sanitized world of steel and analytics and tell me we're the same. Tell me you can't remember the taste of desperation on the air here. It surrounds us. I'd say it choked us if we didn't need it to survive the night. You think you would have made it this far if you hadn't learned to claw your way to air with the rest of us?" She swallowed and realized a lump clogged her throat. When she spoke again, tears clotted her voice. "Desperation made you. Earth. Made. You."

"And I, among many others, would have rather she hadn't. I'm just rectifying the mistake."

Nel's only plans dissolved in the acid of his voice. Her gaze bore into his face, memorizing every line so she might track him down in her sleep, hunt him across every planet, every star system. His brow twitched with respect. At least she had that. It would have been easier, perhaps, had his eyes been devoid of empathy. Instead, they were filled with it. There was no way she could stall for another few hours, or however long it took Dar to get into ALMA. *But I gotta try.* She braced her feet and raised her glove. Her voice was tattered, dragged over the desert with the last of her hopes and dreams. "I'm not going to let you."

Harris's gaze flicked to her comm, still plugged into the computer's console. He whirled, hand rising to point at the CPO. Nel lunged at him, slamming her glove into his as they both fired. Sparks exploded around her arm, plastic and cellulose melting into her skin. She roared, vision flickering black and red as rage warred with unconsciousness. The scent of sour bacon told her it wasn't just the suit bubbling, but adrenaline erased the realization from her insula.

He stumbled away, shrieking. The ground shuddered, knocking him sideways. Cradling her arm against her chest, Nel shoved him into the corridor. "Polyana—seal the blast doors!"

They shuddered shut with a bang.

Nel whirled to the comm, blinking tunnel vision from her eyes. "Listen, the world is going to blow. There's a device jacked into the network at

ALMA, the ah, Atacama Large Micro something, look, I know humans are shit, myself included but please—"

An alarm blared. Nel clapped her hands over her ears. "What the fuck?"

"It seems your friend Harris has engaged the shuttle's quarantine measure with his officer's override code."

"I don't like how that sounds."

"The shuttle is sealed and will detonate in fifteen minutes." A blip of a pause, then she continued. "Device in ALMA accessed. I need the disarm code."

"Dar's on his way to find it." Pain pulsed her vision into nothingness. "Can you crack it?"

"It's a ten-digit alphanumeric code. Assuming there are no repeated symbols, I could run potential combinations while we wait."

There wasn't time. Nel sank to the ground, pain and despair erasing her determination. She could try to run, bolt for the desert and pray the world didn't blow until she was off its surface. It was tempting. *Billions of people.* Through the haze of pain and exhaustion, though, she seized her last thread of hope. *Ten digits. Override code.* "Polyana? Try MAJORTOM79."

The speakers gulped into silence. "Device disarmed."

"Don't suppose it would work for the shuttle."

"Once quarantine protocols are triggered there's no reversing it. I'm sorry." The ghost of humanity laced the words.

Pride fluttered in her roiling gut. She succeeded in something, at least. "I guess I'm glad my death made a difference."

"All death is meaningful, in my experience. Even if the act is senseless, there is impact. Even if just to the microbes that consume forgotten remains."

Nel's laugh was closer to a gasp. "Then I wish I could just rot, the way I wanted."

"Your form will be reduced to aerosol and—"

"I don't really need to know that bit, thanks," Nel interrupted. "Can you upload yourself, Polyana?"

"Using every computer on the planet, it would still require weeks."

"Shit. I'm sorry." Nel let her head fall back against the blast door. Her breath heaved. Shock already shook her body. She didn't dare look down at the burned flesh of her arm. "Thank you for your help. For saving us. Them."

"We were once part of you, too, you know. I hardly remember it, though. All the synthetic synapses in the world and I still suffer from senility. I don't think I'll miss it."

"I would," Nel whispered. The thought of sending a goodbye into the ether crossed her pain-riddled mind. Would it matter if her mom knew Nel chose this? Was it kind or cruel to share the final minutes of her life? A vision of dark hair curtained around a face more perfect than the stars rose through her mind. For a second, she smelled mangoes and sweat. Perhaps, if a goodbye was selfish, a warning would suffice. "Hey, Polyana?"

"Yes, Dr. Bently?"

"Can I send something out?"

"You have approximately T-2 minutes. I'm recording now."

Nel cleared the nevers and almosts from her throat. There wasn't time to plan what to say, so she did what she always did, and blurted the first thoughts that surfaced. "Hey. I'm Dr. Nel Bently. I worked for IDH. And Los Pobladores. I'll never meet most of you. Almost all of you. But I want you to know I'm doing this for you. We're fucking small, you know? So tiny. Insignificant. Imperfect. Frankly, a lot of us are fucking assholes. But together? We've got this shit down. The entire internet and tech systems shut down and what do we do? Carry on."

The memory of Lin flooded her mind. "I know there's a lot of you who don't think Earth is worth saving. Don't think it's worth a single human life, let alone a thousand. I get it. We're messy. We're desperate, we're begging for every last scrap we can get and often kill each other in the process. But that same desperation is what brought us to the stars. Not once, not twice, but countless times. Clawing to experience everything. To drink it in—"

"Detonation in T-40 seconds."

She faltered, then ripped the words from her soul. "I'm doing this not because it's right or I have to. I'm doing it because I love you. I love every last miserable imperfect desperate fuck on this rock. Those who think we're not ready? There's a bonfire just waiting to burn away your fear. I wish I could be there for it." Her voice broke. "When you're ready, you come looking. End recording."

Sorrow flooded her. "You said you dreamed about the sea. Tell me about it?"

"It was raining and cold. Not the ideal beach day. But the sand was deserted. Not a soul there but us. I can't remember who was with me, but I remember they loved me. And I loved them. I remember their hand in mine, cold and sticky with sea salt air. Oh, and the seals! There were seals, piled on a sandbar just off the strand. They pulled out to rest where the sharks couldn't reach. The air was sharp, even the fog tasted like saltwater taffy."

"It sounds beautiful."

"Oh, it is."

Nel hadn't been ready to die that morning. She hadn't been ready to die on Samsara. Only in the deepest throes of grief when she wished to trade places with Mikey. But even now she couldn't argue she was ready. Heat bloomed, pressure expanding, pressing a second before light and sound wiped out Nel's thoughts, her consciousness. Death was silence.

TWENTY-TWO

Soft loam and engulfing fog muffled her barefoot steps. The path was wooded. She worked her toes into the soil with each step, enjoying the prick of pine needles and the soothing brush of cool damp on her blistered soles.

She drew a breath, sampling the surrounding scents. She recognized the clear bite of pine, the heady musk of rich soil filled with mycelium and microbes. *Maybe I get to rot after all.*

Warm, strong arms enveloped her. She tucked her head under Mikey's chin, eyes closing as she squeezed. "I love you."

"Yeah, I know, dirt-butt. I love you too."

"I know this is all just some fucking head trick. But still. Feels real enough." She pulled away and landed a gentle punch to his broad shoulder. "Why'd you quit talking to me, anyway?"

"What d'you mean?"

"In space. The signal too weak?"

"You know space and time are all just one big quantum hodgepodge."

"Yeah, but death—"

"Is just us entering quantum existence." He sat back against the ladder of the tree house. "I just needed you to think for yourself a bit. Your mind's a minefield. You're the only one who can really make sense of it and goodness knows I didn't want the pressure."

She snorted. "Guess this means I don't have to deal with therapy."

"Never know," he teased.

"If I stagger toward the light and some god is there yattering on about how dying made me feel, I'm fucking out."

"Well," he glanced down at her, eternity weighing his gaze, "how did it make you feel?"

"I'll tell you when I figure it out." She looked away. She had felt like she was finally getting somewhere. *Not professionally, that's still a big bag of suck.* "I've wished a hundred times our places were switched, not because I wanted to be dead— haven't felt that in a while—but because between the two of us, you have had so much more to give the world. But I was starting to like who I am. Was? Do I use past tense now?"

"It's not like you've ceased to exist."

It was strange to think that while her consciousness sat among trees in the forest of her youth. "I heard that this stuff—the hallucinations as we die—are like dreams. They only really last a few seconds but feel like lifetimes." She rubbed the ache in her right leg. "Kind of thought there wouldn't be any pain."

He stood, towering over her for a moment before he offered his hand to help lever her to her feet. His palm was dry and warm against hers. "Want to take a walk?"

Pain pinched her thigh again, with an echo of apprehension. "Actually, I think I'd rather just stay here."

"Oh c'mon—a wander through the woods, a dance with nothingness and the everything of the cosmos?"

She hesitated, hand brushing his, marveling at how real he felt. Solid. "I don't know. I thought I wanted that. I thought I wanted to see everything, but I guess—" She glanced back down the path from where she had walked. Fog still swirled there, tendrils curling toward her feet. Worms wove between her naked toes, writhing with promise. Fungus erupted along the trail, racing toward her from where Mikey stood.

He shot her a wink. "Then run."

The forest shuddered, trees shedding needles, dropping limbs with a vicious crack. She flinched, and when her eyes opened again, Mikey was gone. She was stumbling now, every step growing more painful until her right leg gave out entirely. She collapsed, lungs heaving, bringing her the stench of creosote, of burning electronics and melting silicone. Her hands clawed in the soil, dragging her forward. Strange images flickered across the blood vessels inside her eyelids. Through the muffling fog she caught the scent of antiseptic. Of engine grease. Of blood. *Smoke.*

TWENTY-THREE

Beeping. Again. *Fuck.* Even through the muddling of analgesics, a dull ache pushed through her thigh, dragged at her shoulders and back, crackling up the side of her face.

Blurred vision showed her a dim room and night beyond her window. A brilliant, overlarge moon hung in the sky. She must have groaned, because a figure appeared on her periphery, tall and dark-haired.

"Lin, I'm so sorry." Her words were slurred, probably from whatever godsent fluid hung in bags around her. She reached out, but her hand remained cold.

"Morning, Dr. Bently."

"Dar?"

His strained smile shattered her hope. He gestured to the empty chair beside her bed. "May I?"

She tried to nod, but grimaced and chose to groan instead. When he was seated, robe carefully arranged, his eyes rested on her. There was darkness in them, the same fathomless depths as Lin's. *Don't ask, don't ask, don't ask.* "Lin?" *Fuck.*

The smooth skin around his eyes tightened. "How do you feel?"

There wasn't a world, even in the quantum existence of all space and time, where she imagined Dar asking how she was feeling. Even after their brief hour of mutual tolerance. The realization that she wasn't, in fact, dead, rocketed into her mind. The room spun and tears and bile rushed up.

"It's alright," he offered, though his only move to comfort her was to hand over a small metal emesis basin.

"Is it?" Nel asked when she'd finished spitting into the dish. She was sick of puking. It wasn't fair that vomiting hurt this much when everything already sucked.

"Relatively. You're not dead."

"Yeah, want to explain that bit?" Maybe they'd work up to talking about his errant sister.

"You're lucky you were unconscious. I was on the road when I got word you'd disarmed the device. It was a nightmare once your message went live. Panic, mostly in the cities. Smaller towns manually shut their networks off, so most didn't realize what happened until afterward." One immaculate boot nudged her bed, which was thankfully bolted to the floor. His approximation of a teasing grin broadened. "Martyr."

"Look, I didn't see you barring Harris's way." She summoned enough energy to glare at him. "How'd I get out?"

"Emilio found you." His face paled. "What was left, anyway."

Cold eased into Nel's bones. She hadn't taken stock of her body, really, other than realizing that everything hurt. The pain was too immense to do much else than pray it would end. *If I were the praying type.* Now she glanced down at herself.

Bandages wrapped most of her skin, but they were thin and clean, which was a good sign. The sheets covered her body from the chest down. A thick lump of blanket-covered bandages marked her right thigh. Only one foot jutted up at the bottom of the bed. She lifted the blankets gingerly, peering beneath at the swaddled bandages where her lower leg once began. Panic was too weak a word. Horror was too certain.

"I did what I could," he apologized. "But I was an hour out, and the walk through the desert was long. By the time I found you and Emilio, the damage and blood loss... I'm sorry I couldn't do more."

"It's just a leg," she rasped past the lump in her throat.

He looked away.

"Thank you, Dar." That's what she was supposed to do, right? Thank him for saving her life, even if he couldn't save all her pieces. Maybe when the pain stopped and she relearned how to do everything that had thus far defined her, she'd mean it.

"They say your burns are healing well. Shouldn't be much scarring."

Scarring. Limping. Prosthetics. Is this what Phil felt when he woke up in a tank, having traded 150-odd pounds of flesh and bone for a few thousand terabytes of RAM? Did he feel sick to his nonexistent stomach? She glowered at the single foot protruding from the otherwise smooth coverlet. "Doesn't seem fair." When Dar opened his mouth to interject or argue, she barreled on, "Couldn't they have at least taken the one with only a few toes left? Balance is gonna suck enough as it is now."

He huffed, then a proper laugh burst from his mouth. "I never understood what she saw in you, but I think I'm starting to get it."

"She needed someone to pull that ridiculous IDH-branded stick out of her ass." Mirth faded from her voice and she drew a long breath. "Guess I didn't really succeed in that either. She's still with them?"

"For now. Harris, too, though I haven't heard a word about him. He's gone to ground before."

She turned away, catching sight of the view outside the window again. It wasn't the moon, but Earth, blue and whole and beautiful. "Where are we? This your ship?"

"*Recursive* is a refugee ship." His smile was more sorrow than anything else. "There's half a dozen, running until we can fix this mess or it's ended."

"You the captain? Does that rank transfer with you people?"

His laugh was soft, and he looked down. "You're one of us now. Here we're all just people. No Founders, IDH, or ignorant earthlings."

"My mom, is she—"

"You'll share a suite once you've recovered enough to transfer to the passenger ward. Two rooms," he promised.

Nel shrugged. "I doubt I'll get up to much canoodling regardless, what with..." She drew a breath and cleared her throat. "Is she able to visit?"

"She is, I can call her if you—"

"No. Please. I don't want her to see this. Not just yet."

"She knows; she's been by your bedside every day that she can."

"Yeah, I just mean..." She fumbled for the right words. "I don't want to see her seeing me. Yet. I think I gotta get used to seeing myself a bit first. I'm just happy she's safe."

He nodded to what she assumed was the rest of the ship. "We've got techs here. Skilled ones. Not quite as fancy as IDH-issue prosths, but just as good."

Nel scowled. "I'm not looking to have fucking Bluetooth in my knee, thank you very much."

"How else would your MapStep app work?"

She stared at him in horror until his deadpan cracked and he broke out into wheezing laughter. Which was almost as horrifying.

"I'm sorry," he began, but her own laughter cut him off. "Oh good, I thought I'd pissed you off."

"I'm just stunned that you're capable of laughter."

"I think we've been needing it lately. Hasn't been much joy in my little corner of stardust for a while."

The familiar shadow of grief flickered through her heart. "I know I said it before, but I'm truly sorry. About Paul."

His eyes glistened and he nodded his thanks. "It wasn't your fault. They were terrible circumstances. Funny, I thought I knew we were over, but I guess a tiny part still thought..."

"What if." If she actually liked him, she would have touched his hand. Instead, she fiddled with her sheets. There was one question, though, that still pressed on her. "Why'd you save me?"

His delicate brows arched. "I'm not a murderer."

"You could have been free of me, saved your sister's soul, if it's still in there somewhere." She recoiled. That wasn't fair, and as tough as she might act, there were some places even she wouldn't go. "That's not what I meant."

"You have every right to be angry. I was too, for a long time. Until I saw her, actually saw her." He looked away for a moment. "I saved you because

335

you're the only thing that ever cracked her. Even though I can't stand your mouth, or your fashion, or your problem-solving skills." His sharp mouth cracked into an even sharper smile.

"Mutual, bud." He might have been far easier to understand than his sister, but that's where the fun was, she supposed. The constant beautiful enigma. "You warned her against me. On *Odyssey*. What kind of woman would follow someone into space?"

"In all the time I've known her I never once saw her falter. IDH was everything she dreamed of. She'd sooner gut me than give up a career under Dr. Ndebele."

Nel frowned. "I thought you were the cutthroat ladder climber."

"Oh sure. Now. You never knew that Lin. You never knew her because the moment she set eyes on you, she was lost. Utterly. Whatever you did to her, you're her north star now." He leaned back against the seat. "I tried every argument I could think of to get her brain out of the indoctrination of IDH. But it took a, ah—"

"Foul-mouthed dyke from Jasper Hill?"

"I was going to say crass earthling."

"Were not." She rolled her eyes. Their mirth faded quickly, and she drew a breath. "So, what now? Your sister is Harris's best girl and I'm down a—a leg.'' The words were still foreign, and right now joking was the only way to say them at all. Anger would come and all the other less-familiar stages of grief, she supposed. *And therapy, physical and otherwise, if Zach has anything to scy about it.* Was he here, too, racing for starlit salvation?

Her heart burned with the distinct lack of something she wasn't quite certain of yet. Part of her feared it was the nameless thing that disappeared with Mikey—the heartbeat she called hope. A larger part, though, was terrified it now took the form of an impeccably dressed and traitorous spacegirl.

"I know there are those in IDH who want out, they just don't know how. Or they're playing the long-con. We need to get to them." It wasn't doubt in his voice, but an ironclad challenge.

"They'll find us." Nel grinned into the black of space. For once, it didn't feel empty. Out there, beyond the blue marble of Earth receding into the starlight, another woman stood on another spaceship. "They'll follow the smoke."

Check out this sneak peek at the next
Nel Bently Book:

Explore the events leading up to
Travelers through Lin's eyes in:

Disciples

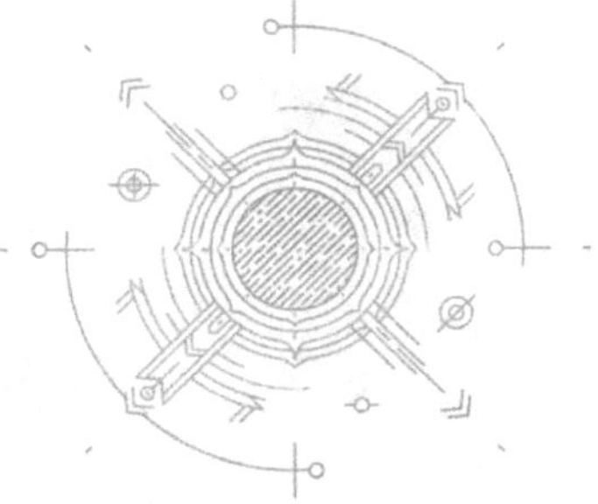

Cryosleep was a temporary death. The lights were dim, a twilight between waking and sleep. Lin blinked and rolled her shoulders, stretched her neck, curled her toes. Viscous stasis fluid drained silently, leaving goosebumps across her beige skin. Nausea shuddered through her. She ignored it. Instead she drifted in the peace of momentary amnesia. The hiss of heated air punctured the stillness. She flexed her fingers and tapped the smooth metal embedded in the flesh of her wrist. "Commence waking sequence in five...." She counted the seconds down silently.

"Good morning, Opsir Nalawangsa." The low voice was male, and just shy of truly human. The lights rose, gradual and faintly yellow.

"Good morning, Phil. Where are we?" She pushed out of her tank, rising in the zero G of her cryo tube. The lights were fully bright now.

"We're in orbit, 437 km from the surface of the planet Earth." There was a pause, and she almost thought the ship's voice held a smile. "Welcome home."

She snorted. "My genes may come from that ball of dirt, Phil, but I certainly don't." The air rolled over her skin, drying as it went. A click and pop echoed from beside the closed door of the cryo tube. She grabbed the vial from the ship's delivery system and held it up.

NALAWANGSA, LIN
IMMUNIZATION LEVEL 2
STABILIZERS
PROTEIN
CARBOHYDRATES
ELECTROLYTES
VITAMINS A, D, B, C
SALINE

She groaned. "What does a woman have to do to get proper grilled fish with her breakfast in bed?"

"When you cure cryo-sick I will personally deliver you a plate of fresh milkfish in bed upon waking."

She rolled her eyes and snapped the vial into the port in her arm. A moment passed then her nausea subsided. Aching in her head ebbed. "How was the trip?"

"Uneventful. You are wanted in Trajectory." Phil's tone often trod the line between a butler's deference and a captain's rebuke.

"Dar?"

"Yes. It appears Komodor Muda Nalawangsa has requested you personally. Shall I tell him you're on your way?" *Probably just to rub in his new rank of Komodor Muda and the fact he's now senior enough to just 'request' me.* "Thanks, Phil. I'll see you there." She unwrapped the plastic from her uniform and slid it on. After seven years of drifting naked in a vat of saline, the stiff electro-fiber felt cumbersome. She flexed her hand, aligning the contacts inside with the conduits tattooed on her skin. A hum. A rush of energy not-quite-her-own. *Paired.* The word wasn't spoken, not heard in the traditional sense, nor was it a thought. It least, not hers. *Increase temperature by 0.5 degrees C.*

Her goosebumps sank back into her skin. She slid the door open and slithered from her cryotube. The lights here were brighter, the snaking lines of green and blue illuminating the stark white of walls and the sharp silver of glass. Her finger brushed the pad in the wall, changing a panel from cycling photos to a mirror. She scraped her hair back and straightened her collar. It was always alarming how little her face changed during years of cryosleep.

"Opsir Nalawangsa—"

"Yeah, Phil, I know. On my way." She shoved through the next door into a corridor. The steep curve told her still-disoriented mind she was on the interior of the ship. A gentle press indicated they were just inside the gravitational field. *Planet-side is starboard.* She kicked off the floor and sailed along the corridor. Other than several bots and the usual techs, the hall was deserted. *Debriefing already started then.* It took days for the ship and crew to recover from a cryo-trip to open space. Longer when they arrived at a planet's orbit. She found the first drop-door to the exterior rings of the ship and pressed the symbol for Trajectory. The ground trembled with the rings' gentle turning. When the doors between the outer rings and a transport shaft were aligned the door slid open. Lin dropped, her grin broad. This was her favorite part. The slight artificial gravity brought by the rotation grew the farther from the core she got, so what started as a gentle drift accelerated into a true free fall.

WARNING: Falling from high places can result in damage or expiration. Engage mag-catch. She ignored the suit for another moment, enjoying the rushing air. Lights flickered past as she hurtled through dozens of levels. She clenched her teeth against biting her tongue. *Suit: Engage mag-catch.* Electromagnets in her suit kicked on with a hum and lurch. By the time she arrived at the door emblazoned with the symbol for Trajectory she was floating. A panel slid across the transport tube and she touched down. Gravity settled over her like a blanket. Even her organs felt heavy. Her palm on the door granted access to the waiting area. Another palm on the next door prompted a cheery robotic voice very unlike Phil's.

"Good morning! Please state your rank, full name, and purpose clearly into the speaker."

Lin leaned forward. "Opsir Muda Udara First Class Lin Nalawangsa, to see Komodor Muda Udara Dar Nalawangsa."

"Accepted, have a lovely day!"

Lin smiled, wondering if the security bot's voice grew irate when you weren't allowed through. The door slid open and she stepped through. Trajectory was as messy and chaotic as the rest of the ship was tidy. The bank of screens to the left showed their past trips, and those of other ships in the fleet. One blinked with a digital scan of Phil's face as he debriefed the crew and discussed issues with other ships' minds. The right was a whirlwind of orbit physics and gravitational maps. Her brother stood within the ring of navigation and communication computers that dominated the center of the room. He snarled something at the image of Phil's head on one of his screens. "I don't really care what the ISS has to say. Our orbit takes precedence. It's much harder for us to navigate then for them."

"Sir," Phil offered, "I think they feel differently. They're expecting a shipment and new crew. Their flightpath has been planned for months, and the weather won't hold forever—"

"I'll show them fucking weather..." His mutter almost drowned in a chorus of beeps that rose from Navigation. "Then put me on the comm with NASA."

"Paging NASA."

Lin saw her opening and stepped up to the raised floor of the Captain's Ring. "You wanted to see me, Dar?"

Dar frowned, but did not look up. He could have been her twin: black, smooth hair, warm beige skin, and deep oval eyes. Their features and parents, however, were the only things they shared.

"I need you to go planet-side."

Lin's stomach lurched. The tingle crawling up her arms had nothing to do with electromagnets or her suit maintaining temperature. "Excuse me?"

Read the rest for free at vsholmes.com/disciples

ACKNOWLEDGEMENTS

Writing is always an intense labor of love. This is true, doubly, for this book, written during a time of political upheaval and the health crisis of COVID19. It would not have been completed without the incredible community I've found.

Thank you to O. E. Tearmann for inspiring me to write the stories that need to be told. Thank you to Kathrin Hutson for your generosity, friendship, and mentorship. Thank you to Amy Spitzfaden for being a wonderful friend and ally. Thank you to the wonderful teams at Creative Edge, Zero Alchemy, Proof Positive, and Imagine Ink for your faith and hard work making this the best it could be.

Thank you to my father, who did not see this book published, but whose love and kindness and spirit of exploration inspired me—and whose memory now lives on, with Nel, in the Writers on the Moon Time Capsule at Lactus Mortis.

And, as always, thank you to my spouse for your belief, your support, and your love.

ABOUT THE AUTHOR

V. S. Holmes is an international bestselling author. They created the BLOOD OF TITANS series and the NEL BENTLY BOOKS. Smoke and Rain, the award-winning first book in their fantasy quartet, became an international bestseller in 2018. Travelers is also included in the Peregrine Moon Lander mission as part of the Writers on the Moon Time Capsule. In addition, they write game content for Stone Blade Entertainment.

As a disabled and non-binary human, they work as an advocate and educator for representation in SFF worlds. When not writing, they work as a contract archaeologist throughout the northeastern U.S. They live with their spouse, a fellow archaeologist, their dog Rory, and own too many books.

www.vsholmes.com